Clan Chief

Highland Heroes Series: Book 2

Theo Mann

Invisible Publishing

Highland Heroes Series

Contents

Chapter 1

S nowflake stared down at a spot on the bare wooden floor. "Well, that's it. She's gone."

Dead Betty choked across the room. "I can't believe it. I can't believe Lily really is gone!"

"Did she really travel back in time?" Zero whispered. "How is that even possible?"

Snowflake zoned out on the spot on the floor where Lily disappeared. Her friend, her comrade, Lily Dindle, and her brother Liam Barnett, vanished from that spot. One minute they were there, and the next, they just.... weren't.

Not even knowing they were going back in time on a top-secret mission to save the President of the United States could change the hollow feeling in Snowflake's chest.

Liam took Lily to ancient Scotland to rescue Lady Rhona Armstrong from a dark wizard who was trying to kill her, but none of that mattered now.

The Last Division had been together for so long. They had bled and fought and died together. They dedicated their lives to each other. Now one of them was gone for the first time since they came back from the Afghanistan war.

Snowflake dragged her awareness back to the present. This wasn't Afghanistan. The Last Division was in Ironforge, a normal suburban house in inner-city Detroit.

She forced herself to shake off her mounting dread. "Well, it's over now. Let's get back to work. We need to retool our rotation, now that there are only four of us instead of five."

She turned away to leave the room. She didn't want to deal with this hollow place where Lily used to be. Nothing felt right and Snowflake knew only one way to fill the hole: she had to keep working. Work and combat solved all her problems.

Dead Betty, Zero, and Echo Boxwood didn't move. They all just kept staring at the center of their circle. Snowflake would have to pull rank on them to snap them out of their trance.

She opened her mouth to start snapping orders when a howling tornado erupted on the same spot. A whirling vortex blurred in the air and then spat out Liam Barnett right in the middle of the room.

He slammed down hard on the wooden floor and a small copper box fell at his side. It bounced once and rolled a few feet away.

Liam landed on his shoulder and curled over before he realized where he was. Soot, dust, and grime smeared his face and smudged his clothes. He glanced around at the four women before he recognized them.

"Liam!" Snowflake demanded. "What are you doing back here?"

His wild eyes skipped from one face to the next. "Lily...the battle..."

"What battle?" Zero asked. "Where's Lily?"

"How could you leave her behind three hundred years in the past?" Betty added. "You should have brought her back with you."

"We were fighting the...." He spotted the box and dragged himself to his feet. "I have to go back. I have to get her out. I promised...."

He moved to pick up the box, but Snowflake dodged in front of him. "You aren't going anywhere until you tell us where Lily is."

"That's what I'm telling you. We were fighting the wizards. They had dragons...."

Snowflake gaped at him. "Wizards? Dragons?"

"She's in danger. I promised I would bring her back and then..." He frowned over his shoulder at the other three. He just now seemed to be waking up to where he was and w hy.

Snowflake picked up the box behind his back. "If Lily is in danger, we're going through to get her. We'll arm up and deal with whatever we find on the other side. Come on, all of you. We can expect trouble."

"You can't," Liam cut in. "Only two people can go through the time portal at a time."

"Oh, right. Betty, you come with me."

"No way. Lily is my sister..." Liam tried to snatch the box away from Snowflake, but she yanked it out of his reach before he got near it. "She's your sister and you abandoned her in the middle of a battle. It sounds like we care a lot more about Lily than you do."

Liam glared at her. "How dare you?"

"Oh, I dare! I dare a lot more than that. You never told us anything about dragons or wizards or anything. I never would have let Lily go into something like that. I should kill you right now for lying to me—to all of us. I should have done it when you first showed up here. Then Lily would be safe and we wouldn't have to deal with you and your lies."

He narrowed his eyes and fumed. "No one is going back there without me. I made a promise to get Lily to safety and…"

"You care more about your promise than you do about your own sister."

"You don't even know how to use that thing," Liam went on, "and you have no idea where to find Lily even if you did. If anyone is going back to rescue Lily, it will be me. Anyway, I'm on a mission for the President. I still haven't completed it."

Snowflake surveyed him more closely and finally relented. "All right, but I'm going with you."

"Lieutenant…" Echo began.

"You three hold the fort here. I'll find Lily and bring her back."

"What if something happened to her?" Zero's eyes darted to Liam. "I don't like the sound of that battle."

"If anything happened to her, then someone needs to go on and finish saving Lady Rhona. We all got called back into service even if Lily is the only one who deployed." Snowflake handed Liam the box. "All right. Do what you have to do."

"But Lieutenant…." Betty protested. "We won't be able to fulfill our mission *here* with only three of us."

"Consider our mission on indefinite hold. Do what you can and keep up your training schedule. If Liam came back that quickly, I could be back in five minutes, too."

"Only two of you can come back at a time," Zero pointed out. "If you and Lily came back, Liam would be stuck over there."

Snowflake shook the objection out of her mind "We'll deal with that when the time comes." She crossed to the cabinet in the corner, pulled it open, and took down a 12-gauge shotgun. "If there are dragons on the other end, I better be prepared."

"You can't, Snowflake," Liam called from behind her. "You can't take any weapons from this time period."

"Why not?"

"You'd corrupt the timeline."

Snowflake snorted. "You're already sending three people back in time for the express purpose of affecting the timeline. I'd say it's fully corrupted by now."

"Besides," Liam added, "shotguns won't do any good against wizards or dragons."

Snowflake glared at him. This guy was really starting to piss her off. "Fine. Let's get out of here."

"Hold on a sec." Betty grabbed Snowflake's arm and pulled her across the room. Betty cast a backward glance at Liam and drew Snowflake far enough away that Liam couldn't overhear.

"What if he's lying, Lieutenant?" Betty whispered. "You have no proof that Lily is in danger, or if she is, that he didn't do something to her."

"Betty's right," Echo added in an undertone. "We have protocols to follow. If someone comes back alone, they're treated as suspect."

"He could be leading you into a trap," Betty went on. "You shouldn't trust him."

Snowflake studied her friends one after the other and then sighed. "You're right. I don't trust him, either, but going with him is the only way to find out where Lily is. If she's in danger, from him or anyone else, someone has to get her out of it. Besides, we're all on deck as far as the mission goes. If Lily can't complete it, that puts the four of us in charge of completing it in her place."

Betty shot another glance over Snowflake's shoulder. Betty's features hardened when she looked at Liam. "Just keep an eye on that guy. I don't trust him."

"Not even Lily trusted him and he's her brother," Echo pointed out. "She should know better than anyone."

Snowflake nodded. "All right. I better go. I want to get there before the battle turns against Lily."

"You'll come back, right?" Zero asked. "You won't abandon our Division, will you?"

"Of course not. Nothing is more important than this. That's why I'm doing this."

Snowflake cast one last look around the group. Anyone else would have hugged these women who had been her constant companions and her only friends for years.

Lily hugged them before she left. Lily hugged Snowflake before she left, but Snowflake didn't feel right about hugging anyone. That wasn't her. She had to stay in command and that meant keeping her distance from her subordinates.

The Last Division hadn't been officially part of the Military in years, but the five women still maintained their command structure. It was the only life any of them knew anymore.

She was supposed to be their commanding officer even though the Last Division had been retired from the military for years. They had maintained their command structure and hugging her subordinates didn't sit right with Snowflake.

She always kept her distance between herself and her comrades. Someone else might have done things differently, but doing it this way sure made it a lot easier to tell them what to do.

None of them questioned the situation until today. Snowflake didn't like Lily hugging her before she left, but now Snowflake faced the prospect of doing the same thing. She was secretly glad looking back that she did hug Lily—or that Lily hugged her. Snowflake wouldn't want to part from her closest friends, maybe forever, without doing that.

Now Lily was gone. She might never come back and Snowflake might not come back, either. Whatever happened to Lily to trap her in the past might happen to Snowflake, too.

She should hug her last three remaining friends. She should show them that she cared about them as more than just their commanding officer, but she couldn't bring herself to do it. She couldn't cross that divide holding them apart. She needed Lily to do that for her

.

Without warning, Dead Betty came forward, put her arms around Snowflake, and hugged her. Snowflake stiffened for a second and then, against her own will, she softened and hugged Betty back.

Snowflake wouldn't have been able to do it on her own, but she was glad now that Betty did it. It sealed something that started a long time ago. It answered a question lurking in the back of Snowflake's mind that she never even realized was there.

What if the survivors of the Last Division only cared about each other because of their past during the war? What if they never really cared about each other at all? What if they only clung to each other out of some injured need to hide from life?

Betty's hug put those fears to rest. Zero and Echo came forward to hug Snowflake, too, and she welcomed them with a glad heart. She hugged them much more closely than she hugged Lily. Snowflake regretted that now, but with any luck, she would see Lily soon and make it up to her.

She pushed Echo back and affection flooded her heart when she smiled at her three friends. This deep attachment for them drowned out the nagging doubts of going into dangers she knew nothing about....and going unarmed, at that.

She couldn't remember ever feeling this close to them. She didn't even mind them squeezing her arms and gripping her shoulders. Their touch connected them in ways Snowflake had never known before. Not even risking their lives during the war and losing their friends in combat compared to this.

Liam watched from across the room. He didn't say anything or intervene until Snowflake turned away. "I'm ready."

He put the box on the floor and pressed the symbols on its sides. The vortex opened in the middle of the room.

Liam grabbed Snowflake's hand as the wind snatched at her hair and clothes. It started to tow her into the swirling mists rotating faster and faster. The time portal opened to drag her in.

Snowflake glanced over at her three friends, but they were already blurring in the spinning room. She opened her mouth to call out one last farewell, but she couldn't breathe. The tornado ripped her off the floor and sucked her into its center.

The next instant, a deafening crash struck her eardrums. The room collapsed and crushed her in darkness.

Chapter 2

Colton Buchanan leaned over the high stone parapet and looked down at the ground far below. The walls merged with the sheer granite cliffs towering to the mountain peaks behind him. The dark grey stone concealed the fortress of Icemeet so no one could see it unless they were standing right in front of it.

No windows or decorations gave away the citadel's location. Guards patrolling the ramparts gave the only clue that this cliff served as the entrance to a vast edifice built into the mountainside.

Colton could see all the way down the mountain to the Boundless from here. The estuary separated Clan Buchanan territory from the city of Kald beyond. The imposing castle of Tyrekirk towered over the landscape.

Tyrekirk imposed Laird Balfour Armstrong's rule over the whole countryside, but his power ended at the Boundless. Clan Creighton might rein across the water, but Clan Buchanan would never bow to the Laird's tyranny. The two Clans had been at war for generations with no end in sight.

Colton propped his arms on the parapet and watched two fast-moving streaks whiz up the mountainside from the faraway planes. The two missiles hugged the ground covering the miles with blinding speed. Only the faintest whisper of movement gave away their position. Their dappled coloring made them blend into the landscape just as well as the fortress did.

Colton straightened up and called to the guards on the turret. "Open the gate! The scouts are returning! Raise the gate!"

Armed men got busy releasing the counterweight. It dropped on creaking ropes to raise a massive granite block barricading Icemeet's only entrance. The ropes twanged and stretched from the strain as the equally giant stone sank to the ground to pull the gate up.

Colton sprang down the steps chiseled into the fortress wall. He reached Icemeet's main courtyard just as the two streaks crossed the opening. They hurtled past the guards.

The counterweight thumped against the paving stones and the guards started to raise it again without a moment's break.

The two streaks only slowed when they made it inside. They slowed enough for Colton to make them out as two large cats.

They strutted the rest of the way into the courtyard and shook out their rough, mottled fur. Their coloring blended perfectly with the rocky terrain outside and they matched the courtyard's stone walls now.

Colton walked straight toward them and they both turned to eye him with sharp, fierce stares. Their eyes displayed the characteristic radiating lines of the Highland tigers. All the Buchanans had the same pattern in their eyes.

Colton got within fifteen feet of them before they both transformed in front of him. They stood upright on their hind legs and their fur vanished under clear skin. The hair on their heads grew longer and their tails vanished. They turned into men as tall, straight, and square-shouldered as Colton himself.

He threw out his arms and called, "Brothers!"

The taller, light-haired man hadn't shaved in a few days. Colton's brother Reid wore no shirt or sporran and his feet and legs were bare under his black kilt. Only a rough leather belt held his kilt on around his muscular waist and a swath of tartan covered his chiseled, muscular chest.

The other was as dark and rugged as Colton, only a few inches shorter. Duncan was the youngest and not as powerfully built as his oldest brother, but he had a more compact, explosive air about him that his bigger, older brothers lacked.

He wore only his kilt and tartan like Reid. Three days' growth of black beard covered more of his face and set off the feral glint in his deep, black eyes.

Duncan and Reid cast a stark contrast to Colton's spotless kilt, furred sporran, and the tailored black jacket covering his immaculate white linen shirt. As acting Chief of Clan Buchanan, Colton had to cut a much more impressive figure than his brothers who had been out living rough on the mountain for days.

Reid strode toward Colton and the brothers embraced in plain sight of all their guards and Clansmen, but no one noticed. The Buchanans had seen it all a thousand times.

Duncan stood off to the side and grinned at his brothers. Colton held Reid at arm's length, clapped him on both shoulders, and then turned to Duncan.

Duncan laughed and hugged Colton just as warmly. "Ye're getting as fast as Reid, laddie," Colton remarked when he finally pushed his younger brother back and savored the sight of him.

"He'll beat me one of these days......when Hell freezes over," Reid remarked and all three laughed.

Colton put an arm around each of his brothers and steered them toward the fortress. "Come along, the pair of ye. We'll get ye under cover and ye can tell me all."

He headed for the arched passage leading into the fortress. The long, ringing stone corridor followed the courtyard and opened on the left side. Arched gaps gave a view out over the courtyard.

Highlanders standing guard on either side of the threshold parted to let the three brothers through. Colton suppressed his curiosity just long enough to get his brothers under the roof.

"Well?" he prompted. "How did it look down there?"

Reid pulled up short under the arch and lowered his voice to a confidential murmur. "Clan Creighton is arming for another invasion. I'd bet me life on it."

Colton's happiness at seeing his brothers again vaporized in a flash. "Ye dinnae say."

"Aye. We both saw the signs. Laird Balfour is bringing in armies from the south and we saw at least a dozen more dragons coming in from the west. There can be no doubt. We can expect another attack sooner rather than later."

Colton turned to Duncan who stood listening with his bright, black eyes. He didn't miss a single word.

Colton didn't have to ask Duncan to confirm his brother's report. The two had been out together for three days scouting the countryside to bring back intelligence on Clan Buchanan's enemies.

Duncan would have seen everything Reid saw. Reid wouldn't be saying this at all if they both didn't agree to tell Colton what was going on.

Colton compressed his lips. "Well, it's naught we havenae seen coming a long way off. We'll just have to step up our preparations to repel them."

"Aye," Duncan breathed. "We've done that a dozen times as well. They can drive us off the planes, but they'll never drive us out of these mountains. We have all the advantage on the ground fighting as tigers. The dragons are the Creightons' only true advantage."

"Aye." Colton frowned and scratched his chin. "It is strange, though.... the timing...."

"How do ye figure?" Reid asked. "They're always getting up some mischief or other. They'll never stop with this nonsense."

Colton slapped Reid's shoulder again and jerked his thumb toward the courtyard. "Come up to the battlements with me, both of ye. I want to...." He broke off. "Och, no. Ye're both beat. Ye'll want food and sleep and clean clothes before ye talk all that business."

"Stuff it, ye mapit!" Duncan spat out. "Ye winnae banish us to the nursery while ye strut about making all yer plans. We're in this with ye, man!"

"Aye," Reid added. "What's food and sleep and clean clothes when we've a war to fight?"

"Ye keep yer clean clothes to yerself, laddie," Duncan finished. "Some of us can still defend the citadel while ye primp and preen."

Colton rounded on Duncan fighting back laughter. He grabbed his youngest brother by the back of the neck, wrestled him into an elbow hold, and jabbed his fingers into Duncan's ribs. "I can still whip yer insolent hide, laddie! If ye fancy yer chances getting mucked up, I can strip off as easily as ye."

Duncan howled trying to fight his way out of Colton's grip. "Ye great lug! Get yer hands off me."

Reid stood off to the side chuckling at their antics. "Ye made that bed yerself, lad. We'll bury yer rotten carcass with honor and grace. Ye have me word on that."

Colton gave his brother a few more firm digs and then let him go. Duncan snarled and tried to lunge for him, but Colton only caught Duncan by the head again and cuffed around the ears.

Colton shoved Duncan away with a laugh. "Havenae ye had enough yet? Ye're more game than I thought. Perhaps ye should stay out on the mountain a few more days. That'll make ye a man."

Duncan finally straightened up, pressed his wrist to the corner of his mouth, and laughed. "I'll best ye one day, Colton. Ye mark me words."

"I'm all breathless with anticipation, lad. Now come inside and get yerselves cleaned up. Ye smell like a cow bier."

All three of them laughed and Colton put his arm around Duncan's shoulder to lead him into the citadel. Duncan leaned against him and Colton knew, as he always did, that everything was fine between him and his brothers. They were joined at the shoulder against the enemy.

They all turned away when a shout went up from the guards on the parapet. Colton knew that sound and it set his nerves on end.

All three brothers spun around and Colton stiffened when one guard pointed over the parapet toward the Boundless. More guards assembled from all over. They were all looking down at the same spot.

"What in thunder....?" Reid growled. "The Creightons had better not be coming over the water now of all times."

Colton stormed back into the courtyard. "What's up?" he yelled up, but the guards didn't hear him. They were all hurrying down the wall toward the gate.

Colton sprang up the steps to the ramparts with his two brothers right behind him. His blood ran cold when he looked down at what the guards were staring at. Someone else was coming up the mountain, but it wasn't another cat. It was a woman.

She looked absolutely awful. Muck clumped in her hair, scratches and bruises covered her face and arms, and her clothes had been torn to shreds. Tears streamed down her cheeks and got mixed up in the grime and filth caking her skin.

She staggered trying to climb the mountain. Her knees gave out more than once and she supported herself on her hands to push onward. She was climbing straight toward Icemeet.

Colton's heart seized and Duncan whispered the one word all three brothers were thinking. "Edeena!"

Colton whirled away. "Open the gate! Send out ten men to bring her in!"

He and his brothers charged down the courtyard. They got there as the gate swung upward to let their only sister inside the fortress. Ten guards advanced and surrounded her. They brandished their sabers toward the Creighton side, but no one came. Edeena was all alone.

She sobbed harder as she got closer and saw Colton and his brothers coming out to meet her. She stumbled one last time and stumbled into a run. She was limping on one leg, but she picked up speed, charged into Colton's arms, and collapsed in a flood of tears.

Colton wrapped his sister in his arms and held onto her for a moment. She was one of the strongest, fiercest, most resourceful fighters in the whole Clan—or she was when she left Icemeet to cross the Boundless to the Creighton side.

What on Earth had happened to her there to bring her so low? Colton didn't want to find out, but he had to. He was in charge of Clan Buchanan. He would be Clan Chief after his father died and all his Clansmen considered him Clan Chief already.

Whatever happened to Edeena, Colton would be the one to deal with it, but not now. He gathered his sister in his arms and clutched her against his chest while he turned and walked back into the courtyard. "Lower the gate—and double the watch! Keep an eye out for anyone coming after her!"

Several of his men called out, "Aye,", but Colton wasn't listening. He had to take care of his sister and he had to find out what happened in Kald.

He didn't expect Reid and Duncan to come back with any report other than the one they brought him. Whatever Edeena had to tell Colton would be much more important and much more dangerous. He had to seriously restrain himself from putting her down in the passageway and questioning her then and there.

He carried her to the passage's far end. Duncan darted ahead and opened the door for him. Colton carried Edeena through the main foyer, past the great hall, up three flights of stairs, and Duncan opened her bedroom door.

Colton laid her on the bed. "Och, there ye go, lassie. Ye're home now and safe. Ye can rest here and...."

She rocketed off the mattress and almost broke his nose sitting up too fast. "I'm so sorry, Colton! Ye'll never forgive me! Just dinnae throw me out! I cannae bear it! Ye winnae send me away, will ye? I didnae mean to. I tried to stop it. I swear to ye I never...."

"Wheest, lass!" he breathed. "No one will be throwing ye anywhere. This is yer home. Do ye think for an instant I'd send me own sister away? Wheesht! Ye're raving."

"Ye dinnae understand ought, Colton!" she choked. "I'm.... I'm mated....to an out-worlder! I tried to stop it! I didnae mean to. I swear I never wanted to.... He forced me...."

Reid bumped into Colton shoving his way to the bed. "Forced ye! Who is the bastard? We'll track him down and...."

"Ye dinnae understand!" She buried her face in her hands and dissolved in tears.

"If he forced ye, ye arenae mated," Colton pointed out. "Ye cannae mate with any man except by love. Our Clan...."

"He's a dead man. That's all he is," Duncan snarled behind Colton's back. "It doesnae matter if he comes from the moon. He willnae last the month with us hunting him."

Colton couldn't bear to see Edeena crying, but her words froze his heart. No wonder she looked so bad. Whatever happened to her across the Boundless must have been catastrophic.

He laid his hand on her shoulder. "Lassie...."

"He used magic!" She threw back her head so all three of her brothers had no choice but to look at her hideous face. Grime and snot glued her filthy hair to her cheeks. Her eyes blazed with a mixture of fury, betrayal, and black despair.

"He used magic to bind me to him! He cast a mate-bonding spell to make me obey him. He made me tell him all I kenned about Lady Ilisa Buchanan and our mission to find her in Kald. He didnae ken the spell would bind me to him for life. I tried to stop it, but it was too late."

Her rage evaporated and left nothing but anguish and heartbreak in its place. Colton stared down at her trying in vain to fight down panic. This was so much worse than he ever feared.

"Who was he?" Reid hissed. "If he's a Creighton...."

"He wasnae any Creighton. His name is Liam Barnett and he came back through time from the future.... with his sister, Lily. They were searching for some Lady Rhona Armstrong and they wouldnae believe she doesn't exist. She's the ancient ancestor of some dignitary in their time and...."

Colton held up his hand. "Stop right there, lassie. Ye're saying a wizard came back through time.... from the future?"

"He cannae be," Reid muttered. "He must be a Creighton. No one on the Buchanan side would dare lay a finger on Edeena."

"I wouldnae have believed it meself if I hadnae seen the time portal with me own eyes," Edeena went on, "but these two were like no others in this land. They talked and dressed strange. They werenae Creightons. I'd lay any odds on that."

She was starting to calm down, now that she realized her brothers weren't going to turn against her, but Colton couldn't clear his thoughts.

He turned away and paced to the window, but the view only brought him face to face with the mountain running down to the planes, the Seat of Armstrong standing tall against the sky, and the Boundless separating him from his enemies.

"How did it happen?" he murmured. "Tell me all."

"They captured us in battle....

Edeena choked on the words again. This must be hard for her, but Colton didn't interrupt or try to take it easy on her. He needed to know everything and he needed to know it now. Every Buchanan life depended on it.

"The outworlders were working with two soldiers from Tyrekirk tasked with guarding Prince Ness's life. They hid him in the slums. They killed Farlan and...."

"Who killed Farlan?" Reid demanded. "Who killed Farlan, Edeena?"

"The sister... Lily....and then they caught me." She broke down in tears again. No one said anything for a minute while she vented her desperate anguish. Then she rallied, straightened up, and threw back her head in defiance. "Anyway, it's all over now. I'll just...."

She looked around the room and her face twisted. Colton couldn't listen to any more of this. He strode back to the bed and towered over her. "Listen here, lassie. Ye'll go nowhere. Is that clear enough? Ye're home now and ye'll stay home. If ye're mated to some glackit from across the water, more's the pity, but ye'll go nowhere—not as long as I'm around."

"Aye," Reid growled and Duncan nodded.

Edeena looked up at Colton and her eyes brimmed with tears. "Do ye mean it, Colton? Ye will nae send me off?"

"Och, no, lassie. It is nae yer fault, but I'll tell ye one thing straight. If that bastard shows his face anywhere I can see him, ye'd best hide in the closet for he'll lose his neck right smart."

"If we dinnae get to him first," Duncan muttered.

"Thank ye, Colton." She started sobbing again. "I dinnae ken how to thank ye lads."

"Ye can thank me by telling me the rest," Colton countered. "How do ye ken they truly came from the future? Clothes and strange speech winnae convince me. Ye must have something more than that."

She nodded and pulled herself together. "Aye—that. Aye. He had a.... the brother, I mean—Liam—the wizard—he had this wee box contraption...." She held up her hands to show how big it was. "It had queer marks all over it and he pressed some of them to open the box. It snapped and opened this tunnel in the air. I dinnae understand it, but it took him back to.... wherever he came from."

"So...he's gone?" Reid snorted. "How convenient for him."

"He was trying to escape the battle with his sister...and I pushed him through the portal. I thought if I got rid of him, I'd be free."

Colton saw her falling apart again and pulled her back with his next question. "What battle?"

"The Laird's wizards attacked. Ness Creighton fought them to defend the party and.... he's dead now. I stayed around just long enough to see and then I fled. Anyway, I saw Liam hesitating and I took me chance. I pushed him through the portal and he vanished along with the box."

"So the sister is still in Kald?" Reid asked.

"Aye. I dinnae ken where."

"Did ye find ought about Lady Ilisa?" Duncan asked. "Did ye make any headway on yer mission at all?"

"Aye." Edeena wiped her nose on her sleeve. "She's in the castle at Tyrekirk. She's the Laird's prisoner and threatened with execution. We were on our way there to free her when the Laird's wizards attacked us."

"That bastard Laird!" Duncan snarled. "I'll cut his head off!"

Colton started to turn away. "We must mount a rescue mission straight away. We cannae leave her to the Laird." He inhaled to give orders to his brothers. He wished he could let them rest after they just returned from scouting the Buchanans' territory, but that would have to wait. This was much more important.

The door exploded off its hinges and Colton's cousin Fergus blundered into the room. "Laddie.... the dragons...."

"Are they attacking?" Colton sprang for the exit and his hand flew to his dirk. "Are the Creightons launching their assault now?"

"Och, no," Fergus panted. "They're bringing in more dragons—about thirty. They're all in the air over Tyrekirk."

Colton allowed himself to relax, but only a little. He pointed to Edeena. "Sort yerself out, lass. I'll be back to question ye in a little while."

She grabbed his hand and kissed it. "Thank you, Colton."

"Wheesht, lassie. Not now."

He pulled away and he and his brothers marched all the way back down to the courtyard and up to the ramparts where they were before.

The dragons Fergus mentioned were still airborne over Tyrekirk and there were at least thirty. Duncan pointed to the south. "Look. They're bringing in more."

Colton's resolve hardened. The Creightons could bring in hundreds of dragons. The Buchanans would never lie down. They would never stop fighting and trying to destroy their old enemy.

Colton harbored no doubt at all about why the Creightons were flying their dragons around the castle turrets. They wanted to intimidate the Buchanans. That stupid frumpit of a Laird thought he could frighten the Buchanans into submission.

Well, it hadn't worked in centuries and it wouldn't work now. If anything, it only enraged the Buchanans and made them hate the Creightons more.

"What the hell is that?" Duncan murmured.

Colton turned around to see what his brother meant. Duncan frowned at a spot off to one side. He was looking half up the mountain beyond the gate. No enemy could be coming from there.

Colton swiveled the other way and hardly believed his senses when a blurry sort of whirlpool opened in the fabric of space. He had almost convinced himself that Edeena was imagining things when she mentioned the wizard traveling through time. Now Colton saw the same thing with his own eyes.

Two tall figures stepped through the opening and a small copper box bounced on the stones at the man's foot. He picked it up and said something to the woman next to him.

They both wore trousers and the man's clothes were dirty and torn.... like Edeena's. The strangers surveyed the landscape and then turned their gazes toward Icemeet. They were too close not to see it along with Colton and all the guards watching from the parapet.

The wind caught the woman's long silken black hair and tossed it across her angular face. She narrowed her dark eyes at the Highlanders standing above her.

Her features hardened in a way that set Colton's hair on end. She wasn't afraid. She was steeling herself for a fight even though she was unarmed.

The man took hold of her arm and tried to pull her away. He jutted his chin toward Kald, but the woman didn't take her eyes off the Buchanans. Everything about her stretched Colton's nerves to the breaking point. Who was she? What was she doing here?

She said something to the man out of the corner of her mouth and set off walking for the gate like she belonged here somehow.

Some of the guards drew their weapons and several archers nocked their bows to aim down at her, but she didn't break off.

Colton almost gave the order to open the gate when a ragged scream split the chilly silence. "Open the gate! Open the gate!"

All eyes turned to Edeena as she tore across the courtyard running for the gate. She reached it before the guards could react. She pulled up pounding her fists against the huge stone.

The guards down on the ground looked up at Colton and he nodded for them to release the counterweight. The gate swung open and Edeena charged outside.

She hurtled for the strangers and flung herself full tilt at the man. She hugged him and then grasped his hand to pull him inside. Colton couldn't hear them from here, but he could just imagine what she was saying to him.

"That filthy, rotten piece of tripe!" Reid hissed. "He's come to the wrong place if he expects a warm welcome from us."

Colton fought his temper under control. "He's Edeena's mate. We'll see if he's sincere, and if he isnae, he can tell us more from Kald, at least."

He turned to the stairs and had to force his way between his brothers. Reid and Duncan glared at the man in undisguised fury. Colton didn't blame them. He said he would slit this bastard's throat if he ever set foot in Icemeet, but Colton couldn't do that if Edeena wanted to keep this man as her mate.

Colton stormed down the steps doing his best to get his thoughts in order. If Edeena was telling the truth, this wizard didn't actually mean to bond her to himself with that spell. He also didn't mean to abandon her. Edeena pushed him through the portal and sent him away, not the other way around.

Now she was out there hugging him and leading him through the gate to bring him into the fortress. Colton would just have to bide his time and find out for himself what this wizard was all about.

He reached the courtyard just as Edeena brought the man under the gate. The strange woman trailed a few paces behind. She watched Edeena and the wizard with the same cold detachment that Colton felt. Whoever this woman was, she had nothing to do with Edeena or Liam Barnett, but that only piqued Colton's curiosity more.

Edeena tried to beam at Liam and then she blushed when Colton walked over to them. "Colton, this is Liam Barnett, the wizard I told ye about. Liam, this is me eldest brother, Colton Buchanan. He's acting Clan Chief of Clan Buchanan."

Colton surveyed Liam up and down. Liam might be a few inches taller, but Colton was too good a judge of character to think very highly of this man. Liam might be fit, strong, and muscular, but anyone could see that Liam wasn't a fighter. He hadn't done very many hard days of training in a harsh environment like Icemeet. He was soft. He was a city boy with shifty eyes and an overabundance of caution.

Colton saw in an instant that Liam recognized a stronger, tougher, and fiercer man in Colton. Liam tried to smile and failed. He had to work hard to meet Colton's eye and Liam didn't offer his hand. "Good to meet you. I've heard a lot about you."

"As I have heard a great deal about ye," Colton growled. "How is it ye dare to show yer face on our land after what ye've done to me sister?"

"Colton..." Edeena began.

He held up his hand for silence. He didn't take his eyes off Liam. "Well? What have ye to say for yerself? Give me one reason I shouldnae kill ye where ye stand."

Liam glanced back and forth between Colton and Edeena. "If you know that much, you know the mate-bonding spell was unintentional."

"Och, it was perfectly intentional," Colton snarled. "Ye kenned exactly what ye were doing at the time."

"I didn't know it would be permanent. I wouldn't have done it if I had known."

"I dinnae believe ye," Colton countered. "I believe ye'd have done it regardless of the outcome. Ye wanted yer information and ye'd do what ye must to get it. I ken yer ilk too well."

"So.... what?" Liam waved toward the gate. "Do you want me to leave? I was just about to go over to Kald and...."

"No!" Edeena cut in. "No. Ye're here and ye'll stay here." She tugged his hand to lead him toward the passageway. "Come inside. We can...."

Colton saw his brothers surging forward to intervene, but Colton got there first. He dodged in front of Edeena, and in a split second, he had his saber in one hand and his dirk in the other. "Not so fast, lass. These aliens are trespassing in our territory and deserve a death sentence for that alone. And as for him...."

He jabbed his saber tip at Liam's neck and cocked back his left elbow to raise his dirk over his shoulder. He would have lunged to cut Liam's head off, but the dark-haired woman reacted impossibly fast.

She had stood off to one side in a relaxed posture. She kept her countenance impassive and calm through the whole confrontation. She didn't seem capable of moving that fast, but as soon as she got in front of Colton's blade, he realized his mistake.

His saber point brushed her hair when she slotted between Liam and Colton's weapon, but she didn't even flinch. Her dark eyes made Colton flinch, though, and he had to stop himself from recoiling as though she'd attacked him.

Reid and Duncan drew their blades just as fast. They moved in to back Colton up, but she didn't even look at them. She stood just as tall as Colton and her eyes drilled him to the core.

"Whoa, buddy. Take it easy. We're totally unarmed." She murmured under her breath in a satin undertone. She spoke in a low, sultry whisper and raised both hands where he could see them.

He stiffened even more at her tone. She might be unarmed, but she was no less a threat like this. If anything, she was even more dangerous for being unarmed.

"Everybody just…. take it easy," she murmured. "We didn't mean to trespass on anything. We were trying to get to Tyrekirk. Something must have gone wrong and we wound up here."

"Ye foul witch!" Duncan spat. "Ye're naught but a fiend like all the Creightons…."

"We don't know anything about the Creightons," she went on. "We only came to find our friend. She vanished in Kald and she's in danger…."

"She's talking about his sister…. Lily," Edeena interjected. "She was the one…"

"Hold yer tongue, lass!" Colton barked much louder than he meant to, but the woman only blinked. She never took her eyes off him. She didn't even look at his weapons or his arms. She read him in his eyes alone.

Edeena jumped out of her skin. "Ye told me, Colton…you promised me…"

"That was ye! Ye're me own sister. As for this waste of flesh…." He glared at Liam over the woman's shoulder. "He killed our cousin. He's as good as dead."

"I'll deal to him, lad." Duncan stepped forward and hefted his saber from the side. The woman couldn't block Duncan and Colton at the same time, but she still didn't balk.

"NO!" Edeena screamed. She jostled the woman from behind and Edeena flung herself between Duncan and Liam. "Don't harm him, Duncan! He's me own mate!"

"Not for long!" Duncan crossed his arm over his chest, seized a fistful of Edeena's dress, and started to drag her out of the way.

She screamed again and Duncan gave her a brutal push. He almost knocked her off her feet.

The woman stood like a rock through the whole procedure. Her unbending stare was really starting to unnerve Colton. He couldn't hack her to pieces—not for all the gold in the mountains—and he couldn't hack Liam to pieces with her watching. Something in her eyes wouldn't let him.

Duncan raised his saber on high and brought it down with brutal ferocity to cleave Liam to death. Liam cringed under his arms from the blow that would end his life.

Colton didn't know what came over him. He thrust his saber past the woman's head. His blade sliced off a lock of her hair, but she still didn't shrink. The blade passed her ear and Duncan's saber smashed down on Colton's weapon.

Duncan froze, but Colton was already pulling his weapon back. "Throw them both in the vault. We'll question them later. Come along."

He sheathed his blade and snatched the woman's elbow. He yanked her away and his brothers attacked Liam from both sides. Colton was right about him. He was a limp dishrag with no combat training or backbone at all.

Colton became aware of a strange tingling sensation running up his arm where he gripped the woman's arm. He should hate her, but he could only stand in awe of the way she conducted herself in the courtyard. Who was she?

He didn't even know her name, but he'd seen no one like her in his life. Not even the women of Clan Buchanan were as tough and determined.

He should have treated her more roughly, but she didn't fight him. She never protested once that he was about to lock her up in the fortress cellar under lock and key until he could interrogate her as a Creighton spy.

Edeena went ballistic and tried to fight Reid and Duncan to get them to release Liam. Her shrieks and curses echoed off the courtyard walls as she screamed at her brothers to let Liam go.

Colton blocked her voice out of his ears. She would say and do anything to defend her mate. She couldn't help it even if he was a rake and a criminal. Colton only regretted that he didn't have the nerve to skewer the bastard on sight, but he couldn't do that with this woman around.

He didn't even really care that Edeena was making such a scene in front of the whole Clan. Colton would handle this another way.

He paused at the great door leading from the passageway into the stairs. The woman stopped there and stood calmly while he looked back over his shoulder.

Edeena punched and kicked and pummeled first Reid and then Duncan trying to drive them away from Liam. What a moppet Liam turned out to be. He let his woman do his fighting for him. He didn't even try to break free on his own account. That told Colton all he needed to know about the scum that forced a mate-bonding spell on her.

He started to turn back to the door and caught the woman regarding him with her piercing black eyes. "Do you really have to interrogate us?" she asked in her low, steady undertone. "I'll tell you everything I know if you just ask. We don't have any secrets to keep from you."

She had a strange way of speaking exactly like Edeena said. He could see she was from another country, and from the way she was dressed, he wouldn't be surprised if she was from another time, too.

He'd seen her come through the portal with his own eyes, hadn't he? He had no reason to doubt Edeena's story, but this wasn't Liam's sister. This was a different woman.

He tried to shrug her comments away. "We have our own laws to follow. Any trespasser on our land earns a death sentence. I'm already making an exception for ye, so dinnae try yer luck."

The slightest twitch tugged the corner of her lip, but she stopped herself from smiling at him. Her eyes told him that she understood. She was far from stupid and she was reasonable enough that he didn't take hold of her elbow when he opened the door.

More commotion echoed from the courtyard. Colton turned back a second time and saw Liam shooting spells and incantations at a bunch of Highlanders who arrived to help Reid and Duncan subdue him.

Colton started to turn back when his cousin Connell strode into view. He approached the fight from one side and cast a spell of his own. Sparkling white light flowed from his fingertips, surrounded Liam's body, and pinned his arms and legs to his sides.

Reid, Duncan, and the others moved in. They picked Liam up and carried him into the passage. He couldn't move no matter how hard he struggled. Connell followed them holding Liam bound by magic.

Colton led the strange woman downstairs like she might be a guest or even a friend. He couldn't explain why, but he trusted her not to fight him or try to escape.

By the time he entered the Icemeet vault several stories below the fortress, he was seriously starting to question whether he should lock her up at all. He halted in front of the barred cells and changed his mind when Reid and Duncan burst with Liam.

Edeena shrieked and raged at them. She kept swinging her fists and landed a cruel punch on the side of Reid's head. "Let him go, Reid!" she shrieked. "Let him go! He's me mate!"

He ducked under the blow and then roared in fury when her fist struck his eyebrow. He straight-armed her out of the way and sent her wheeling into the wall. "Be done with ye! Lay yer hands on me again and I'll thrash ye into oblivion, ye daft cow!"

The woman turned around to watch, but not even that seemed to surprise or alarm her. Neither did she act unnerved by Connell using magic to subdue Liam.

Colton stepped in front of his brothers and unlocked the first cell. He held the bars aside while Reid and Duncan hauled Liam inside.

They flung him down hard on the wooden bench and immediately retreated. Colton slammed the bars shut and turned the key.

Connel's magic evaporated and Liam shot to his feet. "You'll regret this! You can't stop me from getting back to Kald and searching for my sister."

He approached the bars, but he didn't grab hold of them and try to shake his way out like some prisoners would. He stood back, put his hands together, and started to summon his magic again.

Connell reacted instantly, moved his arms in complicated patterns, and muttered incantations. A gauzy film of yellow sparks rippled down the bars of Liam's cell. He charged the bars, but a powerful discharge of golden energy erupted from them and flung him back.

He collapsed on the bench and started shooting spell after spell at the bars, but Connell countered everything and the magic held firm. Liam couldn't escape.

Colton and his brothers watched until Liam finally gave it up and folded on the bench. The three brothers stood by and made sure he didn't try anything again before Colton went over to the other cell.

He didn't like to look the woman in the eye, but after he unlocked the bars and opened the door for her, he had no choice but to face her.

He nodded inside. "In ye go, lassie. We'll question ye as I said and then we'll see what's what."

"You can't go along with this, Snowflake!" Liam yelled. "You can't let them lock us up like this."

She glanced over at him and then looked back at Colton. She measured him with unflinching intent and then stepped across the threshold to enter the cell.

She turned around and held his gaze while he shut the bars and locked them, but he couldn't slam them in her face. He respected her too much.

What kind of a name was Snowflake? It couldn't be her real name, but now wasn't the time or place to ask.

Connell extended his magical protection across Snowflake's cell, too, but Colton could already see that she was no enchantress. She wasn't even interested in escaping.

Colton thanked Connell and sent him back upstairs. Colton, Reid, and Duncan retreated to the stairs, but Colton couldn't help casting a backward glance into the vault before he left.

"Those two are trouble," Duncan growled in Colton's ear. "Ye should have let me cleave the bastard to the gizzard when I had me chance."

"Aye," Reid added. "The longer he stays, the stronger the mating bond will become. We should rid Edeena of him now. Then she'll be free to mate with one of our own kind."

"We'll find out what he kens first," Colton replied, "and as for her...."

His gaze lingered on Snowflake. She hadn't taken her eyes off him since he walked away.

He let the words trail off. He wasn't sure if she would turn out to be his enemy after all or if he would regret not killing her on sight, too.

He did know that his brothers were right about both of these strangers. They were trouble. Whatever ill wind this woman brought with her into his land, he could never go back to the way things were before. She changed everything when she passed through the time portal. Now she was here, for better or for worse.

Chapter 3

S nowflake stayed alert until the vault door closed with the three Highlanders on the other side of it. Only then did she allow herself to turn away, sigh, and start to relax the tension in her neck and shoulders.

"That was really stupid, Snowflake," Liam snarled from the next cell. "You're supposed to be this big war hero. You didn't even fight back. I'm disappointed and that's putting it mildly. I thought you had more backbone."

She ignored him, crossed the cell, and sat down on the wooden bench. Even then, she couldn't bring herself to completely let her guard down. She sat straight up scanning the vault even though there was no one here.

She had to stay on her toes. Those three men.... They were unlike anyone she'd ever met and not because they were all kilted Highlanders with enough muscle each to break a grown man in half.

Liam told her and the rest of the Last Division that his time travel device would bring them to Highland Scotland three hundred years in the past. That part didn't surprise her. She expected to enter a world where men wore kilts and had strange attitudes about women.

None of that prepared her to meet the Buchanan Clan. Liam's device obviously malfunctioned and carried him and Snowflake to the wrong place. Her shock had nothing to do with the time period or their clothes or any of that.

These men were fierce, battle-hardened, shrewd, ruthless, and determined in ways she'd never encountered before. Not even the Afghans she dealt with during the war came anywhere close.

Reid and Duncan looked like a cross between wild animals and ferocious men born for combat. Their bodies showed all the signs of being forged in hardship. None of the three brothers carried a scrap of fat anywhere. Their muscularity revealed none of the soft, sculpted refinement of having been honed in a gym.

Whoever these men were, they had earned every ounce of their strength under the harshest conditions. All three carried the scars of decades of combat. Saber cuts and gashes crossed their chests, arms, and even their faces.

And then there was Colton. His immaculate kilt, sporran, and jacket hid his body from prying eyes, but she never doubted for an instant that he was as hardened and tough as his brothers—probably more so.

His determination when he aimed his saber at her told her loud and clear that he knew exactly how to use it. He didn't earn his place as acting Clan Chief by being soft. Both his brothers obeyed him instantly, even when he contradicted them by sparing Liam's life.

She struggled to organize her impressions of the last few minutes. She had to control herself and her reactions to this situation, especially to Colton.

She spent years in the military. She never once betrayed the chain of command—not outwardly—but in all her time in the army, she never met anyone she respected and wanted to obey as much as Colton Buchanan.

He was a true authority. He didn't need the chain of command to make people do what he wanted. He could treat everyone as an equal and they naturally followed him because of his unshakable sense of power. It came from his innermost being.

Snowflake became an officer and took charge of the Last Division because, in her secret heart of hearts, she didn't believe anyone else was qualified to lead. She thought she was better qualified to lead even than her own superior officers, but she never told anyone that. She never dared to say those words out loud.

Now she met someone who was far more qualified than she was. She wanted Colton to lead her and tell her what to do. She wanted to obey his commands and believe in him, but she couldn't do that. He threatened to kill her and Liam. That made him her enemy. Didn't it?

Liam's voice cut in on her thoughts. "Are you listening to me, Snowflake?"

She woke up from her trance and glanced over at him, but only for a second. She faced the front, which brought her back in line to look at the door where Colton vanished. When would she see him again? Would he be the one to interrogate her?

"Aren't you even going to talk to me?" Liam demanded. "I'm starting to really regret bringing you here."

"You didn't even mean to bring me here. Lily isn't here." She shot him another pointed look until he turned away. "You better tell me everything you know about these people,

Liam. You've already seriously compromised this mission by keeping vital information from me."

He sighed and collapsed back on his bench. "Fine. The Creightons and the Buchanans have been at war for centuries. No one can even remember why. Like I told you outside, the city of Kald is the Creightons' stronghold and the big castle is Tyrekirk. The river between them is the Boundless. It's the boundary between Creighton territory and Buchanan territory. It's the red line no one can cross without inciting a war."

"So you lied about that, too. You said you would take Lily and me to Scotland, but there is no river Boundless in Scotland and this war never happened in Scottish history. Where did you bring us? Where did you bring us really?"

Liam didn't answer. He refused even to look at her.

"That's not all," she prompted. "You said Lily was in a battle against dragons and now...."

Her gaze migrated back to the door as the penny dropped. Something about the Buchanans struck her as animalistic and wild. Not even Colton's spotless clothes and neatly trimmed hair could hide it. In fact, he seemed the most wild and animalistic of them all. He was even wilder than the armed guards outside.

That wildness came from somewhere deep inside him. It radiated from his very pores and she shivered in spite of herself.

"The Royal House of Creighton are the only dragons around here," Liam went on. "The rest of the Clan is just regular people like you and me."

She turned around one more time and fixed him with her most penetrating glare. She was getting mightily sick and tired of his games. "What about the Buchanans? You aren't telling me everything you know about them."

He only held her gaze for a minute before he turned away. "They're Highland tigers."

"What?" Snowflake asked.

"Highland tigers," he repeated more loudly this time. "They're shifters. They can change into Highland tigers. They're bigger than normal cats—maybe about as big as a medium-sized dog—and they're ferocious. Don't ever get into a fight against one of them. Trust me."

She bit back the next words and didn't tell him that she didn't see herself ever trusting him again—ever.

So that explained this feeling she got from all the Buchanans, but especially from Colton and his brothers. That wildness lurking beneath their skin—that primal ferocity threatening to break the surface at any moment—it was very, very real. She didn't imagine it.

"The difference is that they can all do it, not just the ruling family," Liam went on, "Edeena and her cousins came over to Kald when Lily and I were there. They attacked us and we fought them....and it wasn't pretty."

"But you killed their cousin," Snowflake pointed out. "So the Buchanans aren't completely invulnerable."

"Lily killed their cousin." He looked away again. "I used magic to stop Edeena from killing us both and you can see what good that did."

"So you're stuck with her for life?"

He nodded. "The Highland tigers mate for life. Once they bond, the bond can't be broken unless one of them dies....and I'm not even sure if that will work."

"Well, you got yourself in a mess. Now her brothers want to kill you to free her from the bond."

"Don't remind me," he growled. "That has to be the reason she pushed me through the portal and sent me back to the States. She was trying to get rid of me, but that obviously didn't work, either. We're still bonded."

"So what's the deal with Lady Rhona Armstrong—the woman we came here to protect?" Snowflake asked.

Liam shrugged, swiveled around, and stretched out on the bench. "I have no idea. We talked to quite a few people close to the Royal House of Creighton and they all insisted that Lady Rhona doesn't exist. Lily...." He sighed heavily. "Anyway, the only lady we could find out about was Lady Ilisa. Edeena and her cousin went over to Kald to find her. They say Lady Ilisa is a Buchanan and she was married to the Buchanan's Clan Chief—Neill Buchanan. The Creightons kidnapped her and we found out she was being held in the castle pending execution. We thought she must be Lady Rhona so we tried to get inside and save her....and that's when everything went south and the wizards attacked us."

Snowflake finally leaned her back and head against the wall behind her. This mystery just kept getting deeper and deeper, but one thing was certain to her now. She wasn't on Earth anymore—or not the Earth she knew. Liam had taken her somewhere else—another reality, maybe. She would probably never know for certain because he would never tell her the truth—about anything. She wouldn't be able to trust him—ever again.

Snowflake would give anything to know what happened to Lily. Was she even still alive in Kald? Had she been killed by wizards or burned alive by dragons?

Maybe if Snowflake could catch up with her, Lily would have found out something more about Lady Rhona. Snowflake could only hope.

Liam didn't offer any further information. He kept his eyes shut. Maybe he was going to sleep. At least Snowflake knew enough now to explain herself to the Buchanans.

Her mind flashed back to Colton. She really hoped he would be the one to question her. She would be able to tell him the truth and make him understand that she wasn't a threat to his Clan.

Liam was a different story. Colton and his brothers would probably never stop hating Liam as long as he was still alive and mate-bonded to their sister.

Maybe Snowflake's best strategy was to distance herself from Liam. She could make Colton understand that she had nothing to do with the events in Kald that led to Liam and Edeena becoming mate-bonded. Colton would listen. He would understand. She would make him understand.

She looked down at the bench. She should probably lie down and try to sleep, too, but she couldn't stop her mind from racing. She'd gone behind enemy lines before, but this was unlike any mission she ever trained for. It was a game of wits against.... That was the problem. She didn't even know for certain who her enemy was.

The moment she thought that, she knew the Buchanans weren't her enemies. She didn't know who the enemy was, but it wasn't them.

Chapter 4

Colton knocked on Edeena's bedroom door. She yanked it open and scowled at him. "What do ye want?"

"I'm still yer Clan Chief and I'll make me presence kenned when and where I please, lass." He took one instant to make sure she was suitably dressed before he marched into the room. "I want to speak ye about those newcomers. We can do it here like brother and sister or ye can come down to me office and be questioned like a common criminal. The choice is yers."

She scowled at him when he took a stand next to her dresser and faced her. She finally swung the door shut and squared her shoulders. "Very well. Say what ye came to say."

"It isnae me that'll be saying ought, lassie. I want to ken all ye ken about those two."

"I told ye that before. Liam Barnett...."

"I ken all about that. I want to ken the rest."

"What rest is there?"

"Why did they come back through time in the first place?"

"I told ye that as well. They're searching for some Lady Rhona Armstrong that's related to their leader or some such. They say Lady Rhona is in danger from a dark wizard that traveled back in time before them. They say this wizard wants to kill Lady Rhona and change the course of time."

"What else?" Colton insisted.

"That's all there is. Liam and his sister Lily got themselves saddled with two soldiers of the House of Creighton..."

"Which ones?" Colton demanded.

"What difference does it make which ones? They were naught but common soldiers."

"Just tell me the truth, lassie. I'll be the one to decide if it makes any difference."

"Ye're taking this whole Clan Chief business too far, Colton." She sat down on the bed and bounced the mattress.

"There is no such thing as taking it too far. When the fate of the whole Clan rests on yer shoulders, ye can run it the way ye please. In the meantime, ye'll answer me questions. Now who were these soldiers?"

"Their names were Grant and Elliot Ritchie if ye must ken. They were tasked with guarding Prince Ness and a fine to-do they made of that."

"So what happened?"

"I told ye. The wizards killed Ness, I pushed Liam through the portal...."

"And then?"

"Then I fled back across the Boundless and came home. That's all."

Colton pierced his sister with a hard glare. "Ye're lying, lass. I ken ye too well. Now tell the truth or ye'll be down in the vault with the other two."

She looked away and crossed her arms over her chest. "Leave me alone, Colton."

"That's the last thing I'll do." He stalked over to her and towered over her. "This is yer last chance. What happened after the wizards killed Ness?"

She gulped and finally looked down at her hands in her lap. "Grant Ritchie.... turned into a dragon—a big, black brute of a thing. I havenae seen a dragon so big. He defended Lily....and then he flattened the wizards. He tried to save Ness, but it was too late. His brother abandoned him and Grant went off with Lily. That's all I saw before I ran for it."

Colton frowned at her. "Are ye saying one of these common foot soldiers was.... a Creighton?"

"Aye...and I'll wager all I have he didnae ken it beforehand. His brother wouldnae even look at him and.... I swear the lad nearly broke down when he realized what he'd become.... or what he was. I dinnae understand it, Colton. I swear."

"All right, lass. I'm going down to question these strangers meself. I'll thank ye to keep away from Liam until we decide what to do with him."

He headed for the door and Edeena jumped up to rush after him. "Ye cannae keep him locked up, Colton. He's me mate one way or the other. Ye'll have to accept him into the Clan."

He rounded on her snarling through bared teeth. "Accept him into the Clan is what we winnae ever do, lassie. Ye get that in yer head for good and all. If ye insist on staying mated to him rather than watching me and the lads carve his head off, ye'll go out with him and make yer own way. We winnae ever accepted him—no, never."

He watched the words sink into her head. Maybe now she would understand the gravity of the situation and stop blowing her mouth off about Liam.

"Liam will stay a prisoner as long as he's in this fortress. If we deem he's no threat to our Clan, he can go out and ye with him. That's the best ye can hope for."

Colton walked out of the room and shut the door in his sister's stunned face. He was all finished taking it easy on her. She was the one who staggered in crying about how Liam did her wrong. Now she was defending him and saying he had to be accepted into the Clan.

Liam would be accepted into the Clan over Colton's dead body. Colton felt pretty certain Reid and Duncan felt the same way, which meant the rest of their Clansmen would have no problem standing against Liam, too.

Who the hell did Liam Barnett think he was, mating with Edeena and then thinking he could just discard her? No man could get away with that and now Liam had the nerve to set foot on Buchanan land. He deserved to die on both counts.

Colton went back to his office and organized the piles of papers waiting for his attention. Acting as Clan Chief in his father's place was becoming a tiresome chore, but someone had to do it. He would much prefer to run around on the mountain scouting Icemeet's perimeter and preparing for the next war.

He was just getting ready to read a letter from another branch of the Clan living deeper in the mountains when he heard footsteps coming down the corridor outside.

The footsteps halted at his door and then it opened inward to reveal that woman—Snowflake. Colton couldn't think of her as that. That name didn't do her justice.

His cousins Fergus and Alastair flanked her and Colton was relieved to see that they held themselves tense and alert around her. Fergus kept shooting her sidelong glances like he might be readying himself for a fight.

She didn't exactly relax, either. She didn't glance around nor did she stiffen completely, but her bright, snapping eyes told Colton in no uncertain terms that she was ready, too.

He strode over to the door and pulled it completely open. "Come in, lassie. Ye lads can go. I'll take it from here."

Fergus jolted. "Are ye sure ye dinnae want us to hang about? It's no trouble...."

"No," Colton told him. "Get back to the parapet and man yer posts. On ye go, laddie." He waved to Snowflake. "Come in, lassie. There's no sense hanging about in doorways."

Snowflake stepped across the threshold, but Fergus and Alastair didn't budge until Colton swung the door shut in their faces.

She looked over her shoulder toward the door. "Are you sure you don't want to keep them around in case I try to kill you or something?"

Colton laughed in spite of himself. "If ye want to kill me, lass, ye'd best be ready for me to fight back. I dinnae like yer chances even with them gone." He strode over to his desk. "Take a seat. I dinnae fancy a lady fainting under interrogation on me watch."

Now it was her turn to laugh, though she tried to bite it back and failed. He returned to his own chair and faced her across his desk. She looked incredibly appealing when she smiled and her cheeks colored. She was a strikingly beautiful woman underneath that iron exterior.

She didn't let her guard down and she didn't sit. She stayed standing over by the door, but not because she wanted to flee. She eyed him from a distance and he realized with another pang that she was sizing him up. She was measuring him in case they really did end up getting into a deadly fight in his office.

His insides clenched as the truth sank in. She resisted his efforts to put her at ease, but at least she didn't start off hostile. Maybe he still stood a chance to keep this amicable.

He pulled out his own chair and forced himself to sit down under her unflinching gaze. "I understand from questioning Edeena that ye had naught to do with me cousin Farlan's death in Kald. I ken ye werenae in the country at the time and it was yer friend that killed him."

"Does it matter who killed him? *I* understand from questioning Liam that it was your cousin who attacked Lily first. He tried to kill her. If she won and killed him defending herself, then you have no reason to seek revenge."

Colton allowed his eyes to drop to his hands folded on the desk. Even as much as he respected this woman, he realized in that moment that he underestimated her. He was going to have to watch his step here.

"I saw ye come through the time portal with me own eyes, so I have no reason to doubt that part of yer story," he went on. "I also understand that ye and yer friend came back in time to search for Lady Rhona Armstrong.... whoever that is."

"Then you know that Liam and I never intended to come to your territory at all," she replied. "You don't have to impose a death sentence on us for trespassing when coming here was totally unintentional."

"I never intended to impose a death sentence on ye, lass." He waved to the chair across from him. "Will ye kindly sit down? We can discuss this in a civilized manner without shooting accusations back and forth across the room."

She hesitated and studied him for a moment longer. Then she shook her long black hair out of her eyes, walked over to the chair, and sat down. "All right. Discuss away."

He had to bite the inside of his cheek to stop himself from grinning. She really was a rare specimen. "As ye ken already, me name is Colton Buchanan."

"Acting Clan Chief of Clan Buchanan," Snowflake finished. "Edeena said so."

"Now ye tell me yer name so we can be properly acquainted."

"My name is Snowflake," she replied, "but you already knew that. You heard Liam call me by my name downstairs."

"That isnae yer real name, though, is it?" He stood up and paced over to the window. "Tell me yer real name."

"I don't think so. That's classified."

He frowned at her. "What does that word mean?"

"It means it's a military secret. No one knows outside my closest comrades. I can't tell you."

He spread both hands before her. "I'm trying to make this easy on us both, lassie. I have no desire to keep yer locked in the vault...."

"And yet you *have* kept me locked in the vault," she countered. "You aren't trying very hard to let me out of it. You only brought me here to wring me for information which I already told you I would give you willingly."

"I brought ye here to ensure that ye dinnae pose any threat to me Clan and our interests. This country is crawling with our enemies and ye show up here with a man we've all sworn to kill. If ye cannae see I'm trying to trust ye and smooth the way to releasing ye, then ye're not the woman I take ye for."

She didn't answer and he saw her holding her breath. She wanted to shoot back, but she stopped herself.

He took a chance and pressed his advantage. "How can I trust that ye arenae me enemy when ye winnae tell me the simplest information about yerself? Ye ken all there is to ken about me...."

"Not all. You didn't tell me you were a Highland tiger shifter. I had to find that out from Liam."

He stiffened involuntarily and then let his shoulders slumped. "I would have told ye if it came to that."

"Came to what—a fight? I'm sure there's plenty you haven't told me about yourself.... just like there's plenty you don't know about me. Finding out my name won't tell you that."

He let out a shaky sigh. He wasn't used to people standing up to him like this. She dissected his arguments so effortlessly.

He returned to his chair, sat down, and folded his hands in front of her again. "All right, then, lassie. What would ye like to ken that ye dinnae ken already? Ye ken I'm a tiger. Would ye like to see me shift? Is that it?"

Her eyes popped. "What—now—right here?"

"Is that what ye want? Will that convince ye that I dinnae have any secrets from ye?"

She shut her mouth with a click. "That won't be necessary."

"Ye ken me brothers are Reid and Duncan," he went on. "Me father Neill is Clan Chief, but he leaves the running of the Clan to me. Is there ought else ye want to ken about me or me Clan? I'll tell ye. I have no secrets from ye, though it pains me to see that, despite yer assurance yesterday, ye do in fact have secrets from me."

She looked away. That was the very first time she ever broke eye contact with him since he first saw her outside the gate. "All right. I'll tell you my name, but only if you promise never to tell anyone, not even Liam."

Now it was his turn to raise his eyebrows. "Liam doesnae ken yer real name?"

She shook her head. "He better not or I'll kick his ass myself."

"Och!" he breathed. "I didnae ken."

"You didn't know what?"

"I didnae ken ye kept such information from him. I supposed ye two were thick as thieves."

She snorted. "Lily is my friend. Liam is her brother and he's lied to us a dozen times since this whole thing started. Lily is the only reason I'm here and that's the God's honest truth. I wouldn't be here at all if I wasn't worried about her and I didn't have a mission to fulfill."

"All right, lassie." He leaned back in his chair and rested his arms on either side. He was starting to feel even more hopeful about her. "I give ye me word of honor as a Highlander, as a Buchanan, and as a man that I winnae ever tell a living soul yer real name.... assuming ye see fit to grace me with the information."

The faintest hint of a smile tugged at her lips and her eyes sparkled. Her cheeks flushed. That wash of color completely erased the hard, impenetrable reserve that made her seem so intimidating. "My name is Jaimee Abernathy."

He got to his feet and paced back to the window thinking fast. "Jaimee. That's a man's name."

"Where I come from, it can be a name for a man or a woman."

"Abernathy is a Scottish name."

"I don't know about that, but that's my name. Just don't tell anyone."

He turned around and experienced a surge of...was it excitement? A sudden wave of delight and happiness gripped him when he set his eyes on her face even though it had only been a few seconds since he saw her last.

"Why dinnae ye want anyone to ken yer name? Ye have a charming name. Why do ye go about calling yerself a common name like 'Snowflake' instead?"

She didn't blush or look away. Her dark eyes locked on him. "That is also classified.... but if you really want to know, I was in the army. Snowflake is my codename."

He frowned at her—not that he doubted her. He'd never heard of a woman outside Clan Buchanan belonging to any army, but she certainly looked strong enough and determined enough.

When he didn't answer right away, she lowered her eyes to her hands in her lap. Her expression softened in ways he hadn't seen in her yet. She was right. He knew nothing about her.

"My comrades and I were in a war," she murmured in a broken undertone. "We lost a lot of good people until there were only five of us left. We retired from society and dedicated our lives to helping the poor. I...." She threw back her head and looked him square in the eye again. "Lily was one of the five that survived. That's why I have to find her."

It took all Colton's strength to turn his back on her to look out the window. He gazed across the Boundless. The dragons were still circling Tyrekirk.

Colton hardly saw them. He couldn't stop seeing her sitting like that, bowed and changed, while she told her story.

He knew enough about people to know she was telling the truth. She had been in combat and lost the people closest to her. It changed her. No wonder she was so powerful and sturdy despite her hidden pain.

"Anyway," she went on, "we withdrew from the world and from our families. War took its toll on us and we didn't want to fight anymore.... until we got called up for this mission. At first, Liam said it would only be Lily coming back in time and then she disappeared. That's the only reason I'm here—to find her."

He couldn't turn around, much as he wanted to. Her words stung him in ways he never expected. She woke something buried in his heart that he never felt before—something excruciating.

"Aren't you going to say anything?" she asked after a long silence. "I've told you everything."

"I dinnae ken what to say, lassie." He could barely make his throat work. "I feel the same way as ye."

"What way?"

"About the war," he replied over his shoulder. "I cannae hardly bear to carry it on after so many of me Clansmen have died before me eyes. I would gladly give it up and retire from life, but I dinnae have any chance of that. The whole Clan is depending on me and I'll certainly take over as Clan Chief after me father dies."

"My God!" she gasped. "That's awful!"

He tried to shrug it off. "It's me fate so there winnae be any withdrawal for me." He forced himself to turn around and meet her gaze. "I'm grateful for yer confidence. I dinnae need to keep ye locked in the vault any longer, but I must make a good show for Reid and Duncan. I will release ye, but I cannae do it straight away. Be patient a while and I'll do it shortly."

She squared her shoulders and confronted him with all her former reserve back in place. The vulnerability she showed him a moment before vanished as though it was never there. "What did you do with Liam? You took him away. Is he being questioned somewhere else?"

"Aye. Did ye think ye were the only one? Did ye think we'd question ye and not him?"

She raised her eyebrows again. "We? Which one of your brothers is questioning him? Are they torturing him or something?"

"I cannae speak to what Reid is doing with Liam. I suspect Reid winnae be so soft on Liam as I've been on ye." She burst out laughing and a lick of fire went through Colton's guts. "Is that funny, lassie?"

"Let's just say I was soft on you, too."

His heart skipped a beat when her eyes twinkled at him. She was blushing again.

He walked around his desk struggling to keep his composure around her. He motioned to the door. "I'll do me best to make yer stay here as comfortable as possible. Just remember what I saw and be patient. There are larger forces at work and another battle brewing as we speak. I must tend to that first and foremost."

"Why can't you just let me go? I'll leave your territory and cross over to Kald to look for Lily. Then I'd be out of your hair completely."

"I cannae do that, lassie. I cannae let anyone crosse the Boundless with the war heating up. I'm sorry, but it's impossible."

He opened the door, and to his relief, he discovered Fergus and Alastair standing guard in the corridor outside.

She took one look at the two guards and then turned back to face Colton, but her eyes betrayed the slightest hint of something like pain or maybe hope. She questioned him with her eyes. Was he really sending her back to the vault as a prisoner?

He couldn't break the hold of her eyes on him. If she resisted going back to the vault, he didn't trust himself to insist.

Fortunately, Fergus stepped over to the threshold just then. His saber hilt clinked against his leg and the sound distracted Snowflake.

Jaimee. Her name was Jaimee. The name gave him another unaccountable thrill. He knew her real name and it seemed to give him some power he didn't have before. She let him know her true nature along with that name. She no longer hid behind a nickname.

The name meant more than that, though. Colton was the only person who knew it. Not even Liam knew it. It was a secret between Colton and her.

Jaimee. Everything about her flooded him with so much hope and excitement. He hadn't felt this way in years. In fact, he couldn't remember feeling this way ever.

He had to find a way to get her out of the vault. She didn't belong there.

Chapter 5

The two guards flanked Jaimee on the way back to her cell. Liam still wasn't back. The taller guard shot her one of his sidelong glances. He'd been acting fidgety around her since she first showed up here, but neither he nor the other guy threatened her

The shorter one had sandy blonde hair while the taller one had dark hair all over him. It covered his arms and legs in a thick, dark mat.

The shorter one just stood there in a relaxed posture while the taller one unlocked her cell. Besides the fact that they were about to lock her in a basement dungeon, neither of these guys treated her like a prisoner anymore. Did they overhear Colton promise to let her out?

She stepped into the cell and the taller guard locked her in. His dark eyes met hers for a fleeting instant and then he looked away. She recognized that apologetic expression. He didn't like this any better than Colton did. Now she was certain these two men had been eavesdropping on her so-called interrogation with Colton.

She sat down on the bench and let her eyes drift out of focus until the two guards left her alone. They didn't post anyone to stand outside her cell. They must really be lowering their security measures. They wouldn't do that without their acting Clan Chief's approval. Colton must have told them to take it easy on her.

Her conversation with Colton brought up more questions than it answered, but not because of anything he said about the situation between the Creightons and the Buchanans. Colton didn't tell her anything Liam hadn't already told her.

So things were heating up between the rival Clans again. Jaimee would get caught in the middle of another war even if Colton let her go to Kald. She couldn't escape it.

The middle of another war was the last place she wanted to be, but that didn't bother her as much as her meeting with Colton.

He admitted so lightly that he was a tiger—a Highland tiger. She could believe it, now that she'd been so close to him for such a long interview. He was a tiger in more ways than one.

That sense of wild, untamed ferocity blasted out of every inch of him. She wouldn't like to face him on the wrong side of a fight and not because he was so much bigger and stronger than she was.

Something explosive lurked under the surface of all these Buchanans. It must come out sometime and it could only come out in battle. The whole world better look out when it did.

Then there was his admission that he was worn out by fighting and loss the same way she was. Those words tore at her soul. He must really be suffering if he had to deal with all that with no possibility of reprieve.

He had to command his father's forces. He had to handle all the Clan's business and make all the decisions. He would become Clan Chief for real as soon as his father died.

She and her friends in the Last Division had been living in retirement for years. They had kept up their combat training in isolation, but they didn't have to face the enemy.

He had to fight every day and the people dying under his command were his own relatives. This must be so much worse for him than it ever was for the Last Division.

Her heart went out to him. If she could only find a way to help him, to lighten his load, she would jump at the chance. She didn't know much if anything about this war, but he needed someone to help him.

He had his brothers, but he needed more. He needed all the help he could get to carry this burden. One man couldn't do it alone. No one should have to go through what he'd been suffering.

She didn't even mind now that he knew her real name. Telling him broke the seal on a part of her being that had been in hibernation for years. The part of herself that she tried to bury in the past came to life again.

She wasn't Snowflake anymore, even though everyone would keep calling her that. Only he would call her by her real name, but one man made all the difference. She was Jaimee now. She couldn't go back to being Snowflake—Snowflake the soldier, Snowflake the machine, Snowflake the untouchable.

Jaimee was someone softer, someone touchable, someone who could feel something. That part of herself would always belong to him as long as he was the only person alive in possession of that name.

She startled to high alert when a door slammed open somewhere. The two guards returned and then Reid and Duncan came in with Liam and the young wizard who enchanted Liam's cell.

At least ten guards surrounded Liam even though the wizard's magic held him immobile. Jaimee saw right away that Reid did not treat Liam softly at all. His hair was a mess and he had a black eye.

He struggled, jerked his body back and forth, and cursed his captors, but he couldn't move his arms or legs. The magic bound him and he floated four feet off the floor.

The wizard followed behind Liam with sparkling silver filaments flowing from his fingertips. They surrounded Liam in a cocoon of gossamer sparks.

Reid and Duncan stood off to one side while the guards unlocked Liam's cell. Then the wizard floated Liam inside, laid him on the bench, and the guards locked him in.

They went through the whole procedure and the wizard held Liam immobile with magical filaments until he reestablished the enchantment on the bars.

The instant the wizard released him, Liam sprang to his feet, flung his arms toward the bars, and unleashed a crushing bombardment on the magical field. Liam hurled concussions, blasts, and even lightning from his hands.

His assault slammed the bars and the wizard's spells boomed and thumped under Liam's attack, but the field didn't give in the slightest.

The wizard reacted just as fast. He conjured more filaments that snaked between the bars, wrapped around Liam, and smacked him hard against the back wall.

Liam flopped onto the bench and groaned. He tried to stand again, collapsed on his knees on the floor, and bared his teeth at the Buchanans outside, but he didn't get up again.

"Stay down, lad," Reid growled at him. "Connell has more important business than to stand guard over ye day and night. If ye dinnae stay down, I'll tell him to stand here and hit ye again as many times as it takes. Do yerself and him a favor and hold yer wheesht for once."

Liam glared at them and his breath hissed when he panted through his teeth. Connell must have helped Reid and Duncan question Liam. Now he knew better than to attack again with Connell standing there.

Jaimee watched the whole exchange from her bench. She didn't get up to intervene—as if she could intervene.

The same two guards that brought her back from Colton's office stood with the other Clansmen watching Connell subdue Liam. Those two guards definitely changed their stance toward him. Colton never told them to take it easy on Liam. Colton probably told them to be as hard on Liam as possible and why shouldn't they? They hated Liam and wanted to get rid of him.

Reid and Liam faced each other down. Duncan strode over to Jaimee's cell and fixed her with a direct, challenging stare through the bars.

She read his expression as plain as day. He expected her to fight back the way Liam did, but when she didn't leave her seat, he walked off.

Reid took a second longer to break away and the rest of their Clansmen filed out a second later. The door banged shut and left the two prisoners alone.

Liam didn't relax until everyone else left. He finally heaved himself off the floor and keeled over on the bench. He hugged his ribs and groaned. "God Almighty! These assholes are the worst!"

Jaimee didn't say anything. She didn't want to ask what happened to him in Reid's custody. She could already imagine enough.

If she asked him, he would ask her and she didn't want to answer any questions about her interview with Colton. She held that experience close to her heart. She would never tell anyone what happened in his office. She couldn't explain it even to herself.

Liam raised his head and narrowed his eyes at her. "Have you been here the whole time? They didn't interrogate you, too, did they?" His eyes flicked over her face and body. "They couldn't have."

She still didn't say anything. She could make it easier on Liam by telling him about Colton's promises, but she didn't even tell him that she'd seen Colton or that she ever left this cell. Better to let him think she'd been here all the time and that the Buchanans only questioned Liam.

Why didn't she tell him? She never would have dreamed of keeping information from one of her comrades on a mission, especially a mission as sensitive as this one.

Liam had been keeping information from her and the Last Division from the beginning. He didn't tell Lily before she left Ironforge that she'd be facing dragons and Highland tigers and wizards and God only knew what else.

What else was he hiding from her? Was he withholding vital information that could make it possible to complete this mission?

He might be under orders from Washington to sacrifice the Last Division so he alone could fulfill the mission. He might be under orders to abandon the Last Division in the past so none of the five women could tell anyone what the government was up to.

She didn't like thinking that way about someone she was supposed to be on a mission with, but the evidence weighed against Liam. He hadn't been as forthcoming with her as he could have been or should have been. Why should she be forthcoming about something as personal as her interview with Colton?

Chapter 6

J aimee woke up in the middle of the night. She didn't know what woke her up, but once she found herself awake, she couldn't go back to sleep.

She tried to turn over on the bench, but she couldn't find a comfortable position. The hard boards dug into her hips and shoulders until her bones ached.

She sat up, rested her head against the wall behind her, and listened to Liam's long, slow, deep breathing. He was still asleep.

None of the Buchanans returned after Reid and Duncan brought Liam back. The two prisoners had been here alone for hours before they both fell asleep.

Colton's promise that he would free her from this dungeon kept Jaimee's spirits much lighter than they would have been without his promise. She kept kicking herself for not telling Liam, but she couldn't bring herself to say anything to him.

She didn't feel too bad about the way Reid and Duncan treated him. Jaimee couldn't blame them for trying to get some payback for Edeena's situation. Liam made his bed and now he had to lie in it.

It was also Liam's fault that both he and Jaimee had ended up in Buchanan country instead of in Kald where they were supposed to go. Whether the box malfunctioned or got damaged in the battle against the dragons, she could lay that one at Liam's door, too. He should have checked it before he transported himself and Jaimee to a strange land populated with deadly Highlanders.

She was just deciding to lie down again and try to drift off when a soft click snapped her eyes open. She strained to see in the darkness.

A single barred window high on the wall gave the faintest glimmer of light. Starlight gleamed on the floor and showed her the vault door swinging into the chamber.

A shadowy figure glided silently into the room and tiptoed toward the cells. Whoever it was wearing a dress.

"Liam!" Edeena whispered. "Wake up!"

He groaned in his sleep and started to roll over. He turned his back to her.

"Liam!" she hissed louder.

He shot off the bench in a flash and whipped around to stare at her. Jaimee froze to her seat. Did Edeena realize that Jaimee was sitting up listening to every word she said?

"What are you doing here?" Liam whispered back. "You shouldn't have come. You'll get into trouble with your brothers."

"Dinnae worry yerself about that. They arenae capable of harming me no matter what they say. They arenae more than pussy cats."

Liam snorted. "I think they're a little more than that."

"I can convince them to let ye out. Just give me time."

Liam heaved himself off the bench and slouched over to the bars. "First, let me try to break the mate-bonding spell. You wouldn't be helping me without that."

"What about this?" She tried to touch the bars and a rain of sparks showered down in front of her. Connel's enchantment stopped her from making contact with the bars.

"Your cousin only cares about stopping me from getting out of here. The spell might still make it through as long as he didn't specifically block that kind of magic."

He sat back on the floor and started rotating his hands in circles above and beneath each other. He moved his arms around like he was stirring something between his palms.

A glowing ball of light erupted between his hands. It got bigger and gave just enough light for Jaimee to see Edeena's face lit up with hope.

The ball floated out from between Liam's hands, drifted between the bars, and surrounded Edeena. Liam kept swirling his hands around and whispering incantations under his breath.

The ball wrapped around Edeena illuminating her all over. A magnificent smile split over her face and Jaimee had to marvel at how beautiful Edeena was. Jaimee had only seen Edeena distressed and violent before this moment.

All at once, Edeena gave an excruciating groan, clenched her teeth, and pitched over on her side. She lay there twitching and writhing in agony.

Liam shot out his hand to touch her, but the magical field snapped back and he yanked his hand away. "Edeena!" he hissed. "Edeena! Talk to me!"

She gave one more brutal spasm and collapsed on the floor with a pitiful sob. She flung her arm over her face. "It's no use!"

"I'm sorry!" he breathed. "I can't tell you how sorry I am. I would do anything to break the spell. I never would have done this to you if I had known it would go like this."

She hauled herself up sniffing. She wiped her face on her dress hem. "It's all over! Colton will drive ye out and me along with ye. That's the best we can hope for if Reid and Duncan dinnae kill ye first."

Liam snorted and looked away. "Maybe that would be for the best. Then you'd be free to mate with one of your own kind. They all say so."

"No!" She forgot to keep her voice down and glanced over her shoulder toward the door. How did she get rid of the guards so she could sneak in here? "Be patient. I may be able to find a way to release ye from the vault."

"How? Don't do anything to endanger your position here. Your place in your Clan is more important than getting me out of here."

She regarded him through the bars and then turned away. Was she crying in the darkness?

"Promise me," he whispered. "Promise you won't do anything to piss off your brothers.... especially Colton. If he agrees to let me leave Icemeet, I will, but you have to stay behind."

"No!" she exclaimed. "Me place is with ye."

"Your place is with your people. I couldn't be responsible for you returning to Kald or somewhere you'd be in danger. It would be better for you to stay here with your Clan than to leave with me."

"Dinnae say that!" she choked. "Would ye consign me to a life of misery without ye?"

He chuckled softly. "You hate me. You would have killed me a long time ago if the mate-bonding spell didn't stop you from doing it. You don't know what you're saying. Leaving your Clan to be with me would be a much more miserable life than staying here without me. At least here you have your family looking out for you. What do you think you're going to do—travel back to the future with me? I don't think so."

She sniffed again, but she didn't answer. Jaimee's skin crawled listening to this. She shouldn't be listening to these two have a lovers' whispered conversation, but Jaimee couldn't exactly leave the room.

"Go back upstairs," Liam whispered. "You're putting yourself in danger by coming down here. Don't come to visit me unless you have some definite way to break me and Snowflake out of Icemeet."

"I have to!" Edeena hissed. "I'm going out of me mind without ye! I cannae think on ought but being near ye."

He looked away.

"Say ye feel the same way about me," she breathed. "Tell me I'm not the only one. Tell me I'm not alone in this nightmare."

Her voice cracked at the last words, and when he eventually turned around and looked at her, he whispered so low that Jaimee couldn't hear him.

He whispered to Edeena for a minute and she finally nodded, got to her feet, and left the vault. She eased the door shut behind her.

Silence descended over the vault and Liam limped back to his bench. He sank down on it, let his shoulders slump, and heaved a broken sigh.

"Are you sure there's no way to break the mate-bonding spell?" Jaimee ventured.

He didn't jump or spin around. He didn't act at all surprised that she was awake and listening.

"The spell should have worn off by now," he muttered. "I might have already broken it back in Kald, but we're still bonded. It must be something in the tigers' nature. Once it's done, it can't be undone. I wish it could."

"You can't continue this. You ruined her life."

He shrugged and leaned back against the wall, but he didn't raise his head. He looked as dejected about this as Edeena did. "I've done all I can. I know it's bad. It's probably the biggest mistake I've ever made in my life. I would go back and do it differently if only to make it easier on her, but I can't. Whatever happens, we're stuck together as long as we're both still alive."

Chapter 7

Colton stepped into the vault and looked around. Liam wasn't in his cell. Reid and Duncan had taken him away—not to interrogate him again. The brothers had already satisfied themselves that Liam had told them everything he knew.

Connell had helped them squeeze as much information out of Liam as they could want and much more. He had told them everything about his world, his government, his past, and his relationship with his sister.

Liam had also told the brothers all about the Last Division under the influence of Connel's magic. Liam had confirmed everything Jaimee told Colton about being in the army, going behind enemy lines, and losing her entire division except for her four closest comrades.

Liam had confirmed how the five of them had been living in America serving the poor. They had continued their combat and weapons training while keeping constant surveillance on anyone who might draw them back into military service.

The brothers didn't need to question Liam anymore, but Colton asked Reid and Duncan to get Liam out of the way while he talked to Jaimee alone. He didn't want Liam around when he took her out of the vault for good.

She got to her feet when he came toward her door with his keys out. "Is this what you call a state visit?" she asked.

He had to laugh. Seeing her again made him ridiculously happy. He shouldn't feel this happy about seeing an alien and a potential enemy.

She wasn't his enemy, but she was an alien. She wasn't one of his own kind. She was.... well, she was what his people called common. The townsfolk over in Kald couldn't shift into anything.

The Buchanans considered them beneath notice, but he couldn't think of her that way. She fascinated him. He wanted to know everything about her—more than he already knew.

He opened the cell and jutted his chin at her. "Come on out, lassie. I want to talk to ye."

"I already told you everything I know."

"I ken ye did. I dinnae wish to talk to ye about all that."

"What do you want to talk about, then?"

He nodded toward the door. "Come upstairs. We can talk better there."

"We seem to be talking just fine now." She glanced right and left at Fergus and Alastair on her way out to the corridor. She acted surprised that the two men weren't coming along to guard her.

"Would ye like me to show ye around Icemeet?" He guided her to the stairs. "Ye havenae seen much of it."

"That's putting it mildly. I don't think you should do that until you're ready to let me out of prison."

He led her through the fortress with people going about their business everywhere. She took in everything with silent watchful eyes until he turned off into a gallery overlooking the courtyard.

"Ye can see all the way over the Boundless from here." He grimaced toward Tyrekirk. "They arenae flying their confounded lizards about any longer, but they're still there. Mark me words. They'll bring the foul things out against us before long."

She eyed him on the side. "What's this about? Don't tell me you brought me up here to talk about lizards."

He laughed again. Everything about her made him happy—a lot happier than a Clan Chief on his way to war had a right to be.

He leaned farther over the railing and nodded down into the courtyard. "Take a look at that and tell me what ye think."

She leaned over next to him and her satin black hair swept forward to frame her face. She really was beautiful as well as being strong, determined, and incredibly shrewd.

Forty men stood in a square down there. They wore their kilts belted around their waists and their tartans over their chests and shoulders, but they wore no other clothes—no socks, no shoes, no shirts, no jackets, and no weapons.

None of them showed any sign of being aware of the biting cold in the air or the snowflakes swirling in the brisk mountain wind. Snow lay thick on the peaks and in drifts on the parapet, but the men ignored the cold.

Most wore their hair tied back in ponytails behind their necks like Colton and his brothers. A few had let their hair come loose and those that still had it tied back had let it get disheveled and untidy.

They faced the center of the square and they all shouted, bellowed, whistled, and pumped their fists at two men wrestling, punching, and scrapping with each other in the middle. Both men were shirtless and barefooted like the rest.

The two combatants charged each other, closed, and started pounding each other in the ribs, backs, and heads with brutal punches. One of them hooked his arm out of his opponent's grasp and landed a crushing blow on his adversary's cheekbone.

In a flash, the target transformed into a large cat almost as big as a dog. Fur sprouted all over his body and the cat hissed and yowled to wake the dead. His hackles stood on end and his bushy striped tail fluffed up to a thick bottlebrush.

The other man changed just as fast, and in a split second, the two cats locked together in mortal combat. They kicked, clawed, and slashed each other with their fangs.

The men standing in the square went wild and their shouts of encouragement rang off the fortress walls. The cats' screeches and enraged shrieks rose above the noise as the two creatures tumbled over and over on the paving stones.

Tufts of fur flew and the cats bloodied each other something awful before one of them finally kicked the other off. The target cat pitched across the courtyard and struck one of the onlookers.

He pushed it back into the square, but when it faced off against its adversary for the second time, neither cat re-engaged. They regarded each other from a distance while the onlookers yelled at the cats and laughed and joked with each other.

The two cats transformed back into men without warning. They made a few remarks to each other that Colton couldn't hear from this distance. Then the two men strode toward each other, clasped their arms around each other, and burst out laughing as they embraced.

They returned to the square still talking and laughing like they hadn't just been trying to kill each other. The spectators absorbed both combatants, and after some discussion, two different men stepped out of line to confront each other.

The same process followed. The two fighters attacked each other, and in a second, they both changed into cats, too. This fight went on much longer and got a lot dirtier. Both cats suffered more injuries and worse ones that left them bloody.

The fight didn't end until one of the cats clamped his jaws around his opponent's leg. He crunched down on the bone and his victim yowled in pain. The cat twisted away and ripped his leg out of his attacker's jaws.

The stricken cat bolted on three legs to the other side of the square. He burst through the line and took off in a blinding streak for the citadel's many passageways.

The whole square exploded in laughter and Colton had to join in. Jaimee whipped around to stare at him with huge eyes.

The remaining victor cat transformed back into a man and the square collapsed. The spectators charged him, surrounded him, clapped him on the back, and congratulated him on his victory before they returned to their places. They took him with them and two more men stepped out to try their strength and fighting skill against each other.

"It's amazing!" Jaimee breathed when the third pair shifted and started the same process all over. "Now I understand what Liam meant when he said the tigers were ferocious."

"What do you think of their fighting skill?" Colton asked.

She looked up at him and her eyes made his hair stand on end. "Do you mean before they shift or afterward? I can't say anything about afterward, but they seem to be able to injure each other perfectly well."

"And before?"

She shrugged. "I guess they don't really fight long enough for me to judge that."

He gestured down the gallery. "Come along, lassie. We'll go inside and talk."

She didn't say anything while she followed him back to the interior corridor. She was too busy watching the matches down in the courtyard, and when he reached the stairs, she hesitated on the threshold.

She gazed down at the match for what seemed like a long time while Colton studied her on the side. She had completely forgotten he was there.

The third match finished and the spell shattered. She looked up and met his gaze without a blush in sight. Her eyes flashed with the same steely fire he first noticed when she walked through the gate. She was a fighter and her mind revolved around the fights she just witnessed. They were like nothing she'd ever seen, but she couldn't stop thinking about them.

He read it written on her face. She was thinking about what it would be like to fight one of the tigers. Her friend Lily fought them and now Jaimee was facing the same prospect.

He read it when she looked at him. She was finally realizing that he was one of those cats. If she ever fought him, she would be fighting him as a cat.

He tore himself away and led her back to his office. He held the door open for her and shut it after she entered.

He waved to the chair. "Take a seat, lass."

She sat down right away this time and he went to his chair behind the desk. He folded his hands in front of him and then spread them. "Well?"

"Well what? What did you want to talk to me about?"

"Just what I asked ye before. What did ye think of the men's fighting skills?"

"I told you. I don't know enough about how your people fight...and what do you care what I think anyway? I just walked through the door. I'm a stranger—a trespasser."

He didn't take the joke. "It's very unusual for us to meet anyone with yer experience, lassie. Ye've more military experience than anyone I've met in a long time."

"I find that hard to believe. You've been fighting this war for years. I don't know anything about you or your people or the Creightons or your way of life. This fortress must be packed to the walls with people who know a lot more about this war than I do."

"Och, but that's the problem, ye see, lass. They all ken the war through and through. That's the problem."

"I don't understand you. How can it be a problem if they know all about it?"

"I need a fresh pair of eyes," he replied. "I need someone from the outside to come in and tell us what we're doing wrong."

Her jaw dropped and she gaped at him in shock. "You.... what? You want me to do.... what?"

"I want ye to help me train me forces for the assault to come. I want ye to give me yer expert opinion to bring our Clan up to scratch before we engage the Creightons again."

She held up both hands, got to her feet, and started to turn away. "Whoa, whoa, whoa, pal! You can't ask me that! I don't know anything about your people or the Creightons. I can't train your people! I don't have anywhere near as much experience as you think. I've never trained an army...."

"Ye trained yer comrades back home," he interrupted. "Liam told me about it. Ye've overseen their combat and weapons training and ye've organized their intelligence and security measures. That's enough for me."

"Now just hold the phone, pal," she countered. "This is nuts! Your people.... you're cats. I can't train that."

"But ye can train all the rest, cannae ye? Ye've years of experience as commanding officer of this Last Division of yers."

She stared at him with her eyes hanging out of her head. He could see the wheels turning and the conflicting emotions racing across her face.

Colton leaned back in his chair. "Listen to me, lassie. The Creightons are dragons and they're amassing a force of dragons across the water in Tyrekirk. They'll send their dragons over here to lay waste to our forces. That's their only advantage. Get them on the ground and the battle is ours. It always goes the same way. They attack from the air and drive us off the planes. We retreat to the mountain and the weather will turn the tide for us. The dragons are weak and affected. They cannae stand the cold."

Her expression changed again. She shut her mouth. These strategic details snapped her back into practical mode. She was thinking about the battle he described.

"The Creightons are vicious in battle, but that's naught compared to what they'll do if they win. They'll annihilate us down to the last man, woman, and child." Colton waved his hand to one side. "Would ye have us stand by and let them put our people to the torch? They cannae be allowed to win if we can possibly prevent it."

She straightened up. "How *can* you prevent it if they're so powerful?"

"It's just as I've said. We've stood our ground and held our territory as far as the Boundless for generations. We can do it again, but with yer help, perhaps we can swing the scales the other way. We can end them and they willnae attack us anymore."

She shut her mouth and sank back into her chair. She clamped her clasped hands between her knees and turned her eyes to one side.

He recognized that look. She was going over every detail he mentioned. She saw the battle in her mind's eye and measured how to fight it.

"I ken ye dinnae want to go back into battle, lassie. I dinnae want to go meself, but I havenae any choice. The only way to secure the peace for future generations is to defeat the Creightons so decisively that they dinnae launch any more of these offensives against us. What do ye say? Help us. Help me."

Her head snapped around and her eyes locked on him. Did he say the wrong thing?

She let out her breath and her gaze drifted to the window behind him. "I don't know. I was still hoping to go over to Kald to look for Lily."

He compressed his lips. He hesitated to hurt her, but he could never win her help under false pretenses.

"I didnae like to tell ye this, lassie. I didnae like to cause ye any distress, but I see I havenae any choice now."

"What?" she asked. "What could cause me any distress?"

"Yer friend Lily.... she's wedded to the Creighton prince—Grant Ritchie is his name. He's heir to Laird Balfour Creighton. Yer friend Lily is giving her time and effort and knowledge to the Creightons. She's helping them plan to wipe out me entire Clan."

Jaimee stared at him in stupid shock. She couldn't even gasp. Did she even hear what he said?

He got to his feet and pulled a piece of paper from the stack on his desk. He unfolded it and spread it before her.

"This is a bill circulated in Kald announcing their wedding. Some of me spies have seen her in company with Grant and the Laird. Me spies have seen her dealing with the dragons and observing Buchanan land across the water while they plan their assault. There's no doubt Lily is helping them."

Jaimee shook her head fast and passed her hand across her eyes. "That's impossible! The Last Division.... we swore we would never marry or anything! She couldn't marry him. She barely knows him."

"And another thing, lass. He's a dragon himself. Me sister Edeena saw him shift in battle against the Creighton wizards. He's a member of the Royal House of Creighton. He'd have to be if he can shift at all."

"Hold it," she countered. "How can he be a member of the Royal House of Creighton if he's in battle against the Creightons?"

He shrugged. "It appears he didnae ken he was either royal or a dragon until the middle of the battle. Now he's the Laird's right hand and heir to the Seat of Armstrong. It doesnae matter for there's a war on and he's at the center of it all. I can take ye out on the parapet and show ye meself if ye dinnae believe me."

"No....no, you don't have to do that." She stood up and started pacing around the room. "This is insane! She's only been gone for two days."

"I wouldnae be so sure about that, lassie. According to me sources, Lily has been in Kald for nearly eight weeks. She and Liam captured Edeena in Kald two months ago, and after Edeena pushed Liam through the portal, Lily and Grant returned to Tyrekirk. They've been at the castle ever since."

"How is that even possible?" Jaimee choked.

"It would appear the time portal distorted the amount of time between the future and now. Liam returned to the same moment when he took Lily away and returned now. Rest assured me intelligence is accurate. I've confirmed it from several sources. Lily has been at Tyrekirk for several weeks and she and Grant are officially married."

Jaimee collapsed in her chair and buried her head in her hands. "I can't believe it! I mean, I have to believe it, but...."

Colton rose to his feet. He expected her to react like this.

He strode around his desk and picked up her hand. "Ye're in no condition to think on that at present, lass. Come along with me. I have something to take yer mind off all that."

She looked up at him and then blinked down at her hand in his. Her hands felt rough and strong. She hadn't stopped fighting since the war ended. "Where are we going?"

He pulled her to her feet and guided her to the door. "I want ye to come and have dinner with me."

Chapter 8

C olton threw open another door and steered Jaimee into his own bedroom. It was much bigger than his office with huge windows looking out over the western mountains. He could only see the Boundless, Kald, and Tyrekirk by standing right next to the glass.

She froze on the threshold and her clear, all-seeing eyes swept the room. She took in the bed laid with a thick, black bearskin throw, the heavy black velvet curtains surrounding its canopy, the couches set in the corner, a collection of armchairs, and a table near the window.

"What is this place?" she half-whispered.

"This is me own room." He let go of her hand and went over to the table. He started gathering up more piles of papers he left there. "I supposed we'd be more comfortable here than down in the dining hall.... but if ye prefer to eat with me Clansmen, we can go there instead. I'm sure they would be delighted to challenge ye to a match of yer own if ye're game."

She only blinked at him in stupefied astonishment. He tapped his papers into order and put them on the dresser. He went to a cabinet against the wall and pulled out a bottle. "Would ye fancy a drink?"

She still didn't answer. She surveyed the room again. She looked so dazed that he was just starting to wonder if he might have made a serious mistake in bringing her here.

Just then, someone tapped on the door and Colton's young cousin Louisa entered. She smiled first at him and then at Jaimee, who stared at the girl like she didn't recognize another woman.

Louisa started talking the minute she walked in. She chatted nonstop while she set the table. "Fergus says to tell ye that Gavin and Fletcher ran off again, laddie. Fergus says Gavin stole another sausage from the kitchens, and when Bryce set out to give him a thrashing, Gavin pointed the finger at Fletcher and Bryce found out. The whole disaster is boiling over to the guards, laddie. Fergus says, if ye dinnae sort it out, there'll be none left to man the parapet."

Colton had to laugh and Jaimee jumped out of her skin. "Dinnae mind the lads. I'll deal to them as soon as I get a chance to go downstairs."

"Aye." Louisa glanced over at Jaimee and Louisa's eyes twinkled. "I'll tell Fergus it may be a week or two before ye...."

"Get off with ye, ye trollop!" he snapped. "Mind yer tongue."

Louisa laughed and left the room. She came back a second later and laid a bunch of covered dishes on the tablecloth she'd laid out.

She gave Colton and Jaimee another knowing look and left. A second later, he heard her laughing out on the landing.

His cheeks started to burn. He could just imagine what the servants would be saying about him having dinner in his private room with Jaimee.

He covered up his embarrassment by pouring two drinks and taking them over to the table. He put one glass next to Jaimee's chair. "Come on with ye, lass, and get yerself something to eat. I understand the fare in the vault isnae worth sneezing at."

He pulled out her chair, but she still didn't move. She stared at the table, the dishes, him, and then around at the room again. A wild, frightened look came into her eyes. She acted as though eating with him might harm her somehow.

He tried again. "Are ye hungry, lassie? I dinnae expect ye to make any decision on an empty stomach."

She finally snapped out of her trance and came over to the table. She wouldn't look at him when he pushed her chair in for her.

He took his own seat, tossed back half of his drink, lifted the covers off the dishes, and talked to her while he served her. "Anyway, as I was saying, our Clan hasnae ever had any problem fighting the Creightons on the ground. It's a simple matter of swarming them with cats and tearing them to pieces. It's the dragons we have to worry on."

She cleared her throat and started to thaw out. "Um...what exactly do you want me to do to train your people.... that you aren't already doing yourself?"

"I want ye to look them over.... let me ken what ye think.... tell me if ye see any holes in our training routine...."

"What exactly is your training routine?" she asked.

Now it was his turn to blink at her. "Well.... now that ye ask.... what ye saw in the courtyard...."

"That's it?" Her voice started to rise and her astonishment of a moment before vaporized. She was crystal clear now and her tone made him wince. "So.... you wrestle and scrap in the courtyard.... How is that supposed to help you on the battlefield?"

Now it was his turn to clear his throat. "Well...."

"What's your battle plan? What are your defenses? What's your strategy for when the dragons attack your people on the open planes between here and the Boundless?"

He stared at her, stunned. This was not what he was expecting at all. She looked straight back at him waiting for him to answer her questions. Every passing second that he didn't answer twisted the knife deeper.

Her eyes flicked down at the food and drinks spread before them. That fleeting movement of her eyes woke him from his trance and he cleared his throat again. "Ye see? This is why we need ye. We need a fresh pair of eyes and a fresh mind with new techniques." He looked down at the table, too. "Ye havenae touched yer drink. Did ye think I poisoned it or ought?"

"Oh! No. I don't drink. Sorry. I didn't mean anything by it."

"Well?" he prompted. "Will ye do it? Will ye take over training us?"

"Us?" Her eyes popped. "I couldn't train you and your brothers. That would be out of the question."

"Why? If there's ought lacking, we'll need to fix it. That's precisely what I need ye for."

The words slipped out before he thought about them. As soon as he said those words, his cheeks flushed. He couldn't meet her eyes with those words hanging in the air.

I need ye. He did need her. He needed her for a lot more than her military experience.

He didn't realize he needed anything. Now he saw how poor and empty his life had been before she came. What had he been doing by himself all this time? How did he survive trying to do everything alone?

She didn't notice what he said. She puffed out her cheeks, looked down at her plate, and picked up her fork. "I don't know. I'd have to think about it."

"What is there to think on?" he asked.

"For a start, if I help you, that means I'll be staying here. I would have to give up the idea of going to Kald to find Lily."

"I've told ye where she is. She's in Tyrekirk with the Creightons."

"So is Lady Ilisa. You're trying to get her back, aren't you?"

He pointed his own fork at her. "Are ye saying ye'd go there as our agent to find out what happened to her? If ye do, I'll let ye go."

"You.... would let....me go?" she repeated with exaggerated slowness. "So I'm still a prisoner."

He threw all caution to the wind. He had to get her on his side no matter the cost. "I'll make ye a bargain, lass. Help me train me Clan and ye'll be living like this instead of wallowing in a cell as our enemy." He waved at his room.

"Would you release Liam, too? Would you stop holding him as a prisoner and set him at liberty to come and go as he pleases?"

He tried to shrug it off. He should have seen this coming. "Very well. If ye insist, I'll free him, too."

"Are you sure? I wouldn't want you to do anything to compromise your principles."

He squirmed in his seat. He became painfully aware of her eyes drilling him to the marrow again. "He's me sister's mate, so it isnae much of a stretch. If that's yer condition, I'll agree to it for yer sake."

She burst into a huge smile that lit up his world. "Thank you."

"Then.... ye'll do it? Ye'll train us?"

"Sure." She started looking around with a much sunnier expression on her face. "If you're right and you really don't have any defensive strategy, then that can't continue. If all these people are in danger of being incinerated by dragons because of it, then yeah, I would have to do something about that."

He refilled his glass and raised it to her. "Thank ye, lass. Ye have me gratitude."

"I left the army to help civilians against attacks like this. This is right up my alley."

"Yer.... alley?" He frowned at her. "I dinnae ken yer meaning."

"Never mind." She bent over her plate, forked a piece of meat, and put it in her mouth. Her eyes flew wide open. "This is incredible! What is it?"

"That? It's naught but beef."

"I've had beef and it never tasted like this." She cut off another piece and chewed it. "This is delicious."

He laughed. All his reservations dissolved now that she was letting her guard down around him. "It's Clan meat. It's what we eat every night."

"You never gave me this in the vault." She skewered a potato, bit into it, and cocked her head on one side. "The food we usually ate in the Last Division wasn't all it was cracked up to be. I can see that now. I guess I just got used to it."

He inclined his head to one side and studied her with his brow furrowed. "Ye have a strange way of speaking, lass. I dinnae ken what ye're saying."

She smiled at him again, and this time, her cheeks colored. Was she as happy to be sitting here, talking and eating, as he was? "Don't worry about it. It's just.... we didn't put much effort into our food back home. I guess I didn't realize what I was missing...until now."

He stuck his chin out at her glass. "Perhaps ye'd like to risk all and take a drink."

She burst out laughing. "I don't think I'm ready for that yet."

"One step at a time. I'll have ye on the floor in a week or two."

She laughed again and his heart turned a somersault. Was he making her as happy as she was making him?

She twirled her fork through her food and took another bite. He studied every move she made, every hint of emotion betrayed in her expression. Everything about her fascinated him.

She started eating faster and talking faster. "The key is going to be stopping the dragons. The Creightons are just normal people without the dragons, which means the cats will be able to take them."

"Aye," Colton replied.

"Which means we need some way to neutralize them in the air. If we can keep our people on the planes, we can drive the Creightons back over the Boundless. We need to find a way to stop them from crossing."

"Aye," he confirmed.

"You said they usually drive you into the mountains. You said you use the climate conditions to overcome them, but that obviously isn't enough. They must think they can overcome those conditions and finally defeat you. I can't think of any other reason why they would keep mounting these offensives."

He didn't reply this time. She was talking to herself more than him. Her eyes darted back and forth seeing things that weren't there. Her mind whirled planning, strategizing, and calculating.

This was exactly what he needed her for. He needed her to see everything he wasn't seeing.

He had been running this Clan for so long that he no longer saw what was right in front of his face. The job of managing the whole Clan had become so overwhelming that he concentrated everything on that alone.

He didn't have a moment of free time to think of the larger picture. He was too close to the Clan and too entrenched in the way they had always done everything. He couldn't see its flaws.

He let her talk and only offered enough encouragement and input to keep her going. She barely heard him but he heard her. He heard her loud and clear.

She was calling Clan Buchanan 'we'. We need to neutralize them in the air. We need to find a way to stop them from crossing the Boundless. Nearly every sentence she uttered started and ended with 'we'.

His heart flipped again. Could he have just found the missing piece of himself—the one crucial piece that would make him complete?

She finally talked herself out and sank back in her chair. "Wow!" she breathed. "We really have a lot of work to do."

He nodded down at the table. "Are ye ready for a drink now?"

She burst out in musical laughter and her cheeks turned bright pink. "I probably should, but I'm still not ready yet. I'm sorry. I shouldn't let it go to waste, but old habits die hard."

"Not to worry, lass." He grabbed her glass and tossed the liquor down his throat. "Perhaps next time."

She beamed at him with her cheeks glowing. "So.... there's going to be a next time?"

"If ye behave and dinnae wind up in the vault again." He stood up and took her hand. "Come along, lassie."

"Where are you taking me—back to the cells?"

"I told ye I'd free ye if ye agreed to help us." He led her outside and down the corridor to another room at the far end of the landing.

He opened the door and conducted her inside. Her eyes widened even more than when he took her to his room. "What is this?"

"It's a guest room, but it hasnae been used in years. Ye're the first guest we've had in.... well, since I can remember."

She surveyed the room in stunned silence. The furnishings in here were much nicer than his. A multi-colored brocade throw covered the enormous bed. The curtains and canopy hangings were thick burgundy velvet and rich oriental carpets made the floor soft and inviting to step on.

The windows gave a broad, sweeping view over the planes, the Boundless, and all of Kald spread out beyond.

A fire crackled in the fireplace and an enormous wooden tub billowed steam into the room. Heated rocks at the bottom sent up eruptions of bubbles to the surface.

Fresh clothes had been laid out for her—clothes Colton had picked out himself. He made sure she had trousers, a clean shirt, and a leather jacket that would fit her. He had questioned Edeena about what kind of clothing Lily wore. Edeena was adamant that Lily never wore a dress the whole time she was in Kald.

Colton's spies informed him that Lily had started wearing dresses only after she moved to Tyrekirk with Grant. She had to wear them, now that she was Lady Lily Armstrong, but she never wore anything but trousers while she was out on the street.

He took a calculated risk and assumed that Jaimee would be the same. He watched her expression when she recognized the clothes and he knew he made the right choice. She must have dreaded the moment when she had to take off her own clothes and put on a dress.

He made up his mind then and there that, if by some miracle he got lucky enough to take Jaimee Abernathy as his life's mate, he would never even suggest that she wear a dress. If she decided to of her own accord, that was her decision.

He would be more than happy to mate with her the way she was. If she was half as good at training his men as he suspected she was, then wearing trousers would be the more appropriate attire anyway.

"Ye'll stay here from now on, lass. I'll see ye bright and early tomorrow morning on the courtyard and we'll get ye started."

He couldn't resist. The feel of her hand in his felt too good. He didn't give himself a moment to hesitate. He raised her knuckles to his lips, kissed her hand, and walked away.

Chapter 9

J aimee stood alone in the guest room looking around at everything again and again. She couldn't stop turning in a circle taking in every detail of this incredible room.

She had been prepared when she left Ironforge to fight dragons, face evil wizards trying to kill her, and any number of other dangers. Even after she wound up in Icemeet, she had been holding herself ready to fight at a moment's notice.

Now she found herself in this room instead. Her brain hadn't yet caught up to reality.

It was much nicer than Colton's room, but something in the stark, somber austerity of his room somehow made her more comfortable. This room looked like the presidential suite at the top of a giant skyscraper. It was too nice for her. She wasn't used to this kind of luxury.

The crackling flames blasted heat into the room. It warmed her and further softened the tension she'd been holding at bay since she first set foot in this country.

The steam coming from the tub broke down the last of her resolve. She went over to the tub and trailed her fingertips through the scalding water. It looked too inviting to pass up and, in a split second, she couldn't take resist anymore.

She shut the door and returned to the tub stripping off her clothes. She discarded them on the floor, but she still felt grimy and disgusting. She hadn't taken a bath or shower since she left Detroit.

She had to climb into the tub slowly. It was beyond hot—almost too hot to stand. She couldn't walk away, though, not without cleaning herself up and enjoying this rare moment of total relaxation.

She reclined in the water and all the knots and strains in her back and shoulders started to melt in the heat. Her head fell back and her eyes sank closed.

She drifted in bliss and found her thoughts migrating back to Colton. He sure was good-looking in a rugged, feral way and she really enjoyed talking to him. He was a fantastic listener and took in every detail that she said during dinner about the Buchanans' defenses.

She had been right about him. He was a born leader. No wonder the rest of the Clan wanted him to take over as Clan Chief when his father died. He was already doing the j ob.

He saw his own failings, too. He recognized that the Clan needed new blood, new perspectives, and new strategies. That made him a better leader than nearly everyone she'd ever worked with in the army. He wasn't too proud to admit that he needed help.

His words played again and again in her mind. *I need you. Help me.* Those words caused a reaction in her heart and soul. She wanted to help him.

She tried to shake those thoughts out of her head. It was the innocent civilians she wanted to help. She wanted to save all these people from getting decimated by the dragons.

She tried to concentrate on the defenses again and wound up thinking about Colton instead. He was the one she wanted to help. She wanted to give him what he needed. She didn't want him doing this alone anymore.

He understood about being tired out by war, but he had no choice but to keep going. If that wasn't worth her coming out of retirement, she didn't know what was.

She couldn't go back to Ironforge and leave him to handle this alone. No one deserved that.... but staying meant walking away from everything she knew. It meant turning her back on everything the Last Division stood for.

She forced herself to sit up and open her eyes. She wasn't going to stay here. She was on a rescue mission to find Lily and take her back to Ironforge, too. Jaimee wasn't here to save Colton from anything, let alone himself.

Then she remembered. Lily was married. What if Jaimee went through this entire rescue operation only for Lily to decide to stay? What if Jaimee got injured or killed in this strange world of the past—all for nothing?

Lily wouldn't have married Grant at all if she ever intended to return to present-day America. She might have thought she couldn't get back to Detroit after Liam disappeared. She might decide, once she realized that Liam and Jaimee returned to save her, that she wanted to go back after all. Lily might be delighted to have Laim and Jaimee rescue her.

That would never happen. Lily would never leave Grant. Jaimee couldn't tell how she knew this, but some part of her gut told her it was true.

Lily had turned her back on the Last Division. Lily had thrown off their vow of isolation and retirement. Lily had given herself to a man, a people, a life beyond the Last Division. She wouldn't come back from that.

Up to two months had passed in this time period since Lily left Detroit. That was plenty of time for her to meet a man, fall in love, and marry him, especially after her brother vanished and she thought she had lost her only way to go home.

Still, what could make Lily join forces with the Creightons? Lily had better instincts than that.... or so Jaimee thought

If Colton was telling the truth about the Creightons and their plan was to wipe all these people out, maybe Lily wasn't Jaimee's friend after all. Maybe Lily never really took the Last Division's mission seriously.

Jaimee's mind switched back to Colton. If Jaimee chose to stay in this time with him, she would never go back to her own time period, either. She would have to cross some invisible line inside herself to even consider it—and she wasn't considering it. It was out of the question.

Jaimee sat up and got busy washing her hair and body. She found a cake of soap in a wooden dish resting on the edge of the tub. She soaped up in her usual businesslike way. She was on a mission here. She had a job to do that didn't include turning her back on everything she held sacred.

Colton was a nice guy. He was a strong leader and incredibly attractive, but that didn't mean anything. Jaimee wasn't going to get with anyone, especially not someone three hundred years in the past.

She rinsed her hair, climbed out, dried off, and put on the clothes that someone had left for her. She held up a pair of leather pants that were buffed softer than velvet. She had never seen anything so beautiful, and when she slipped them on, she no longer doubted that Colton was the one who left them for her.

Her stomach flipped when she thought about him picking these out for her. He must really care if he left these for her instead of a dress. She was the only woman in the whole fortress who wore pants, but he obviously didn't care. He accepted her for who and what she was.

He did a lot more than accept her. He encouraged her and valued her unique skills and experience. He wanted her to bring those skills and experiences to his Clan. He thought they enriched his Clan and strengthened his position. That's why he wanted her.

He wanted her and not just for her military experience. She knew that from the way he was acting. She would know it even if he didn't explicitly kiss her hand just now. He wanted more and the Buchanans mated for life.

She tried one more time to shake those thoughts out of her head, but it still didn't work. She couldn't stop thinking about him.

She wasn't going there with him or anyone else. She would finish this mission and go back to Ironforge. Lily might betray the Last Division's oath, but Jaimee wouldn't. She couldn't. She was the Last Division's commanding officer. She couldn't let the other three down. If she didn't uphold their oath, how could she expect anyone else to?

Darkness was falling outside by the time she finished getting dressed. Now that she finished her bath, exhaustion was starting to catch up with her.

Her body ached from sleeping on that hard bench for three days. This bed enticed her to sink into its plush folds and drift away. She sat down on the mattress. Her eyelids already weighed a ton.

She pulled back the covers when a knock startled her. She spun around and stared at the door when a second knock came.

She opened the door expecting Colton. Jaimee stiffened when she came face to face with Edeena.

"Hello," Jaimee began.

Edeena's eyes darted into the room. "So ye're staying here now, are ye?"

"Your brother told me to stay here."

"Making yerself comfortable, though. I can see that." Edeena swept past Jaimee, strolled over to the tub, and turned in a complete circle inspecting the room as though she'd never seen it before.

Jaimee returned to the bed and sat down. She was too tired to play games with anyone right now. "What can I do for you? You're my first visitor, so......nice to see you."

"Dinnae give me that line of codswallop! Liam is suffering down in the vault and ye lounge around in here like some royal princess! How can ye accept this room without trying to help him?"

"As a matter of fact, I am trying to help him. I just talked to Colton about it and he promised to free Liam, too."

Edeena blinked at her and then threw up her hands. "Ye're spinning me a yarn. Colton would never agree to that."

"He asked me to help him train your people for the next Creighton invasion. He asked me to use my military training and experience to give your Clan an edge. He gave me this room in exchange for my help and he also promised to free Liam."

"Ye!" Edeena gave a sick laugh. "What can *ye* do for our Clan that me brothers arenae already doing? We've held the Creightons at bay for centuries."

Jaimee shrugged. "That's what I said, but he thinks I can turn the tide so you do more than just hold them at bay. He thinks we can stop them from invading at all ever again."

"That's a load of bollocks!" Edeena snapped.

Jaimee turned back to the bed and pretended to straighten the pillows. Maybe that would send Edeena a message that Jaimee wanted to go to sleep. "Why don't you tell your brother that? He's acting Clan Chief. I'm sure he'd be delighted to hear that you think his ideas are so stupid."

"And ye believe him that he'll free Liam if ye do this?" Edeena snorted again. "Ye're soft in the head."

"I believe him. I take him at his word. It surprises me that you don't. He wouldn't make a promise like that unless he planned to keep it."

Edeena looked away.

"Anyway," Jaimee went on, "I doubt your brothers will ever forgive Liam for what he did to you. They won't stop trying to get rid of him, which means Liam will be in danger even after Colton frees him from the vault. Helping Colton is probably the best way to help Liam. Don't you think?"

Edeena shrugged. She wouldn't look at Jaimee. Edeena strode over to the window to gaze across the Boundless. "I suppose so."

"Tell me more about your brothers. If you know some reason why I shouldn't put my faith in Colton's promises, you better tell me now."

"Och, aye," Edeena murmured over her shoulder. "He's good for his word. If he promised, he'll do it."

"What about the other two—Reid and Duncan?"

"Reid is Colton's man, the same as Duncan. They'll follow him to the ends of the Earth and no question."

Jaimee nodded at nothing. "I gathered that."

"What I want to ken...." Edeena turned around to confront Jaimee again. "....is *when* Colton will free Liam from the vault. If he made that promise.... When *did* he make that promise?"

"I don't know. Maybe an hour ago."

"Liam is still down there pining away. Colton should have released him by now."

"Not necessarily. Colton promised to free Liam on the condition that I help him train your people. I haven't done that yet."

"But he gave ye this room," Edeena argued. "If this whole thing hinges on ye helping our people, ye should be in the vault, too."

"Look. I don't claim to understand Colton's thoughts or why he does anything. He's your brother. You understand him a lot better than I do. Why don't you go ask him yourself?"

"I couldnae do that!" Edeena exclaimed.

"Why not? He seems like a reasonable guy."

"Not where Liam's concerned," Edeena muttered. "I havenae seen Colton like this with anyone besides the Creightons."

Jaimee snorted. "Good point. Now I want to ask you something."

Edeena spun around. "What is it?"

"I want to know everything you saw and heard Lily do when she was with Grant Ritchie."

Edeena gave another sick laugh and this one she aimed straight at Jaimee. "Och, ye want to ken how yer friend could fall in love with the great, ugly black lizard."

"I'm talking about *before* she knew he was a great, ugly black lizard—before any of that. What happened? How did they meet?"

"How should I ken? I wasnae there."

"But you were there at the end. You saw him shift."

"Aye." Edeena's gaze drifted back to the window. "I saw that much."

"What happened after.... after Lily saw him shift? Was she horrified? Was she disgusted? Did she treat him like a great, ugly black lizard?"

"She couldnae. She was in the middle of the battle and then.... after Ness died...."

"Who's Ness?"

"The prince, of course—the Creighton crown prince that Grant and Elliot Ritchie were tasked with protecting. They were naught but common foot soldiers—or so they thought—and the wizards attacked Ness and...."

"The Creightons.... attacked their own crown prince?" Jaimee exclaimed. "What the hell for?"

"How should I ken? Does it matter why? Grant, Elliot, and Ness got into a battle against the Creighton wizards. Ness defended Lily and lost his life doing it. Then Grant shifted and finished off the wizards....and then Elliot left...."

"What do you mean—he left?"

"He turned his back on his brother—his own flesh and blood. He pushed Grant away and Elliot walked off alone."

"Then what happened?"

"Lily stepped in and took Grant off. I didnae see ought else."

Jaimee's eyes drifted toward the window, too. Edeena painted a pretty telling picture of what happened after the battle. So Lily was the one who took Grant away. She must have already started to care about him before that.

Jaimee could imagine the scene. Lily wasn't disgusted and horrified by Grant shifting into a big, ugly black lizard, but Elliot sure was. Jaimee didn't blame him. That must have been a shock for everyone, especially Grant.

Jaimee's heart twisted thinking about Lily. She must have really cared about Grant... .and now she was married to him. She was living as a lady in Tyrekirk and married to the heir to the Seat of Armstrong.

"Is there ought else ye want to ken about yer friend the lizard-lover?" Edeena sneered.

"No. That's all I want to know. Thank you."

Edeena glared at her waiting for Jaimee to say something else. "Well? What do you mean to do about Liam?"

"I already told you. I plan to help Colton train your people. Once I do that and earn his goodwill, he'll be much more agreeable to freeing Liam—or rather, he'll be about as agreeable to freeing Liam as Colton is ever going to get."

Edeena snorted and headed for the door.

"You remember what I said," Jaimee called after her. "Even if I get Liam released, that won't change your brothers' feelings toward him. They'll still try to get rid of him any way they can, even if that means killing him."

Edeena shot her a hateful glare. "That's me own business and none of yers."

She stalked out of the room and Jaimee sank back on the bed with a sigh. She sent up a silent prayer to Heaven asking that no one else would interrupt her while she was sleeping.

She crawled under the covers and the gentle crackle of the fire soothed her shattered brain. She collapsed and fell instantly asleep.

Chapter 10

C olton paced up and down in front of his men. They were all fully dressed according to his orders—unlike their usual attire. They usually went around barefoot and shirtless, but today, he wanted them looking shipshape for when Jaimee showed up to start training them.

He appraised their tartans, their weapons, and the state of their shoes, but he restrained himself from making any comment on the cleanliness or lack thereof. He couldn't expect his Clansmen to change their whole way of life overnight just because Jaimee showed up. He was already pushing his luck by asking them to dress properly.

They stood in five or six ranks of forty each. Their number filled most of the courtyard and this wasn't the whole Buchanan force. Most lived in the mountains. They only came down to Icemeet when they needed to defend the Clan's territory from Creighton invasion.

He halted at the end of the line where Reid and Duncan waited for him. They looked much neater than the rest of the assembled men. Both of them had washed and combed their hair, shaved, and they wore clean shirts and tartans which was a whole lot more than Colton could say about the rest of his Clansmen.

Colton turned around to take his place at Reid's side and cast one last critical glance down the line of Highlanders. He never noticed until now how scruffy, dirty, and mismatched they were. They looked like peasants or mountain men—because they were.

Colton always considered their rugged character their strength—their one true advantage over the crisp, disciplined Creighton army. He admired the Buchanans for their earthy nature and their defiance of society and refinement.

Now it struck him as low, common, and ragtag. What kind of an army was he trying to run here? He dreaded the moment when Jaimee came out and saw the Clan like this—and this was so much better than the way they usually looked.

This was a terrible idea. He shouldn't have asked her to train his people. He turned to Reid to tell him to disband the men when the passageway door burst open.

Jaimee strode out into the courtyard, took one look at the men, and headed straight for Colton. It was too late to turn back now.

She didn't look at the men for more than that one fleeting glance and she didn't turn up her nose at them. She didn't even seem to notice how ragged they looked—or that they had put on their shirts, socks, and shoes for the occasion.

She halted in front of Colton, raised both hands, and let them fall. "Reporting for duty, Sir. What would you like me to do first?"

He bit back a grin at her introduction. "Ye dinnae have to call me that. Ye're the one in charge here."

"I am?" She glanced over at Reid and Duncan. "Are you sure about that?"

"Aye. I'm sure about that." He took hold of her elbow and swiveled her around to face his men. Several of them had turned their heads to watch and listen to the conversation.

Colton steered her down the line he had just spent the last ten minutes reviewing. Now was the moment of truth, the moment when she realized just what a sorry bunch of losers the Buchanan Clan really was.

He started forward with her at his side. Reid and Duncan followed them closely.

"Now then," Colton began. "Give me yer unvarnished opinion so we can all get to work. We havenae had any refined instruction from anyone who kens what they're doing as well as ye."

He halted in the middle of the courtyard while she scanned the men. Now she could see exactly what condition they were in and how grimy they were. Many were unshaven and only a handful had bothered to straighten their hair.

"What am I supposed to give my opinion on?" she asked. "I can't tell anything from seeing them standing in line."

He checked himself before he answered. He didn't believe at first that she didn't care how messy and unkempt they were.

"What do ye need to ken that ye cannae see, lass?" he asked. "I dinnae ken yer meaning."

"I need to see them fighting. I need to see them actually engaged in some kind of combat before I can give my opinion on what we need to do."

He frowned at her. Didn't she even care what they looked like or how clean they were?

"Why don't we start with the sparring you showed me yesterday?" She waved at the men. "You were doing some kind of wrestling match."

He couldn't stop frowning at her. "Are ye sure, lass? Ye dinnae have ought to say about......?" He broke off.

"About what?" She surveyed the men again. "I can't tell anything from them just standing here."

"Very well." He raised his voice and boomed across the courtyard. "Break ranks!"

The men dissolved into a chaotic jumble with everyone going in a different direction. Most went to the outer courtyard walls and started unbuckling their weapons, kicking off their shoes, stripping off their shirts, and throwing everything into piles in corners.

Colton studied Jaimee's reaction and got another shock when he saw her visibly relaxing and even smiling. Was this what she really wanted—this loose, clannish familiarity? Could it be that she didn't have any intention of turning them into a disciplined army like the Creightons?

He glanced behind him at his brothers and found them gawking at Jaimee as though she'd lost her mind. At least Colton wasn't the only one who had been expecting the worst.

About half the men returned to the courtyard wearing nothing but their kilts and tartans. They swung their arms back and forth limbering up for their matches. A few squatted down to flex their hips and some rolled their heads on their necks.

"Form up!" Colton called and they assembled into a square. The rest of the men slouched around the walls, crossed their arms, and started talking casually, laughing, and occasionally calling insults and jokes to their comrades in the square.

"Who's first?" Colton called.

"Hold it," Jaimee interrupted. "Don't start yet."

"Why?" he asked. "Ye said ye wanted to see them fight."

"You promised you'd free Liam if I did this. He's still in the vault. Keep your bargain."

He had to grin at her audacity, though he couldn't figure out why he expected anything less. "As ye wish, lass. Come along and we'll fetch him together."

He gave Reid a nod and Colton and Jaimee went downstairs to the vault. He had to stop himself from getting overly familiar with her too soon. This was a business arrangement. He had to bear that in mind until it became something else.

Liam got to his feet when Colton and Jaimee entered the underground dungeon. Liam glared at Colton in barely suppressed fury, but Colton ignored him. He was doing this for Jaimee. Colton didn't give a rip about Liam.

Colton unlocked the cell and motioned Liam out. "Out ye go, lad. Ye're a free man."

Liam's eyes darted over to Jaimee. "What's the catch?"

"The catch is that I've agreed to train the Buchanans in their upcoming campaign against the Creightons," Jaimee replied. "So if you still want to go to Kald to look for Lily, I'll have to stay here."

"But that's by the by," Colton interjected. "We already ken where Lily is so ye winnae need to search for her. She's at Tyrekirk married to Grant Ritchie. Ye can go straight there and begin helping them arm against the Buchanans. That's what ye want, am I right?"

Liam glared at him again. "I don't want anything except to find my sister and Lady Rhona Armstrong."

Colton shrugged. "Have it yer own way. I'm done with ye, but I warn ye. If ye go out that gate, ye winnae come back so long as I've the breath in me body to run ye through. Ye mind yer step in the future, laddie." He turned on his heel and went back to the door. "Come along, lass."

She stayed where she was and scanned Liam up and down. Before they could move or speak to each other, Edeena charged in. She rushed Liam and threw her arms around him. "Finally! Come along. I'll take ye upstairs and get ye cleaned up. Och, it's a misery!"

She led him out of the vault. Jaimee turned around to watch them out of sight. She ended up facing Colton. "Thank you. I really appreciate it."

"Dinnae thank me yet, lassie. He'll prove a thorn in our sides before long." He waved toward the door. "Come along. We've more important business to attend to."

They returned to the courtyard where the men were already scrapping the way they did yesterday—the way they did every day. This time-honored tradition never changed and Colton chuckled when he saw the cats rolling, kicking, and tearing each other's fur out.

He had to pull his head back into the game when he saw Jaimee's sharp eyes measuring their every move. She narrowed her eyes watching them tumble over each other.

"Well?" he prompted. "What do ye think?"

She turned away from the wrestling match. Another square of forty men had formed across the courtyard. Two men circled each other holding their weapons—a saber in the right hand and a dirk in the left.

These men were also shirtless and barelegged like the rest. They inched around each other looking for an opening when, without warning, one of the men flew at his opponent in a blinding streak. He dropped his weapon, transformed into a cat, and soared straight for his opponent's head.

The other man dropped his weapons, too, and caught the cat in his bare hands. He flung the creature across the courtyard and the cat slammed into one of the bystanders.

The cat hit the ground and the second combatant scrambled to retrieve his weapons. The cat barely touched down before he sprang up. He hardly flexed his legs before he launched in a yowling blur toward his opponent.

"Stop!" Jaimee bellowed. "Stop!"

All eyes turned to her, including the men in the wrestling match. A tense silence fell over the courtyard and several of the Highlanders glared at her.

"What's the problem, lassie?" Colton asked. "They're only doing as ye asked. Ye wanted to see them fight."

She stepped into the courtyard and addressed the two combatants. "You're supposed to be training with your weapons. You can't do that if you're always changing into your tiger forms." She pointed at the cat. "You—come back over here and face him as a man. Don't shift."

No one moved and a few people glanced over at Colton.

"You won't be fighting another cat when the Creightons attack," she went on. "You need to work with your weapons....and you—"

She broke through the square and went over to the wrestling match. "You solve all your problems by shifting. That might be enough to keep you alive, but it won't defeat the Creightons." She strode back over to Colton. "Tell them."

"All right, lassie." He pointed to the two men that had been wrestling as cats a moment before. "Do yer match over without shifting this time."

"Ye're barmy!" one of them huffed. "What's the point in that?"

"It's as she says. Ye cannae learn to fight as men if ye're shifting always." He stepped away from the square. "Do yer match over and let's see ye do it without shifting."

He returned to Jaimee's side, but she didn't look happy that he intervened on her behalf. Her smile evaporated and she barely paid attention to the match at all when the two men started circling each other again.

They closed and it only took a few seconds before one of them lost control and shifted. The cat sank his teeth into his opponent's arm and it was all on.

Jaimee sighed and turned back to the other square where the men were trying to train with their weapons, but the same thing happened.

Her shoulders slouched and she rounded on Colton. "Look. This isn't going to work."

"Why no? They're learning."

"It isn't that. You want me to take over here? You want me to believe I'm in command of these men and telling them what to do? I can't do that with you standing around telling them what to do in my place." He laughed out loud, but that only made her glare at him. "What the hell is so funny? Do you think this is all a joke or something?"

"Not at all, lass. I'm only laughing because I'm glad ye're here."

"Well?" she demanded.

"Well what? What is it ye'd like me to do? Ye cannae blame these people for thinking of me as their Chief when I am that."

"I need you to leave. I need you to leave me alone with them so they aren't always looking to you to confirm that they're supposed to do what I say."

He couldn't stop chuckling. She really was the feistiest woman he'd ever met. "As ye wish, lassie." He bumped Reid's shoulder. "Come along, lads. We arenae welcome in our own house any longer."

He walked away snickering to himself. Her scowl only made him happier. He led his brothers into the stairwell and exited on the upper gallery where he could watch without being seen—except that she saw him right away.

She frowned even more, but at least none of the other men noticed him watching.

All eyes turned to her and she switched back to command mode. She paced up and down the courtyard and raised her voice to a harsh, clipped shout. "Now listen up, people! I can't teach you how to fight as cats, but that doesn't mean anything. There will be plenty of times you can't fight the Creightons as cats, and even if there weren't, your weapons will do you a hell of a lot more good against them than your teeth and claws. You need to train with other weapons besides your teeth and claws. You need to be at least as well-trained as they are. Now watch."

She elbowed her way into the square where the men had been using weapons. She approached two men on the opposite side and took a dirk from each of them.

She spun them around in her hands and passed her sharp eye over the Highlanders lined up opposite her.

"You!" She pointed at a huge man nearly twice her size. "Come on."

She waved him into the center and all the assembled Clansmen gathered around to watch. They formed a second square around the first and watched the bout three men thick.

She raised both dirks and started circling her much larger opponent. The man drew his saber in one hand and his dirk in the other. The onlookers elbowed each other and whispered behind her back.

"She's insane!" Duncan muttered under his breath. "Ye didnae have to kill her, laddie. She'll be dead in a moment. Ewan will cut her in half."

Colton didn't answer. The confrontation looked so heavily weighted against Jaimee that he half-agreed with his brother. Colton would have given up for dead anyone foolish enough to tangle with big Ewan Buchanan, but Colton had a sneaking suspicion this fight wouldn't go that way.

Ewan puffed out his chest to make himself even bigger. He crouched and dug his bare toes into the paving stones. Jaimee hunched over and cocked back both arms pointing her dirks at him.

Ewan charged her and brought his saber down in a crushing chop at her head. She lunged for him, crossed her dirks above her head to catch his blade, and kicked upward with impossible speed.

She could kick as high as her own face and she nailed Ewan square in the chin.

"Och, no! She did not!" Reid hissed.

Colton stood rooted to the spot watching. He couldn't move or even breathe. Ewan's head snapped back and Jaimee attacked him with incredible ferocity.

She still held his saber in place on her crossed dirks and she kicked him again in the chest this time. He staggered away and his saber blade scraped sparks on her dirks.

He recovered his balance and charged her again. He hacked with his saber and she wound up to kick him again. He reared back to avoid the blow, but she didn't aim for his face or body.

She kicked his right wrist and his saber went flying. It clanged on the paving stones and skidded out of reach.

She pounced and headbutted him hard in the nose. He toppled and she sprang on top of him with agility Colton had never seen before in anyone—cat or human.

She landed on one knee pinning Ewan's dirk hand to the ground. She slammed her opposite foot on his empty saber hand, and in a flash, she had her dirk at his throat.

The whole crowd sucked in a breath and everyone froze—all except Jaimee, who panted and gasped for air through gritted teeth. Her hair scattered across her face that had transfigured into a demonic mask of fury.

Ewan stared up at her in stark, staring terror. "Dinnae, lassie.... dinnae...."

She shuddered as though she was just seeing him for the first time. She dragged herself to her feet, went back to the other side of the square, and returned her weapons to the men she took them from.

"You see?" she called over the crowd in a gasp. "It doesn't matter how fast you are or how big you are or how well armed you are. Only training matters. You need to be ready for anything, including for your enemy to change into dragons while you're in the middle of fighting them."

"That's all very well, lass," another man called from across the square. "How do ye plan to win against a tiger if one attacks ye? Yer speed winnae stand ye then."

She turned around. She didn't turn quickly enough to see who had spoken, but Colton saw. It was Bryce Buchanan, another of Colton's cousins. Bryce was older than the three Buchanan brothers and he usually took the lead on security matters.

She scanned the faces on that side of the square, but she didn't ask who challenged her. She ran her forehead across her shoulder and nodded. "All right. Which one of you wants to fight me as a tiger—no weapons, nothing. Just you in your tiger form against me."

Bryce snorted and gave himself away. "Ye wouldnae stand a chance, lass. We'd tear ye to shreds."

She must have recognized his voice because she fixed him with a deadly glare. "Do you want to bet on that?"

He laughed in her face and Reid muttered in Colton's ear. "She's late for the graveyard, this lassie. She winnae last the day the way she's going."

"I bet you any odds you want that I can beat you," she went on. "You fight me as a tiger and I'll fight you like this." She spread her arms as though she really needed to show herself to these men. She had their complete undivided attention. "If I win, all of you will obey me the same way you obey Colton. You do what I say, train the way I say, and never, ever challenge my authority again."

"And if I win?" Bryce demanded. "What will ye do for us?"

"If you win, you won't have to worry about me because I'll be dead. Right?" She straightened up and looked him straight in the eye. She didn't even blink.

"Och, no, lassie!" Duncan whispered. "Ye dinnae want to do that. Ye dinnae want to fight Bryce. I winnae stand this."

He turned away to go back down to the courtyard. He was going to stop the fight, but Colton grabbed his brother's arm and held him back.

He didn't see how Jaimee could win against Bryce, but Colton saw now why she had to do this. She had to prove herself to these men. She had to earn their obedience and her own authority over them. This was the only way. They wouldn't take her seriously if she didn't win.

Chapter 11

Bryce stepped out into the square, passed his weapons to his nearest Clansmen, and faced Jaimee in the center of the courtyard. "It's yer grave, lassie, but if ye beat me, we'll obey ye and train the way ye say with no challenges. Are we all agreed?" He glanced around the square of listening men.

They all nodded and several called out, "Aye, lass."

She took a step nearer to him and Colton's breath caught watching her square up to Bryce. He wasn't as big as Ewan, but that only meant Bryce had as much muscle compacted into a smaller form.

His curly hair had come undone from its tie behind his neck. It spilled around his rugged face. His weathered, beaten visage somehow looked more dangerous than his younger Clansmen. He was the only man his age who still fought with them and he could whip nearly all of them.

Jaimee yanked off the jacket that Colton had given her. She rolled up her shirt sleeves and took a wide stance facing Bryce down.

Bryce did the same thing and they both eyed each other with matched hostility.

"Ye cannae allow this, lad!" Duncan insisted. "Ye must stop this. It's her life ye're toying with."

"She'll toy with it her own self," Colton replied. "She cannae do ought unless she wins."

"Is this yer way of eliminating her?" Reid asked, but Colton didn't answer.

He couldn't tear his eyes off her, and in that moment, he knew she was going to win. He had no idea how because she didn't know what she was getting into. Watching the Highland tigers fight each other was one thing. Actually facing one in open combat was another matter.

The tigers could fight each other all day long. A tiger against an unarmed human was no contest at all.

He would normally consider any human fighting the tigers unarmed as good as dead, but he couldn't think of her that way. She'd beaten big Ewan Buchanan so easily and so quickly. Colton was starting to think Bryce might be the one on his way to the graveyard.

That wouldn't happen, though, because Jaimee wouldn't kill Bryce. She cared too much about human life—even shifter life.

When the attack came, it took her completely by surprise. Bryce shifted with mind-blowing speed. He shifted in the blink of an eye and rocketed off the ground without bending his legs or giving any warning.

One minute, he stood before her as a man. The next instant, the tiger hurtled toward her head and extended his claws. Bryce's hair-raising yowl echoed around the courtyard.

Most of the assembled Highlanders shrank back from the fight to give Bryce all the space he needed to tear Jaimee apart. Duncan tried one more time to break away to go downstairs and stop the fight.

Colton clamped his fingers on his brother's arm and yanked Duncan back a lot harder than he meant to. He couldn't let anyone intervene in this.

If Jaimee lost this fight or even died, she would do it making a statement to the rest of the Clan. She couldn't be part of this without staking her claim right here and now.

Duncan finally got the message and returned to the railing to watch. He and Reid kept muttering comments, but Colton couldn't hear them.

Jaimee saw Bryce sailing toward her face. She raised her hands to grapple with him, but she couldn't stop his weight from falling against her. He landed on her head and his body covered her face.

He sank his claws into her scalp and kicked out with his hind feet. His hind paws ripped down her shirt and scored her chest and neck.

The whole courtyard exploded with the men yelling, cheering, and shouting encouragement to both fighters. The square dissolved into a loose gathering of men surrounding the battle. Even the guards on the parapet turned backward to watch.

Jaimee yelled in pain, but she didn't fall. She seized the giant cat by the fur and yanked him to and fro, but she couldn't dislodge him. He kept kicking and shredding her while he whipped his head from side to side. He dove for her and sank his fangs into her head.

She let out an enraged bellow that set Colton's every nerve on end. He had to struggle much harder with himself than he ever did with Duncan not to break into a run, bolt down to the courtyard, and stop the fight before it got any worse.

Bryce twisted his body in all directions. He hooked her clothes and skin, ripped her to ribbons, and stained her shirt with blood. She screamed, and with one almighty wrench, she finally dislodged him from her scalp, but not before he carved wicked scratches down her face. Blood ran down her cheeks and made her look hideous and monstrous.

She thrust the cat away at arm's length and wrestled to hold him at bay. Bryce's furious thrashing jerked her nearly off her feet and her shoulders strained trying to keep her hold on him.

He finally fought his way around in her grasp and sank his needle teeth into her hand. She gave another spine-chilling yell, but she still didn't let him go. She dropped on her knees and pinned him on the ground with his fangs still embedded in her wrist and thumb.

She got one hand free, hauled off, punched him hard in the head, and now it was Bryce's turn to scream. He reacted in an instant and whipped out of her grasp. He rotated sideways and scrambled to get away from her. He bounced off another patch of ground and collided with her in a flying tackle.

He hit her full force and knocked her flat on her back. He pounced on her chest and dove his bared fangs for her throat.

She stuck her arm in front of his face just in time and his teeth closed on the same arm he bit before, but she didn't yell out. She gnashed her teeth in a death snarl, grabbed one of his forelegs, and ripped it sideways. She would have snapped the joint if his cat body hadn't been so flexible.

She hauled him off and slammed him down on the paving stones with brutal force. The whole crowd cringed as one and Colton could see his Clansmen wincing.

The cat shrieked in pain and fury, but Jaimee was already scrambling off the ground. She levitated without seeming to struggle at all, and in a split second, she was on top of him. Bryce tried to get away by contorting onto his stomach.

He almost succeeded, but she was a fraction of a second quicker. She reached him just as he coiled all four limbs under him to spring away.

She never made it off her knees, but she didn't have to. She lunged for him, stabbed the webbing of one thumb on the back of his neck, and pinned him. The rest of his body whipped and thrashed in all directions, but he couldn't get away.

She punched down with merciless ferocity and smashed her fist into the back of his head. She pounded his head face downward into the paving stones and his body flopped unconscious on the ground beneath her.

She arched back her arm to punch again, but she stopped herself in time. The cat lay beneath her locked left arm. Bryce was out cold and blood flowed from his mouth where his fangs had hit the ground.

She crouched over him heaving for breath. She kept her fist upraised for what seemed like an eternity. Dead silence fell over the courtyard and all the Clansmen stared at her in dazed shock.

She finally looked up as if seeing them for the first time. Her shoulders quaked as she struggled to breathe. She had done it. She beat Bryce, but at a terrible cost.

Blood saturated her new shirt and caked her face and hair. Gore streamed down her arm and dripped from her elbow. Colton shivered when he thought about the state her arm must be in.

She leaned back on her heels and then lurched to her feet. She swayed there scanning the crowd. Did she think any of these men would be stupid enough to step forward and challenge her again?

No one moved. They wouldn't dare. A bargain was a bargain. She defeated Bryce. That meant they had to obey her the same way they obeyed Colton.

Duncan ripped out of Colton's grip and charged into the fortress. His receding footsteps woke Colton from his stupor and he went downstairs.

He emerged in the lower passage and entered the courtyard just as Jaimee staggered out of the square. The Buchanans parted to let her through.

She stumbled approaching the passage. She cradled her injured arm and blood streamed down her cheeks. She veered sideways and Reid ducked around Colton to catch her.

He lowered her onto a bench inside the passage just as Duncan returned carrying an armload of bandages and a jar of healing ointment.

"Och, lassie!" Duncan breathed. "Ye're in a right state!"

She looked straight up into Colton's eyes. The wild madness of a second before was starting to fade and some of the softness came back into her features. "I had to, Colton. I had to."

"Aye, lass," he murmured. "Ye had to and ye did. No one will challenge ye again. Ye can bet on that."

He only had to look into the courtyard to know he was right. All his Clansmen stood around watching the brothers attend to her injuries. None of the men had moved. They didn't return to their training.

"Louisa is coming to bring ye a clean shirt, lass," Duncan told her. "Let me clean ye up in the meantime. Och! Will ye look at this?"

He peeled back her sleeve to reveal the punctures on her wrist and arm. Bryce had torn open the muscle on the back of her hand and several deep holes leaked blood all the way up to the elbow.

She winced when he started wiping the blood off her hand and repositioning the flesh in the right places. She clamped her mouth shut and turned her face away while he smeared the cuts with ointment and wrapped her whole arm in bandages.

Louisa came out of the fortress and screamed when she saw Jaimee. "What on Earth have ye been doing with yerself, lassie? Och, Colton! How could ye let the lads thrash her so?"

"It's she that's done the thrashing, lassie. Go on inside, the pair of ye. Ye come out when ye're ready to carry on. I'll...."

"No!" Jaimee pushed herself off the bench and got to her feet. "I want to continue. I earned this. Don't send me away, Colton. I have to continue."

"Och, listen to this daft woman!" Reid muttered. "She's off her duff!"

"I said no!" she insisted. "I did this so I could train your Clansmen. I'll change my shirt and wash my face....and then I'm coming straight back out here. Tell them, Colton."

Colton sighed. He should have known it would go this way. He *did* know it would go this way. "Och, lass, ye'll be the death of us all. Very well. Go on with Louisa and get yerself cleaned up. I'll go deal with Bryce."

Her eyes slid over to the courtyard where all the men stood watching her. "Will he be all right?"

"He'll be just grand," Duncan replied. "He'll be surlier than ever when he comes to and has to admit he's been beaten by a lassie."

She blinked at him in a daze and then blushed. "I didn't mean to hurt him. It's just.... he's damn tough, you know?"

Reid laughed and the sound of his voice broke the spell. "He is that and ye beat him with no weapons or ought. Ye earned yer place, lassie."

She finally allowed herself to smile at him and turned away to follow Louisa inside. Colton shared a knowing glance with his brothers and then he strode out into the courtyard.

He walked over to Bryce. The cat still lay flat on his face where Jaimee left him. Colton bent over to pick him up, but Alastair got there first. "Let me, laddie. I'll see to him."

"Thanks, lad," Colton murmured. Now he had no choice but to face his Clansmen. They gathered around him still hushed and subdued after what happened.

"What are we to do now, laddie?" Fergus asked. "Do ye still mean for her to train us?"

"Ye all agreed to the bargain," Colton replied. "Ye agreed to obey her and accept her authority if she beat Bryce. Is there a coward among ye that'd go back on yer word after what ye've just seen?"

No one answered him and quite a few people looked away.

"This is naught to do with me any longer," he told them. "Ye all struck a bargain with her and now ye'll honor it as Buchanans and as men. No more challenges. Ye'll all...."

The passage door opened. The noise interrupted him and everyone turned around to see Jaimee returning. She was wearing a clean shirt and she had washed her hair and face, but she still looked much the worse for wear. Scratches covered her face and vanished inside her collar.

Her sleeve covered most of the bandages around her arm, but they still surrounded her hand in a white club. She hesitated when she saw everyone staring at her. Then she squared her shoulders and strode out into the courtyard.

The Clansmen parted again when she crossed to where she'd dropped her jacket. She picked it up and started putting it on. She had to hold it with her fingertips since she couldn't close her hand completely.

Colton took the hint and went back to the passage where Duncan and Reid were gathering up what was left of the bandages. Colton walked away without looking back.

He went straight back up to the gallery and his brothers joined him a second later. They looked down at Jaimee standing amongst the assembled Highlanders. She spoke to them in an undertone that Colton couldn't hear. What was she saying to them?

They hung on her every word and a few of them nodded. A second later, Alastair returned without Bryce and rejoined his Clansmen.

Jaimee pointed at two sides of the courtyard and the men reformed their squares. One of the squares practiced with their weapons while the other went back to their wrestling matches.

Colton watched for a long time, but not one of the men shifted into his tiger form. Hour passed after hour and still no one shifted. Only once, one of the men lost control, but he shifted back in a blink.

Jaimee was across the courtyard at the time and didn't see it. None of the men mentioned it to her, but Colton didn't think she would have commented even if she did see.

She strode around both squares calling instructions and giving the men pointers on their technique. She had plenty to say about how they handled their weapons, but she was just as involved in the wrestling. She even demonstrated throwing some much bigger men. She expertly knocked them off balance and pinned them with no trouble.

The sun was starting to go down by the time Reid tapped Colton's elbow. Colton turned around to see what his brother wanted and discovered that Duncan was gone.

"The messenger from Easthollow is waiting on ye inside, laddie," Reid told him.

Colton snapped out of his trance. He had completely forgotten about all the other business waiting for him in his office. Reid and Duncan must have left hours ago while Colton got entranced watching Jaimee work.

He hurried away, but his mind remained behind. He wished he could have stayed down on the courtyard to see and hear everything, but that would have defeated the purpose of having her in the first place. She had to do this herself.

Chapter 12

Jaimee crossed the courtyard and picked up a dirk one of the Buchanans had left lying on the ground. She recognized the weapon. It was one of Alastair's. After spending all day in the courtyard with these men, she now knew nearly all of them by face and name.

She had been watching Fergus and Alastair fighting earlier. Alastair had finished a saber fight against Fergus and then put his weapons down when he went to the wrestling matches next. He must have forgotten to take his dirk with him.

She turned the weapon over in her hands examining the blade. It was made of a curious combination of metals she had never seen before. Fergus had executed several powerful hacks at Alastair. Alastair used this dirk to deflect the attacks, but the blade showed no sign of damage, chips, or even any scratches.

Fergus startled her by slapping her on the back. "Dinnae get in any more fights on yer way to the dining hall, lassie. None of us wants blood in our food."

He laughed loudly and headed for the passage to leave with his Clansmen. "Fergus!" she called after him.

"Aye, lass." He turned back still smirking.

She held up the dirk. "What metals do you use to make your blades? Where do you get the raw materials to forge these?"

"That? It's naught but a bit of fliuralt."

"What?" she asked. "I've never heard of that."

"Aye. Our lads mine it in the mountains." He pointed at the high peaks surrounding Icemeet. "Ye should go on and ask Boyd."

"Who? There was no one out here today by that name."

"Och, no! He's our blacksmith. He forges all our blades. He can tell ye all ye want to ken about fliuralt."

He walked away and left her standing there still studying the dirk in her hands. So the Buchanans used some kind of metal no one else knew about. This meant something—something important. She just couldn't figure out what it was.

Either way, it confirmed for her that she wasn't in the same dimension as normal Scotland—not the Scotland connected with the world she knew. This world used different elements, different species, different history—different everything.

She started to turn away. Her arm was really starting to hurt. She probably shouldn't have gotten in a fight against one of the Highland tigers, but she had to prove herself somehow.

It worked, too. All the men listened to her and obeyed her for the rest of the day. She even noticed an improvement in their fighting skills, now that they had to actually practice instead of just shifting all the time.

She turned the blade over in her fingertips trying to decide what to do with it. She wanted to keep it, but that wouldn't be right. She should return it to Alastair. He wouldn't want to lose a weapon as fine as this.

She was on her way to the dining hall anyway. She would return it to him there. She turned to the passage to leave the courtyard and stopped dead in her tracks when she saw Colton coming toward her.

He was alone for once. Reid and Duncan weren't with him, though she had to change her opinion of them after they helped her dress her wounds earlier. She never dreamed they could be so kind to her after she just knocked out their Clansmen in front of everyone.

She almost wished Reid and Duncan *were* with Colton now. She tried to ignore the fact that he stood on the gallery watching her all day, but he made her nervous. She worried at first that he might be judging her ability to teach his Clansmen anything. They were all fierce fighters in their own right.

An hour into the day, she had to admit the truth. Every time she glanced up, she saw him gazing down at her with approval. Was he checking her out?

He strode up to her and burst into a huge smile. Now she knew he was checking her out. "Och, ye've made a powerful first impression on the lads, lassie. They're all down at the dining hall talking about yer victory over Bryce. They'll be talking about that one for months."

The blood rushed to her cheeks. "Great. I was hungry. Now I'll have to skip dinner."

"Not a bit of it. Ye must make yer appearance and let them make a fuss over ye. It's only right after ye triumphed the way ye did."

"I don't think so." She held out the dirk. "Maybe you could go down there and give this back to Alastair for me."

He frowned. "Arenae ye hungry? Ye must eat something."

"I don't have much of an appetite."

"After that day? I dinnae believe ye, lass."

"I'll figure something out. I don't want anyone making a fuss over me."

"If ye dinnae fancy going to the dining hall, perhaps ye'd consent to share yer dinner with me again. No one will make a fuss over ye in me room."

She snorted. "Except you, right?"

Now it was his turn to color and he lowered his eyelashes. If she ever doubted that he wanted something more with her, that blush confirmed it. "Ye have me number, lassie."

"I don't think that's a good idea," she replied.

"It's a splendid idea. What could be better?"

"I don't want to make a habit of it. I'm only here temporarily. It would be a really bad idea for you to get attached to me."

He only laughed. He looked like a completely different person when he laughed. He didn't look as much like a tank about to explode at any second.

"Why is that funny?" she asked. "You know it's true."

"It isnae funny. I'm laughing because I like what I see in ye. I'm delighted at the way ye handled the men today. It was a stroke of genius on me own part if I do say so meself."

"Yeah, you're a genius—modest, too."

They both laughed and she had to fight down that lifting feeling of excitement in her chest. She couldn't start feeling this way about him. It was a recipe for disaster.

"If ye dinnae fancy eating with me, perhaps ye'd fancy yer chances sparring with me instead." He waved toward the empty courtyard.

Her eyes fell out of their sockets. "You want to spar—now?"

"Why not now? No one will see."

"Maybe not now. I'm injured, you know."

He laughed even harder. "Go on with ye, lass. Ye can thrash me with one hand tied behind yer back."

His eyes twinkled so temptingly that she actually thought about it. Should she? "If the men find out, you'll never live it down."

"And neither will ye. If I beat ye, it may undermine yer authority with them."

"That's it." She put the dirk on the ground and yanked off her jacket. "You're on. I'm gonna stomp you into next week."

He laughed at her some more. "Ye keep living the dream, lassie. What'll ye wager I throw ye in the first minute."

"You bastard!" she hissed. "I'm gonna teach you a lesson you'll never forget."

She strode out into the open courtyard. This might be a terrible idea, but that infuriating glint in his eye and his rye smirk wouldn't let her back down. She had to show him she could best him.

He went over to the wall and pulled his tartan off his shoulder. He let it hang and shot her challenging grins while he unbuttoned his jacket. He dropped it on the ground and then pulled off his shirt.

She hesitated when she saw how big he was. His clothes hid his bulk. He was much bigger and more chiseled than she realized. He was almost as big as Ewan, but much leaner and his shoulders were even broader.

He kicked off his shoes, pulled off his socks, unbuckled his saber and sporran, and laid them on top of his jacket along with his dirk.

He didn't put his tartan back on his shoulder. He tucked it into his belt and came toward her naked from the waist up and bare-legged like his Clansmen.

She experienced another torch of adrenaline seeing him like this. He messed up his hair when he pulled his shirt off and he looked much more feral. All his manners and refinement went out the window. She was facing a block of pure, untamed mountain power.

She side-stepped into the courtyard. Was she really going to try to wrestle with this man? She only had one hand. What was she thinking?

"How do I know you won't shift in the middle of this?" she asked.

"I promise I winnae. Does that satisfy ye?"

She didn't answer. She circled him and she took a deeper stance. She would have to adjust her tactics to deal with the difference in their sizes and weights. He was obviously much stronger as well as bigger and heavier.

He wiped the smirk off his face and bent his knees to lower his weight closer to the ground. He brought his hands up and tucked his chin to his chest. His eyes flashed with deadly, raw determination and she tensed for the first close.

His intense glare erased the last of her doubts. He was preparing himself for a serious match. He didn't underestimate her, nor was he intimidated by the prospect of her beating him. She could go all out without offending him.

He inched to the right and she did the same. What if someone came back and saw them grappling? Would the whole Clan come running to see the outcome? What would she do then? Would it mean something to the Clan if she beat Colton in combat?

She should have established the rules and conditions before she agreed to this, but he didn't give her a chance to reconsider. He darted forward and feinted grabbing her before he backstepped out of her reach.

He made two more feints to throw her off track before he rushed her. He caught her in a second and all her energy erupted. She was back in combat and everything depended on winning.

He tackled her around the ribs and would have flattened her, but she didn't fight him. She let him pick her up and he turned her around to throw her, but she struck back and swiped her leg around his knee.

She hooked his foot off the ground so they both stood on one leg. He tried one more time to yank her sideways and she let him. She hefted his leg higher and flung her weight against him.

She toppled him along with herself and twisted onto her side trying to slam him to the ground. She tried once to grab his arm, but he was too big and too strong for that. She couldn't budge his grip around her ribs, so she switched her strategy and went for his neck and head instead.

Both their bodies crashed onto the stones and he grunted in pain. She struck without warning and nailed her elbow into his face. In a split second, she was on top of him and used his grip around her chest to her advantage.

She lunged for him and pinned her elbow against his throat. The hand of that arm was useless anyway so she used her elbow.

She crushed his neck, but she wasn't banking on the rest of him. He kicked out and flipped her off easily. She somersaulted away and both of them vaulted to their feet in seconds.

They faced each other breathing hard and both of them even more mindlessly bent on defeating each other. He was quicker than he should have been for a guy his size, but he impressed her with his ability to control himself. He didn't shift accidentally like the men.

She held off waiting for his next engagement, but he didn't engage. He hung back and waited for her to do it. He waited so long that she couldn't delay anymore or she would lose her nerve.

He must have come to the same conclusion. He charged her at the same instant she rushed him. They closed in a desperate struggle for dominance. Both of them tried to sweep each other's legs, consolidate holds on each other's arms, necks, and chests, but they both parried every move the other made.

He got his elbow around her neck, but she evaded and slipped out of it. She ducked, hooked her arm around his leg, and flipped him, only to get turned over and pinned by him in turn.

She escaped from that, too, and when they both scuttled clear to face each other on their feet, they started circling again.

She got a fleeting glimpse at his eyes and didn't recognize him. He had gone over into some mindless trance of wild madness. Did he even know what he was doing anymore?

They stopped facing each other and traded feints for a while. He jabbed out one massive arm to grab her, but she ducked out of the way. Then she dove sideways in a fake tackle, only to pull back and throw him off balance.

All at once, he burst out laughing and his whole aspect transformed before her eyes. He straightened up, lowered his arms, and laughed out loud. He hugged one arm over his stomach and slapped his thigh.

Her befogged brain mistook his laughter for some kind of ruse and she attacked. She took advantage of him lowering his guard and she dove for him. She collided with his middle, hooked his leg, and toppled him in a flash.

He smashed down on his shoulders still laughing. "Aaargh! What are ye doing, lassie?"

She gritted her teeth and pounced on him swinging her fists. He reacted instantly, but he didn't stop laughing. He thrust out one arm, blocked her punch, and knocked it aside. Quicker than thought, he rotated onto his shoulder and followed through with his other arm.

He snatched her wrist out of thin air and guided her sideways to drop her on the ground at his side.

She shot upright to find him back on his feet, too, but he didn't attack her back. He held up both hands. "Hold yer horses, lassie. Stop." He chuckled some more.

"What's the matter?" she hissed. "Are you ready to surrender?"

He laughed again. "Let's call it a draw before one of us gets seriously hurt. We'd be lying out here bleeding half the night and no one would find us."

He lowered his arms and straightened up. The pale light of the setting sun shone on his chest and shoulders. His hair had come completely undone, but seeing him like this didn't change her first impression of him. He was beyond powerful with that deadly tiger energy simmering beneath the surface.

He held up both hands. "We can declare ye the winner if ye insist."

"No way! I didn't win."

"Neither did I." He extended one hand. "Shall we call it a draw?"

She eyed him preparing for the next attack, but it never came. She frowned and then lowered her hands. "All right."

He stuck his hand out even farther. "Am I too low for ye to shake me hand, lassie? Ye're torturing me."

She scrutinized him for another moment, but those words did something to her. She shook his hand and winced when he squeezed her injured hand too hard. "A draw," she agreed.

He burst into a huge grin. "Wonderful. Ye can thrash me another time if ye really must."

She had to laugh. "Can I thrash you in front of your Clansmen?"

"Och, no! If ye do that, they'll all want a go."

She hesitated and then blurted out, "Thanks for making yourself scarce today. I appreciate you not standing over me......at least, not where they could see you."

"Ye're welcome. Ye were right. They cannae learn from ye with me around."

"They aren't lacking in enthusiasm. I can see that, even if they do need a lot of work."

"Aye? What do they need?"

She shrugged. "Just practice, really. They don't have as much practice as they might if they weren't so concerned with winning."

He laughed again. She'd never seen him so happy. "What's more important than winning, after all that?"

"You know what I mean. They can't solve every problem by shifting. If you're going to rely on shifting to win this war, I'm out of a job."

He strolled over to his clothes and started putting them on in reverse order. She almost regretted the moment when he put his shirt on and she lost sight of his body.

"Ye're right that we can drive the Creightons off by doing the same old thing. We need something more—something decisive to turn the tables on them."

"That reminds me." She crossed the courtyard and came back with Alastair's dirk. "What can you tell me about how these weapons are forged?"

"Ye talk to Boyd about that. He can talk ye into an early grave about forging weapons."

"What is fliuralt? I've never heard of it."

He arched one eyebrow at her while he buttoned his jacket. "That isnae possible, lassie. It's a common metal."

"It's common in these mountains, isn't it?"

"Aye. Of course."

"But it isn't common anywhere else.... like across the Boundless, maybe?"

"What are ye saying, lass?"

"The Creightons don't forge their weapons with fliuralt, do they?"

"What if they dinnae? They can forge all manner of weapons out of some other metal and kill as many Buchanans as they wish."

Jaimee shook her head still studying the dirk. "I don't know what I'm saying."

He finally buckled on his saber, picked up his socks and shoes, and waved toward the citadel. "It's getting dark. If ye arenae hungry enough to go get yer dinner, let me walk ye back to yer room."

"Aren't you going to put your shoes on?"

"Och, no! I cannae stand them. I only wear them as I'm acting Clan Chief. I have no choice but to get up in these fancy clothes or I'd be walking around barefoot and shirtless with the rest of the lads. I wish most days I hadnae been born first. Then I'd be out on the mountain running wild like Duncan and Fletcher."

She studied him on the side. She'd never heard him talk about his duties this way. He always conducted himself with such decorum. It must be hard to want to go off into the mountains but to be stuck inside running the Clan's affairs instead.

She could see so much more clearly now how his position hid his true nature. He let it out in the courtyard just now. He would probably never do it again, especially not if anyone else was around to see.

She thought at the time that he kept their fight private for her sake. Now she realized he was doing it to protect his own standing. He had to show everyone that he was being a responsible Clan Chief instead of a wild boy running around barefoot.

He must have sacrificed a lot for his Clan. As soon as he got back to his room, he would put his shoes back on, comb his hair, and go right on doing it. He would never let his Clansmen know how much he ached for a different life.

She suffered another stab of desire to help him, to lighten his burden. She was already doing that, but he needed more. He needed a mate—a mate for life who wouldn't run off to Ironforge as soon as this was over.

He stopped in front of her bedroom door and turned to face her. Another glint of fire sparkled in his eye, but he didn't laugh or even smile. That glimmer of light meant something different now.

"I'm grateful for yer help with the men, lass," he murmured. "I'm hopeful about this campaign, now that ye're guiding us."

She tried to shrug it off. "I'm only one person. I can only do so much and we still have to contend with the dragons."

"I'm still grateful." He picked up her hand. She expected him to kiss it again, but he didn't. He only squeezed her fingers. "I had fun sparring with ye tonight, lassie. Perhaps ye'd like to take a thrashing another time."

"Perhaps you'd like to get your head smashed in," she snarled.

He burst out laughing again, this time loudly enough to draw a glare from one of the maids who happened to be passing on the landing just then.

"Ye'd certainly have to do that behind closed doors. Me Clan would execute ye if ye did. Good night, lass."

Chapter 13

J aimee went into her bedroom and shut the door. She really was hungry, but she couldn't bring herself to go down to the dining hall. She laid Alastair's dirk on her bedside table. She would have to return it to him tomorrow.... or whenever she saw him n ext.

She sat down on the bed. Her arm throbbed and she wouldn't find any Ibuprofen here. She just had to grit her teeth and wait for her arm to heal.

She still felt Colton's fingers pressed into her skin and her heart fluttered remembering everything that happened between them. Adrenaline fired her guts when she thought about seeing him with his shirt off.

She had her arms around his bare chest just a few minutes ago. She grabbed his legs and rubbed her body against his. She had been lying on top of him with nothing but his kilt between them.

Her cheeks flamed and she turned away, but there was no one here to see her embarrassment. No one knew that she and Colton had been wrestling on the ground or that she touched his body like that.

Was that why he didn't want anyone to see them together? Was he ashamed of what they did? He didn't act ashamed.

He looked incredible in his clean, crisp clothes the first time she saw him in the courtyard. He impressed her with his power and rugged energy then, but that was nothing compared to tonight.

The tiger energy hiding just beneath his skin came to the surface so much more powerfully tonight when he let his guard down. He didn't hide it behind manners and gentility. He let her see just how wild and brutal he could be, but he never hurt her. That was the last thing he wanted.

Then she remembered the way he looked down into her eyes after she defeated Bryce. He understood that she had to prove herself. He understood her in ways she never expected any man to understand her.

She knew he was putting the moves on her in his own rough way. She should stop it. She shouldn't let it develop into anything if she was only going to leave him. She didn't want to do to him what Liam did to Edeena.

She wouldn't have the same excuse Liam had. Jaimee knew exactly what she was doing. Colton needed to mate for life, but she didn't want to stop. How long had it been since she got the attention of a man—a man whose attention she really wanted—a man who was her equal in combat and whom she respected in every other way?

Just thinking about him excited her. She loved talking to him, joking with him, and even sparring with him. She wanted to do it again. She wanted to see if one of them could actually win against the other.

She was really starting to like him. Could she walk away from that? Could she stand to return to Detroit so he could marry someone else? The thought made her sick to her stomach and not because she was hungry.

Someone knocked on her door and she groaned. She didn't want to go another round with Edeena. "Who is it?"

A man's voice boomed through the door. "It's Liam."

Jaimee sprang to her feet and pulled the door open. "Hi. How are you?"

He pushed into her room without asking for permission. Then he grabbed the door out of her hand and closed it also without asking for permission.

"What are you doing?" she demanded. "I was just about to go to sleep. I'm tired."

"You can't! We're leaving. We have to get out of here tonight."

Jaimee froze. "Leave! What do you mean?"

"I've been waiting all day to catch you alone, but you've been so busy I didn't get a chance. It's dark outside, so we can go now. We can get across the Boundless and return to Kald the way we planned."

"You mean.... you would walk out on Edeena all over again?"

He waved that away. "Our mission is more important."

She snorted and threw herself down on the bed. "I don't think so. I gave Colton my word I'd...."

"Oh, don't start with that giving your word nonsense! You're on a mission for the President of the United States. Whatever you told Colton comes second to that."

Jaimee stiffened. "Your word might not mean anything to you, but I got you out of the vault on the condition that I would help Colton train his Clansmen. I just got my arm mangled by one of those cats. I won't leave, now that I finally earned their respect."

She held up her bandaged arm, but he barely noticed. He went over to the window and squinted toward Kald. "That's why tonight will be the best time to go. They won't be watching, now that you earned their trust."

"So you want me to violate that trust? You're as bad as Colton says you are."

He ignored that, too. "What are you waiting for? Come on. Let's go."

"How do you plan to get out of the fortress? The guards at the gate would have to open it for you, and if they see us fleeing, they'll alert the Buchanans. We can't leave."

"I can use my magic to fly us over the walls. We don't have to use the gate."

She shook her head, punched her pillows with her good hand, and reclined back on them. "You have an obligation to Edeena. You're the one who got her into this mess. You might not have intended to mate-bond with her, but you did, so you still owe her something. You're responsible for her. You can't just abandon her all over again."

"Fine. I'll take her back to Kald with us if that's the way you feel."

"No way. She'd be in mortal danger there. At least here she's with her family. You can't put her even more at risk than you already have."

Liam rolled his eyes to Heaven. "Please. The Buchanans hate me. They want to kill me to break the bond."

"Whose fault is that? Maybe if you tried to get along with them and show them that you really have her best interest in mind, they would change their attitude toward you."

He glared at her from across the room. "You really aren't going? You're just going to turn your back on our mission?"

"I'm not turning my back on it. You said yourself you thought Lady Rhona might be another name for Lady Ilisa."

"What does that have to do with anything?"

"The Buchanans think Lady Ilisa is a Buchanan. She was married to Neill, the Buchanans' Clan Chief."

"So what if she was?"

"Then the mystery of who she is and who she was married to is here, not in Kald at all. I mean, how could a Creighton be married to the Chief of Clan Buchanan?"

"How the hell are we supposed to find out?" Liam demanded. "No one has seen Neill Buchanan in years. I've been asking around. He's a recluse. Not even Edeena has seen him since she was a girl."

"We won't find out at all if we leave. If we stick around a little longer, we might be able to question him. He might be able to tell us if she really is Lady Rhona in disguise."

He groaned and hung his head. "This is a terrible idea. You know that, don't you?"

"Both you and I have obligations in this fortress. Leaving now would be cowardly, and even if it wasn't, it would be contrary to our mission. Get comfortable and stick it out a little longer at least until we can fulfill our obligations to these people."

He snarled at the walls around him. "I hate this place! I hate being stuck here when Lily is over there with *them*."

"If Colton is right, Lily is perfectly safe over there. She's married to a prince and living as a lady in a castle. You should be more concerned about Edeena."

He grumbled some more and scowled out the window, but Jaimee was in no mood to sympathize with him. He made his bed and now he had to lie in it. She wouldn't let him run out just because he didn't like it here.

She also wouldn't let him use their mission as an excuse to betray Edeena again. He'd already done enough damage as it was.

Chapter 14

C olton stepped out of the passage and the snowy wind bit into his exposed arms and chest. His bare feet chilled on the paving stones.

He cast his eye around the courtyard and found about sixty people crowded body to body from wall to wall. Clan Buchanan's fighting force stood around talking while they waited to go out on their training expedition in the deep mountains north of Icemeet.

Colton spotted Jaimee standing by the gate. Fergus, Alastair, Ewan, and Bryce all stood around talking to her.

Bryce had become exceptionally attached to her since she beat him in front of the whole Clan. He had taken it upon himself to appoint himself her personal lieutenant.

He had made it his job to keep all the other Clansmen in line. He claimed she needed him to stop everyone else from acting up even though the other men wouldn't dream of stepping out of line with her around.

She had taken his efforts in good grace and a very affectionate relationship had sprung up between them, a relationship only equaled by the attachment all the other Clansmen felt toward her.

A group of female archers occupied the opposite corner and they kept close to each other. These women trained together apart from the men. The archers hadn't been involved with Jaimee's training sessions. Colton was looking forward to seeing her earn the archers' respect the same way she'd earned everyone else's.

Edeena should have been with the archers. She usually went out with them whenever the Buchanans called the archers into service, but Edeena was staying home this time.

Colton had given her several stern warnings impressing on her that he was placing her solely responsible for Liam's conduct while Colton and his brothers were away. Colton put her in charge of making sure Liam didn't run away or do anything to sabotage the Clan.

He strode over to Bryce and Jaimee. "Are we all ready?"

"Ready, lad," Bryce replied.

Colton couldn't help smiling when he faced Jaimee. "Are ye ready, lassie?"

"I'm as ready as I'm ever going to get." She glanced behind him toward the archers. "If *they* can handle it, I can."

He laughed in spite of himself. He couldn't remember laughing this much in years. "They'll be running as tigers, lassie. They can run faster than any human."

"Well, I guess I'll just have to run faster, won't I?"

"Try to keep up." He threw back his head and called up to the guards. "Open the gate!"

The counterweight started to descend and all the Clansmen pressed back against each other to make room for it. The gate creaked up and a shout went through the assembled Highlanders.

Men streamed out of the fortress and Colton got swept up in the stampede. Everyone burst into a fast run straight up the mountain. Colton worked his legs against the steep climb and the heat pumping in his veins dispelled the cold. He was back in the harsh elements testing himself against the mountain and his Clansmen.

Excitement and raw power coursed through him as he picked up speed. The strain on his legs spurred him to run faster and push himself harder. He reveled in his own strength and the chance to test himself. He'd been cooped up inside Icemeet for far too long.

His kilt kicked against his knees as he ran and the cold embraced every part of him. He might as well be naked out here with snowflakes biting his skin and face.

Snowflakes. He glanced over his shoulder and picked out Jaimee running with the rest. She kept pace with them, but the archers were gaining on her. The archers had been the last to leave the courtyard and he could already see the gate lowering back into position. Everyone was outside, which meant there was only one way to go: up the mountain.

The archers drew level with Jaimee. She took one look at them and cracked a grin. She picked up speed with her long, midnight hair streaming behind her. Wild excitement flashed across her face and some of the archers grinned back at her.

Like lightning, the five archers nearest her transformed into tigers. They dropped on all fours and set off bounding up the mountain. Their furry paws barely touched the harsh stones and they outstripped her, but she only laughed and ran faster.

She watched the cats streaking ahead and her flinty eye fixed on Colton. His adrenaline spiked off the charts when her features hardened and she adjusted her course to intercept him. He couldn't let her win this race.

He spun forward and shifted in a heartbeat. He lunged forward and landed on his hands, but they weren't hands anymore. His paws touched the ground and he rocketed ahead running with the wind.

The Clansmen ahead of him had already vanished into the dense trees farther up the mountain. They evaporated into the forest and skimmed along the ground as light as fog.

He lost sight of Jaimee and the archers. There was no way she could keep up with the tigers. He plunged into the shadows, hurled branches, ducked around rocks, and dove under bushes. He overtook Bryce and Alastair and then all three of them were running level with Reid, Duncan, Ewan, and the rest.

Colton ran for what seemed like a long time before the trees opened into rock again. He scanned the countryside searching for the pathway to the Clan's meeting place....and then he saw her.

Jaimee appeared behind the trees farther up the mountain. She was nowhere near the others. She had run around the forest to avoid it completely. He saw in the blink of an eye that she was miles closer to their destination than any of the others.

Bryce and Alastair didn't see her at all. Duncan gave a low growl in Colton's ear. That crazy woman had beaten them all. They might be faster and stronger and more familiar with the mountain, but she had outsmarted them. None of the Buchanans was close enough to catch her in time.

She dove sideways and vanished behind some rocks. She plunged down a side canyon behind the mountain. How did she know? This was her first time leaving Icemeet and she had never ventured into the mountains before. How did she manage to find the quickest route to the Buchanans' secret hideout?

It didn't matter now because she was already in the canyon. The rest of the tigers filed onto the path. It would wind for miles over rough country before it descended through a different chasm to join up with Jaimee's route.

The archers emerged from the woods. They probably thought they had left her behind. The whole Clan was in for a shock when they reached the hideout and found her there waiting for them.

Reid, Duncan, Bryce, and Alastair set off to follow their Clansmen, but Colton's heart wasn't in it anymore. He had been so certain of his victory and now she had beaten him. He had to find a way to best her.

He shook those thoughts out of his head and a lightness came into his heart. He would have laughed if he had been in his human form, but the Highland tigers didn't laugh. This lightness carried him on much quicker.

He didn't have to best her. He would congratulate her with good grace. He was too glad that she was making a place for herself among his Clan. If she kept winning these victories, maybe she would decide to stay.

He shouldn't give himself false hopes, but he found it impossible not to. He couldn't imagine life without her. Did she feel the same way?

He was a bigger fool than Liam and Edeena if he let himself fall for her. She had already told him to his face that she didn't plan to stay. She would leave and break his heart. Then he wouldn't be good for anything, especially not leading his Clan.

Just thinking about her made him too happy. As long as she was here, he could only admire her and encourage her to keep winning. He respected her too much to do anything else, even if he never claimed her as his mate.

The tigers fell in a single-file line running down the steep defile. The frontrunners kept up a brutal pace. They still thought they stood a chance to beat those behind them. Little did they know.

They finally turned a corner and raced into an open area sheltered by towering pine trees. The harsh wind scouring the mountaintop had bent the trunks and flattened the branches to form a roof.

Piles of bundles stood in a line to one side where the Buchanans had stashed their supplies for this exercise. Jamie sat on a crate to one side running her sharpening stone down the length of her dirk. Bandages still surrounded her hand up to the elbow, but she never let her injuries slow her down.

She looked up in mock surprise when the tigers strode into the clearing. Then, one by one, they shifted back into men. The Highlanders stood in a row glaring at her.

A second later, the archers caught up and they shifted, too. "What the devil is *she* doing here?" Colton's cousin Adaira snarled.

"Did ye cheat, lassie?" Bryce boomed.

She raised her eyebrows. "How could I cheat? The race was from Icemeet to here. What do you think—that I spread my wings and flew here?" She laughed at her own joke.

"How did ye manage it, then?" Ewan demanded. "Ye were behind us all the way."

"You think so?" She went back to sharpening her dirk, raised it to her eye, and sighted down the blade. "Well, then I should still be running over the mountain instead of sitting here."

Colton pushed past his cousins and strode into the clearing. "Admit it, lads. She beat us all fair and square." He went over to the piles of goods and started rifling the food stores.

"Ye arenae going to stand this, lad!" Bryce snapped. "She's pulled some witchcraft or some ought. She couldnae beat us. Ye'll have to adjudicate the outcome to ensure she didnae cheat."

"Adjudicate?" Colton burst out laughing. "Och, ye'll get no adjudication from me—not today. She's beat the lot of us and no mistake about it. Now hold yer noise and help me prepare our supper before we all catch our deaths."

She beamed up at him and he found himself smiling back at her.

"Ye winnae side with an alien against yer own Clan, Colton," Adaira insisted. "How do ye ken she didnae pull a fast one on us?"

"How do I ken? I saw her with me own eyes, that's how. She circled the forest and took the steeper incline through Hermit's Nest. She came out from behind the trees for a fair ten seconds and I wasnae the only one who saw her." Colton turned to his brother Duncan. "Ye saw her yer own self, laddie. Tell them ye did."

"Aye," Duncan murmured. "The trollop didnae bother with the forest at all. She came out on the ridge just long enough to see us all scrambling our way through the gully and then she was gone."

"The foul witch!" Adaira growled and some of the other archers started laughing.

"That's the end of it!" Ewan threw up his hands, stormed into the camp, and flung himself down on the ground next to a tree trunk. "I winnae pit meself against her again as long as I live. Ye can mark that one down, lads. I'm done—finished."

A few more people laughed and the group broke up. They spread out around the campsite and started unpacking their supplies. The talk turned to other matters and everyone forgot about Jaimee's latest victory.

She shot a quizzical look up at Colton, but he couldn't stop smiling at her. She had won another round thanks to him and Duncan supporting her.

He returned to the supplies and started getting their evening meal ready. Those were the terms of the race—whoever reached the campsite first got to sit on their backside and relax while the losers cooked and made camp.

The archers started unpacking the goods nearest to Jaimee's spot. Colton didn't look over at her again, but he heard the other women talking to her and then laughter broke out again. So that part was taken care of, too. She had beaten the archers in a fair contest of strength and wits. Now they were all friends.

He kept working until he found the slabs of meat for the party's dinner. He set up a chopping board to cut the meat, but when he heard Jaimee's voice in the hubbub, he looked up.

Adaira and her sister Bonnie were standing over Jaimee. "We need to get into that crate ye're sitting on, lassie," Bonnie told Jaimee. "Ye'll have to budge yerself and do yer lording somewhere else."

All three of them burst out laughing. Jaimee's cheeks glowed when she stood up, put away her sharpening stone, sheathed her dirk, and vacated the area so they could tear into the crate.

She took two steps away, turned back, and watched them at their work. "Should I stand here and tell you how to pitch the tents?"

The other two laughed. "Pitch yer own tent, lassie," Adaira countered. "We curl up and sleep on the ground. Only a lady like ye can sleep in a tent tonight."

Jaimee laughed along with them, but a second later when they were occupied with their task, she cast another questioning glance around at the men. She spotted Colton watching her and her expression changed.

She hardened her features in another stern mask of determination. He could read the thoughts going through her mind without asking what she was thinking. She was making up her mind to sleep on the ground, too, even though she had no way of keeping herself warm. If the Buchanans could do it, she would do it, too.

Colton went back to his chopping, but his mind started churning for a way to help her. She didn't have any fur, nor did the Clan bring any tent or blankets for her. Everyone had completely forgotten about her.

He kicked himself for not thinking of this before, but no human had ever accompanied the Buchanans on one of these expeditions before. He had never set foot in these mountains with anyone but his own kin. They all knew how to handle themselves. None of them needed bedding or protection from the weather.

Chapter 15

Colton finished cutting up the meat and carried it over to the fires his Clansmen had started to cook their evening meal. Duncan and Alastair had already started boiling water and they had set up spits to roast the meat.

Jaimee sat aside warming herself against the chill. She held her bandaged hand out to the flames and the light glowed on her cheeks when she laughed.

"Aren't you going to shift and tear the raw meat apart with your fangs?" she teased. "You don't need to cook it."

"We could," Alastair countered, "but as ye insist that we train as men, we havenae any choice but to eat it the old-fashioned way."

"It tasted better this way at any rate," Bryce rumbled. "Ye cannae beat the juicy flavor of roasted meat. Ye dinnae ken how cold and stringy it is eaten raw."

She made a face and everyone laughed. "I think I'll skip it."

"Go on, lass!" Duncan seized a hunk off of Colton's cutting board and shoved it in her face. "Give it a lash! Ye'll love it."

Everyone laughed and Jaimee joined in. She was such a good sport. She never took their friendly ribbing seriously. "Let me guess. You go and eat grass to get rid of your hairballs, too. Just make sure you do that somewhere I don't have to watch."

More laughter broke out, and when Colton caught her looking at him, he colored and looked away. He kept apart from her for the whole meal. Besides, the archers were crowding around all trying to talk to her. They obviously wanted to catch up on getting to know her after their Clansmen had been with her all this time.

A few people drifted away from the fires as the night wore on. They made their excuses and vanished into the darkness. They would shift and curl up in the trees and rocks for the night.

Jaimee stayed where she was and Colton saw her delaying for as long as she could. She must be dreading the moment when she had to leave to find a place to sleep. Maybe she was ashamed of not being able to take care of herself on the mountain the way the Buchanans did.

Colton waited until only two or three men remained before he sidled over to her and squatted down. "We can make ye a bed here by the fire to keep ye warm, lassie. We cannae have ye catching cold out here. The temperature drops at night and can get right cruel."

"I don't need a bed here. I can take care of myself. Don't worry about me."

"Ye dinnae ken these mountains, lass. Ye'd be dead by morning with no cover."

She smiled at him. Was that genuine affection in her eyes? "I won't be. I'll be fine. Trust me. I can handle it."

He shook his head, but she didn't give him a chance to insist. She stood up and the firelight made her cheeks glow even more from this angle. "Thank you for sticking up for me after the race. I really appreciate it. Good night."

She walked off into the darkness and left him sitting there in turmoil. He couldn't let her put herself in danger. He blamed himself for overlooking her needs. He would never forgive himself if anything happened to her.

He stood up and walked after her. He had to struggle to see in the dark, and in the end, he gave up trying and shifted. He tracked her by smell and then picked out her shadowy outline.

She strolled down the same pathway he and his Clansmen had taken to reach their hideout. She took her sweet time in no particular hurry. She didn't seem to mind the cold.

He caught up with her and shifted back into his normal form. "What are ye doing out here, lassie? Ye'll get yerself lost and not be able to find yer way back to the camp."

She kept walking down the defile. "I told you I'll be fine."

"Where do ye think ye're going, lassie? It's pitch dark out here."

"I just wanted to take a look around."

She turned a bend in the path and stopped. She stepped out onto a rock outcropping and he understood why she came all the way out here in the dark. This corner of the mountain gave a full view of the planes, the Boundless, and Kald.

The wind hit both of them in the face. Tyrekirk sparkled with lights coming from dozens of windows.

Colton took one look and stiffened. "Will ye look at that? There's a light on the planes. The Creightons are crossing the water." He turned to climb down from the rock. "We must get back to the fortress immediately. We must ready our defenses to repel...."

"Hold it." She laid a hand on his arm and a charge of electricity went through him. "It's only one light. It's too small to be an invasion force. It might be nothing."

He crouched down next to her and strained his eyes, but she was right. He couldn't make out anything but that one light. "I'll fetch Reid and Duncan to take a look."

"I have a better idea. Come on."

Before he could stop her, she took off at a run down the mountain heading back the way the expedition came. She ran like anything and he had to push himself to catch up with her. Did she really plan to run all the way back to Icemeet or beyond?

She wound through the mountain paths like she knew them. He was just wondering again how she did it when she sprang up on a different outcropping.

This one jutted to the west and gave a view of the planes from a different angle. She dropped down flat on her stomach and peered down the mountain.

The light coming from Tyrekirk reflected off the Boundless. Now both Colton and Jaimee could see the planes clearly.

Colton dropped down next to her and the rock chilled his chest and stomach. How was she not freezing out here?

Then he heard it. Voices drifted across the planes and up the mountain followed by laughter. "It's Fletcher....and Gavin. What are those lads doing outside the gate?"

She elbowed him, and when he looked at her, she grinned at him. "Now aren't you glad we checked instead of calling the counterassault? They're just fooling around. They're kids. They're running around the way you said you wished you could."

He scowled down the slope at the two boys. Neither of them was over seventeen. So they were out for a lark in the middle of the night and why shouldn't they be? The Buchanans could still go where they pleased on their own land.

The two boys took a big risk camping right under the Creightons' noses, but as soon as Colton thought about the danger, a surge of pride pushed his annoyance away. Good for them for showing up the Creightons.

The Buchanans had every right to camp right up to the water's edge if they wanted to. If an incident like that triggered the invasion, so much the better. The Creightons would learn their lesson one way or the other.

She nudged him again. "Let's get out of here. We don't want them thinking they did anything wrong."

She inched back on the rock and Colton pushed himself up. He followed her back toward the camp, but the closer they got, the more reluctant he was to return.

"I've been thinking, lassie," he began.

"Don't do anything rash," she quipped over her shoulder.

"Ye've nowhere to sleep tonight. Come along with me and I'll keep ye warm. Ye'll freeze to death in this cold."

She spun around so fast her hair whipped her face. "Keep me warm—how?"

"I'll wrap around ye. Me fur will keep the cold out for both of us."

She blinked once and then laughed. She dipped her eyelashes and blushed. "I don't think that's a good idea. People will talk."

"No one will ken—just ye and me. I blame meself for not arranging some blankets or some such thing to keep ye warm. Ye're the first human who's come with us. I didnae think...."

She laid her hand on his arm and squeezed. This time, he could no longer deny that she really meant it like that and the thrill running through him blew his mind in half.

"Listen. I really appreciate the offer, but it isn't a good idea. You need someone you can mate with for life and that isn't me. I'll be going back to my own time pretty soon. You should keep your distance."

"I dinnae want to keep me distance, lassie." He didn't give himself a second to hesitate. He cupped both her cheeks, took a fraction of an instant to lock his eyes on her, and kissed her. "I dinnae want any distance between us at all."

She didn't tear away from him. In fact, her lips softened against his and she kissed him back, even if it only lasted a second.

He held her face in his hands experiencing a flood of emotion unlike anything he'd ever felt in his life. She was beyond beautiful, but that beauty radiated from the inside. She was everything he ever wanted in a woman—in a mate.

His thumbs caressed her cheeks and his fingers laced into her hair, but she still didn't pull away. Did he dare to kiss her again—deeper this time?

His heart threatened to explode out of his chest and his stomach hurt from the tension. He kept waiting for her to react, but she didn't.

He finally couldn't stand the silence any longer. He forced himself to speak, but he couldn't make himself heard above a cracked whisper. "Do ye ken how I feel about ye, lass? Do ye ken how I want this more than anything?"

She lowered her eyes and broke contact, but she didn't remove her face from his grasp. "Yeah, I know, but I can't. I wouldn't be doing you any favors and.... If I was going to get with anyone, it would be you, but I don't think I could even if I wanted to."

"Why?" he whispered. He really wanted to kiss her again. Even the fact that she was turning him down made him ache for her.

"The Last Division...we swore off love and marriage and children and....and everything. We took an oath to hold ourselves apart from society."

He dropped his hands instantly. The words did something to him. He couldn't touch her like that anymore with those words hanging in the air between them, but it was more than that.

The way she said it made it impossible for him to transgress her integrity. He respected and admired her too much. "Aye. An oath is still worth something if it comes to that."

"I'm sorry. I've never met anyone like you. I wish I could. I really do, but there are too many factors against us."

He nodded and turned away. "Aye. I understand, lass. Ye dinnae have to say any more."

He set off for the camp much more determined. He didn't have to hold back. It was done. She'd made her decision, and if she took an oath not to get involved with anyone, he could only respect that.

He made it ten feet before he turned and murmured over his shoulder. "It doesnae change how I feel."

The night swallowed those words. He didn't know for sure if she even heard him, but it didn't matter. He said them. Now they were out there in the world living a life of their own.

The two of them came in sight of the camp. The fire still flicked between the tree trunks. He set off not expecting to speak to her again tonight when she startled him.

She spoke in a barely audible murmur, but the words shot to his guts with a torch of fire. "I feel the same way about you."

He was so surprised that he didn't know what to say or do. His legs kept walking while he tried to decide what he should do....and then he was in the camp. He stopped next to the fire. Everyone else was gone.

He glanced over at her trying to get his brain to function, but the moment had passed. Whatever he was going to say, he couldn't say it here. Someone might hear him.

"You better get some sleep," she told him. "We have a big day tomorrow and everyone will be looking to you to be in charge."

"Aye. What about it, lassie? I cannae let ye to freeze out here. If ye want me to fetch some more wood, you could sleep here...."

She grinned at him and went over to one of the bundles lying to one side. She came back with a roll of blankets and a thick fur throw tied into a neat package.

He blinked at it and then at her. "How did ye get that here?"

"You might not have been thinking about how I was going to stay warm, but I did. I figured you'd all be curling up in the snow keeping warm with your fur, so I stashed this in our gear."

"How are ye doing all this, lassie?" he breathed. "How do ye ken all about these mountains and all the paths and all? I cannae understand it."

She laughed quietly. "Let's just say I have to keep one step ahead of you slouches. I wouldn't be very qualified to train your people if I played the damsel in distress, would I?" She started untying her bundle and turned away to slip off into the darkness. "Good night."

"Lass!" He grabbed her arm harder than he meant to and instantly softened his grip, but that only made him more painfully aware that he was touching her. "I.... I'm pleased.... very pleased that ye're training me Clan. I couldnae be more delighted with yer conduct thus far."

She smiled and blushed again. "Thanks. I'm trying to do my best. I hope I can do your Clan proud. Good night."

She tugged out of his grip very gently and politely. It was just as well that she did because he didn't think he could let go of her if he tried.

She slipped away, and before he could get his mind running again, she was gone. He longed to go after her again. Being out of her presence felt like the end of the world, but she already gave him her answer—as if he didn't already know.

The Buchanans had a taboo against mating with aliens. Now he knew why. They were bad news, but he couldn't think of her that way. She was the best thing that ever happened to him and certainly the best thing that ever happened to his Clan.

He couldn't even think of her as an alien anymore even if she was human. She had integrated into the Clan in ways no one could imagine. She had made so many friends and earned so much respect that he couldn't fathom her ever leaving.

His heart thrilled when he remembered her words. *I feel the same way about you. If I was going to get with anyone, it would be you.*

He was first for her. Only her oath stopped her from giving herself to him and he could live with that as long as he was first.

Chapter 16

Jaimee paused on the mountaintop when she came in sight of Icemeet. After a week of training in the mountains, the Clansmen and archers ranged before her in their cat forms. They streaked toward the gate as it groaned open to let them inside.

A confused flood of emotion made her hesitate—not that she didn't want to return to Icemeet. She was really starting to love the place. She felt even more closely bonded with these people after their week of living rough in the mountains. That was the problem. She cared about them too much.

A surge of exquisite agony gripped her insides when she laid eyes on Icemeet. It had become the home she never had. She never felt this way about Ironforge.

She never felt this way about the Last Division, either. She staked her whole life on her four comrades, but she never let them into her heart the way she let in the Buchanans.

She couldn't even remember the moment when she decided to let it happen. It happened without her even realizing it was happening. They won her over even more than she had won them over. She didn't want to go back to Ironforge.

She should. She should leave right now to spare Colton any more heartache than she was already causing him. She would have to be blind not to see that their bond was leading him to disaster.

He took every opportunity on their expedition to be near her, to talk to her, to organize with her, and to engage with her. They were both in charge of the exercise. They had to talk to each other all the time. They spent every evening sitting around the fire with the other Clansmen, laughing, joking, sharing stories, and enjoying each other's company.

Her heart flipped for the hundredth time remembering his eyes, his smile—everything about him. She shouldn't feel this way about him or any man, but she did.

The tigers raced into the courtyard. She was the only one left outside. A second later, Colton came striding through the gate in his human form, but he didn't look human to her anymore.

She'd seen him shift so often that his tiger nature seemed like the real Colton. He was wild, unchained—a living part of the mountain. He never wore a shirt or shoes during the whole exercise. He ran barefoot and fought bare-chested like his Clansmen. His hair went wild and the stubble on his jawline made him look like half an animal most of the time anyway.

All the Clansmen let their civility go on the exercise. The archers did the same thing, though they didn't run around half-naked like the men. Everyone let their wild nature out. They fought harder, ran faster, and acted rougher than she'd ever seen anyone act.

That only bonded her to them more tightly. They didn't hide their nature from her. Having an outsider see them like this broke down the walls even more. They trusted her in ways they had never trusted anyone outside their own Clan. They didn't have to tell her so. She saw it in their behavior every hour of every day.

Colton squinted up the mountain to where she stood. "Are ye coming in, lassie? We need to close the gate."

That clinched it. She trotted the rest of the way down the slope and followed him inside. She fell in next to him on their way into the fortress, but he didn't smile or joke the way he did on their expedition.

He scowled at the maids and servants going back and forth in the passageways. Everyone was busier than ever now that the fighters from the expedition had returned.

"I suppose it's time we organized the defenses," he remarked. "We havenae any notion when the Creightons might make their move."

"I've been thinking," she replied. "I was wondering if you'd introduce me to your father. I was hoping I could ask him about Lady Ilisa. If she's the same person as Lady Rhona, he might be able to give us information about how to find her."

Colton stopped on one of the upstairs galleries. It overlooked the courtyard where some of the Clansmen were sorting their supplies to put everything away.

At that moment, Liam and Edeena passed on another tier across the courtyard. They didn't see Jaimee and Colton watching. "So that blighter is still hanging about," Colton snarled. "It's just as well. I dinnae have time to hunt the bastard down with all the rest of this business going on."

Jaimee didn't reply. She was the one who told Liam to dig in at Icemeet for the long haul. So much for leaving to spare Colton. Now she was stuck here, too.

She should remove herself from his world. That would be the right thing to do. "Listen," she began again. "I don't think it's a good idea for me to continue to train your Clan."

"What?" He spun around and glared at her. "Of course it's a good idea for ye to continue. What do you mean by that?"

"I meant.... what's going on between you and me. Training your people only brings us into contact with each other—a lot more than we would be if I wasn't training them. It isn't fair to you...."

"Och, dinnae talk on that, lassie! Ye're training them."

"What about you? Aren't you at least a little worried about what's going to happen between us?"

"That's neither here nor there. Training me Clan is more important than ye and me.... if there's to be a ye and me at all. Dinnae say ought about breaking off. Dinnae even think it."

"All right. If you feel that way...." She went back to watching Liam and Edeena. They crossed the gallery and went back inside. There was nothing more to see.

He interrupted her thoughts. "Have dinner with me again tonight, lassie."

She gasped and stared at him with her mouth open. "You're insane! After everything that's happened, that would be the worst thing we could do."

He smiled, but it was a sad smile. "Ye come and have dinner with me. It's naught but a meal. It isnae a marriage proposal."

"Are you sure?"

He laughed, but it wasn't his usual hearty laugh. This must be really bothering him.

"All right. I'll come."

"Excellent." He perked up right away and his expression cleared. "Do I need to send an armed escort at the proper time?"

Now it was her turn to laugh. She shouldn't be accepting this invitation. She also shouldn't be feeling this happy about spending time alone with him.

He touched her elbow and walked off beaming. That expression gave her even more pause. Being with her and spending time with her shouldn't make him this happy, either.

She saw them both teetering toward something that could only end badly, but she found it impossible to stop herself. Some gravitational force drew her to him.

No matter where she went or what she did or who she talked to, she always wound up coming back to him. She didn't seem to be able to do anything else and.... they just seemed to belong together. Was that so bad?

She returned to her room, took a bath, and changed her clothes. Her arm had been feeling better while she spent time on the mountain. She hadn't taken the bandages off since she first fought Bryce, but when she got out of the tub, the saturated fabric fell off on its own.

She examined the knotted scabs crisscrossing her hand. They were still sore and only beginning to heal, but the punctures on her forearm seemed fine.

She flexed and rolled her fingers. The tears didn't come open, so she left the bandages off. They had dried by evening. She could move her hand freely.

She went down the hall and knocked on Colton's door. She had spent every night for the past three weeks with him in one way or another, but she had to fight down nerves.

She burst into a grin when he opened the door wearing a clean kilt along with his usual spotless shirt, jacket, socks, and shoes. "You're wearing your straitjacket again."

He rolled his eyes and pretended to groan. "Dinnae tell anyone. I'm in disguise."

She laughed, stepped inside, and scanned his room with approval. She really loved this room. It made her much more comfortable than the grand guest room she was staying in.

"Come over here and get something to eat, lassie. Ye've been on hard tack for a week. It's time ye let yer hair down and enjoy yerself."

She turned to the table to find it already laid out. He was in the act of pouring a drink for himself. Then he poured a second one and placed it next to her plate.

She chuckled on her way to the chair he pulled out for her. "Are you planning to get me drunk?"

He frowned down at her. "Why would I want to do that?"

She blushed and looked away. "No reason."

He sat down and raised his glass. "Here's to ye, lass."

"Why are you drinking to me? I didn't do anything."

"Aye, ye did something. Ye did more than something." He took the cover off a steaming roast grouse surrounded by small potatoes and a few local vegetables that Jaimee still didn't know the names of.

She watched him serve her and then himself. This couldn't go on.

She propped her elbows on the table and leaned over to him. "Don't you think it's time we talked turkey about our situation?"

"Turkey?" he repeated. "I dinnae ken what that is."

"I mean we should talk frankly about.... you know, you and me."

"Isnae that what we've been doing all along? What more is there to say?"

"For a start, why am I here having dinner with you if there's nothing more to say? Why do we go on with this charade if it's all pointless?"

"Who says anything about it being a charade.... or pointless? I enjoy yer company. Can ye blame me if I'd rather have dinner with ye here than with a pack of me noisy Clansmen down in the dining hall?"

"Don't you think it's courting disaster for ye to keep having dinner with me like this? It isn't like we could ever be together."

He put the cover back on the dish, picked up his fork, and looked down at his plate, but he didn't start eating. He pushed the vegetables back and forth for a while. Her heart lurched when he finally looked up and met her eye.

"I didnae like to put too fine a point on it, lassie, but I suspect it might be a bit too late for me. I've already gone off the deep end over ye. I dinnae think it matters at this late hour if I invite ye to dinner here or not."

Her shoulders slumped and she looked down at her plate, too. "I wondered if you might have."

"Ye dinnae have to worry about me, lassie. I'll handle me own end of things. Ye carry on with yer plans and leave me to handle mine."

"How can you even say that? Do you really think I'd walk out on you like this? There must be something we can do."

"Ye just said there was no way we could ever be together. Did ye change yer mind just now?"

"Well, there isn't, is there? You can't travel back to the future with me. You'd be miserable there. At least here you have your family looking out for you."

He snorted. "Me family cannae do ought for me, lassie. What's done is done. There's no going back."

"So what are we going to do?"

"It isnae any question of what *I'll* do. I dinnae have any choice in the matter. Me Clan needs me. I couldnae leave even if it was possible. The only question is what *ye'll* do and ye've already stated outright that ye're going home. I dinnae blame ye. I winnae give up me Clan and kin for ye. There isnae any cause for ye to give up yers for me."

She pursed her lips and looked away. He said it so directly. He never minced words. He never fed her any fluff or pulled his punches. It was one of the things she most respected about him. She could always count on him to tell it like it was.

"Never ye mind, lass." He downed another glass of his drink and started eating. "It will be all right....and I'll be all right. We havenae gone the whole distance so the situation isnae completely irretrievable."

Those words twisted her guts. He didn't have to use the crudest possible language to say exactly what he meant. They hadn't actually mated. He would be devastated after she left, but he would get over it.

When that happened, he'd be free to mate with someone else. Jaimee couldn't stand that. She looked up at him and gulped.

"What ails ye, lass?" he asked. "Ye look like ye've seen a ghost."

Without thinking, she grabbed her glass and pounded half of it. She wasn't prepared for the scorching fire that exploded her brain and she gagged. She coughed and spluttered as the drink torched a fiery path to her stomach.

Colton's eyebrows flew up staring at her. "Slow down, lass, or I'll be cleaning ye up off the floor with a towel."

She almost spewed her drink laughing, and just as fast, she bolted the rest of the drink.

"What's gotten into ye, lass?" he exclaimed. "Go easy on yerself."

She shoved back her chair and paced over to the window. "This is insane!"

"What's the rub?" he called after her. "Ye said ye wanted to talk turkey or whatnot. Isnae that what we're doing?"

She halted at the window and shook her head at the snowy landscape outside. She had to clear her head and that drink didn't help, but she needed to do something. She couldn't be thinking about staying here—not permanently.

The same old excuses streamed across her mind. The Last Division. Ironforge. The President of the United States. The mission. Liam. Lily. Lady Rhona Armstrong.

All the old demands and obligations and promises crowded in on her. They all demanded that she be what they wanted her to be and that she do what they wanted her to do.

In a split second, they became nothing more than the wind scuttling snowflakes over the rocks outside. What did they mean in the end? Nothing. They meant exactly nothing.

What did she have left if they meant nothing? He said he wouldn't give up his Clan and kin for her. He didn't expect her to give up her Clan and kin for him.

Who was her Clan and who was her kin? She always thought the Last Division was her only family, but all of that disappeared after she left Ironforge. If all her old connections meant nothing, then Icemeet and Clan Buchanan was all she had left.

She shook her head again, but the same truth kept burning into her mind and heart and soul. It wouldn't go away no matter how hard she tried.

She grasped at all her old anchor lines. The mission. Her oath. The war. The Last Division.

She had never found anything more solid to anchor herself to. Those things gave her the only stability in her life.... until now. Now all those old links dissolved in the fleeting winds of circumstance.

They left her anchored to something even more solid, something deeper and stronger, something that would never move. Icemeet would never budge. It would always be here for her along with these powerful people.

These people were stronger, sturdier, and tougher than the whole US Army. They were everything she admired about the Army and Colton was the leader of the whole Clan.

He exemplified everything she looked up to, everything she wanted to be, everything she wanted to dedicate her life to.

She trembled when he came up behind her. "What's on yer mind, lassie," he murmured. "If I've offended ye with what I said, only tell me and I'll rectify the matter. I only meant to be as straight with ye as ye were with me."

She shook her head again, but on the inside, she felt herself drowning. "You didn't offend me."

"What then?" He took her elbow to turn her around and face him. "Dinnae turn yer back on me, lass."

She couldn't ignore him any longer. She turned around, and when she looked into his eyes, she knew. She still tried to fight it, but her gut told her the die had already been cast. It was like he said. What was done was done and it could never be undone.

He didn't have to ask. He must already know because he slipped his warm hands on either side of her face. His hands had become rough and callused during the past week, but they only comforted her more like this.

He pulled her into his mouth and she wrapped her arms around his neck. She gave herself over to kissing him and the feeling boiling up inside her felt nothing but.... right. This had been coming for days—weeks even. Why did she waste the energy trying to fight it?

He pulled her against him and his hands slipped behind her back. His arms encircled her waist and he lifted her up to meet her. Their mouths closed in a timeless connection. He was as solid and unmovable as the mountain itself. She could throw herself against him with all the madness of a hurricane. He could take it.

He exhaled into her nostrils and she smelled him. She felt his body in ways she didn't when they were wrestling in the courtyard. She had become more and more aware of his body every day that they spent together on the mountain. Now she could no longer deny the unique masculine nature hidden under his clothes.

He put her down and their lips glided apart. She found her anchor point in his steady gaze, his bottomless black eyes staring down to the very bottom of her soul.

Her body overflowed with so much tension and agitation that she didn't know what to do with herself. She wanted him more than she ever imagined possible. She wanted to cry from this agonized heartfelt yearning for him—for something so much deeper than his body.

She couldn't kiss him again even though she ached to. She craved nothing but to be near him and to know everything about him. She wanted to be the one he depended on, the one who helped him carry all his endless responsibilities, but she couldn't be.

He didn't try to take it any further. This kiss meant so much more than the one they shared on the mountain. She gave herself fully this time, but neither of them could take the next step. That would be asking too much for both of them.

"I should probably go," she breathed.

"Aye," he replied. He didn't have to say what they were both thinking. If she stayed in this room one more minute, neither of them would be able to stop what was about to happen.

She had to summon all her strength to break away and leave the room without looking back. Shutting the door behind her and walking away was the hardest thing she ever did in her life, even harder than leaving people behind to die in enemy territory.

Chapter 17

J aimee strode down the corridor toward her own room. She really needed to go get something to eat. She didn't want to go to sleep hungry, but she couldn't face seeing the rest of the Clan in the dining hall after what just happened with Colton.

Now what was she going to do? How could she face him again after kissing him like that? She owed it to him and to herself to leave Icemeet, but the more she thought that, the more she just kept not leaving.

She needed to shut herself in her room and lock the door while she thought long and hard about what she was going to do. She needed to come to some decision, but this fluttery excitement in her stomach didn't make it easy.

She couldn't be getting this excited about a man she planned to leave heartbroken and devastated, possibly for the rest of his life—and that was saying nothing about herself.

How could she go back to a life of enforced celibacy and isolation at Ironforge after kissing him like that? She would spend the rest of her life fantasizing about him. She would fall asleep every night imagining herself with him. She would spend her life living in a dream world where she and Colton were together, building a life together, and leading their Clan together.

Their Clan. Her Clan. Did she really want to cross the line and start thinking of the Buchanans as her Clan and kin?

I suspect it might be a bit too late for me. I've already gone off the deep end over ye.

Those words described her just as much as they did him. The Buchanans were already her Clan. They were her Clan and kin so much more than the Last Division ever had been. She felt more loyalty for the Buchanans than she ever did for the Army or the Last Division or even her own native country.

She would be betraying her Clan and herself if she went back to Ironforge now. She would be betraying everything she held sacred....and for what—for an oath that meant nothing anymore? Could she really do that? The thought made her sick.

She approached her bedroom door when someone caught her by the arm. She spun around to find Liam steering her sideways into an alcove down the corridor. "Liam! What are you doing?"

"Well?" he whispered. "What do you think?"

"About what? I just got back from the training expedition."

"You've wasted enough time training the Buchanans. You've earned their respect and now you can ask for something in return."

"Like what?"

He smacked his lips. "Come on, Snowflake. Everyone sees you spending all this time with Colton. You can use your influence to get him to introduce you to his father. As soon as we meet with Neill, we can get to the bottom of this Lady Ilisa mystery."

She turned away and stepped out into the corridor. She didn't want to talk to Liam right now. "I'm not going to manipulate Colton. You can forget about that right now."

"That's what we're doing here, isn't it? You said we should stick around here to find out what Neill knows about Lady Ilisa." Liam hurried after her. "Hey! You're the one who said our mission was here. What happened to that?"

She rounded on him spitting tacks. "There are some things that are more important than the mission, Liam. Jesus, how can you be so thick?"

"There's nothing more important than the mission. How can you even say that?"

"What about your responsibilities? Huh?"

"What responsibilities? My only responsibility is to the President, our mission, and Lily."

"What about your responsibility to Edeena?"

He rolled his eyes and groaned. "Not that again! I'm only here because you said we had a chance to question Neill."

"If that's the only reason you're here, then we're finished. You go carry on the mission by yourself. I'm done with you."

She turned her back on him and headed for her bedroom. She didn't trust herself not to smash his face in if he said one more word to her about any of this.

He hustled over to her to keep arguing about it, but the instant she put her hand on the doorknob, a loud metal bell started clanging out in the courtyard. Gruff male voices shouted out there, and in an instant, something very big and very hard smashed into the walls not far away.

Liam jolted back and looked up at the ceiling. "What is that?"

"It's the assault alarm!" Jaimee spun away. "The Creightons are launching the invasion!"

She charged for the stairs, but he caught her and held her back. "You can't go out there, Snowflake! You can't risk your life for these people!"

"Get your stinking hands off me!" She yanked her arm free and ran into at least thirty Buchanans rushing to get out of the fortress.

They sprang down the stairs with Jaimee right with them. Most of the Buchanans shifted before they got to the bottom. They transformed, launched off the stairs, and sailed down to the lower levels. They landed on their springy cat legs, shifted again, and rushed outside.

A stream of men and women stormed into the courtyard. Men crisscrossed the parapet while others snatched weapons from the storeroom by the gate. The counterweight swung down and the Buchanans flooded out of Icemeet to confront the threat.

Jaimee dashed up to the parapet. The guards were all scrambling to load catapults, spear-launching engines, and position the rest of the Clan's defenses on the walls.

She took one look down at the planes and her blood ran cold. Hundreds of soldiers poured across the Boundless and gained the opposite bank.

They charged up the slope toward Icemeet, but that wasn't the scariest part. Four giant dragons wheeled in the air overhead. Two still soared over the planes, but the other two had pushed as far as Icemeet.

A huge green monster tilted over the fortress and unleashed a torrential jet of flame on the walls. The fire smashed into the upper keeps and Jaimee heard women and children screaming in there.

That sound electrified Jaimee's being. She'd spent the last few weeks preparing for this. She couldn't let these foul monsters harm the Buchanans.

She stormed down the parapet pointing at everyone. "Launch the defenses! Take aim and fire!"

The guards swiveled a siege engine like a giant crossbow to aim it at an incoming dragon. The creature stooped over the plane, angled his wings, and lowered his head. His eyes narrowed to slits and he flexed his great wings picking up speed.

He swooped up the mountain and arched his neck to fire on the planes where the Buchanans were arrayed to defend their homeland.

"Fire!" Jaimee roared and the guards released a massive spear. Jaimee had designed the machine and the spear with Boyd Buchanan, the blacksmith. Now the spear flew straight and true. The dragon didn't see it until it was too late.

The dragon reared back trying to get away and the spear plunged dead on into his chest. He let out a spine-chilling shriek that echoed far and wide. The mountains rang with that scream and it announced to the whole world that the battle was on.

Reid raised his saber on high and bellowed his war cry. All his assembled Clansmen joined in and they set off at a fast run for the planes. They met the Creighton army in a devastating clash of arms that exploded the whole world apart.

Jaimee spun away. She couldn't stay up here while the Clan was down there fighting for their lives. She caught one glimpse of the archers drawing on the opposite battlements. Edeena was with them and they loosed a hail of arrows on the Creightons far below.

Jaimee didn't wait around to see anything more. She dashed down the stairs, snatched her weapons from the storeroom, and raced outside.

She ran into a brutal battle of Buchanans against Creightons. The three remaining dragons came wheeling back laying down scorching carpets of fire on the Buchanans, but at that moment, one of the catapults released.

A flaming ball of burning tar hurtled from the fortress walls. It would have landed and exploded amongst the Creighton forces, but it struck a dragon instead.

The creature pitched over backward and the Creightons checked their attack. The soldiers tried to push farther up the mountain, but the Buchanans held firm.

Jaimee's heart soared when she saw the Creightons weakening. She had been right about the two Clans. The Buchanans had always relied on fighting as tigers. The Creightons weren't prepared for the Buchanans to change tactics and fight as men instead.

The Buchanans sensed their enemy flagging. Jaimee raised her saber and hacked into their ranks. "Forward! Drive them back across the Boundless!"

Reid appeared out of the mayhem. He and Duncan slashed their way forward and the whole Clan followed their lead. They drove the Creightons back toward the estuary and a few of the enemy stepped into the water. The Buchanans were winning!

Jaimee's battle frenzy started getting away from her. She stabbed, slashed, and chopped in all directions. Her saber and dirk became a part of her arms. She moved faster than thought.

The Buchanans almost pushed into the path of their own aerial bombardment. Another curtain of arrows whistled down from the skies. Jaimee, Reid, and Duncan had to hold their people back to keep them out of danger.

A second later, five more catapult charges smashed into the ground thirty yards in front of them. The balls detonated and sprayed fire through the Creighton ranks.

"Forward!" Reid roared and the Buchanans charged to finish off the invaders. They forced their way right to the water's edge when a scream made Jaimee look over her shoulder.

She hesitated when she saw four brilliant blue dragons flanking the Buchanans from the west. The dragons came out of the mountains mowing down everyone and everything in their path.

They combined their fire burning their way into the Buchanan ranks. The defenders at Icemeet fired again and again, but the dragons were coming in too fast.

People started breaking away from the Buchanans' rear. They started to flee back up the mountain. "Stand your ground!" Jaimee yelled, but the Clansmen couldn't hear her over the noise.

A deafening rumble caught her ear. She glanced toward the Boundless and the world dropped beneath her feet at what she saw.

Lily Dindle led a charge of hundreds of Creighton soldiers coming out of Kald. They covered the ground to the Boundless and crossed it in an instant.

Jaimee stood rooted to the spot staring at her friend and comrade—the woman Jaimee thought was her friend and comrade.

Lily wore leather pants and a leather jacket like Jaimee's, but these were black and polished to a high shine. They were too nice to have come from the mountains. They gave Lily a distinctly cosmopolitan look.

Lily carried a saber and dirk, too. The sight of her leading the Creighton forces into battle against the Buchanans snapped the last anchor line holding Jaimee to everything she once knew. This woman was not Jaimee's friend. Maybe Lily never had been. She was an enemy, an enemy of Clan Buchanan.

Lily's eyes found Jaimee's and Lily hesitated, too. The two women stared at each other across the Boundless.

At that moment, another shriek resounded over the countryside from one of the dragons. Jaimee didn't see which one it was. Explosions, the thump of flame, and the clash of steel deafened her from behind, but only one person mattered in this battle.

Lily's features hardened at the exact moment when Jaimee made up her mind. Lily raised her weapons and Jaimee charged her in a rage.

The two women met in a bone-crushing collision. Jaimee brought her saber down to cut Lily in half, but Lily blocked it and drove in with her dirk. She would have gutted Jaimee, but Jaimee parried and slashed Lily across the side.

The two women closed struggling for the upper hand. Jaimee bared her teeth and snarled in Lily's face. Jaimee tried to knock one of Lily's weapons aside, but both women were equally well-trained.

A deep rumble lower than hearing trembled the ground. Jaimee caught a glimpse over Lily's shoulder of the Creighton forces crossing the Boundless. Jaimee couldn't waste any more time on Lily. Jaimee had to get back to defending Buchanan territory from this invasion.

The ground shook again and she saw it. An absolutely massive dragon as black as coal strutted down the Boundless on the Creighton side. His giant wings blocked out the sky, but he didn't launch.

His long tail dragged on the ground and he turned to glare across the water at the Buchanans. He arched his sinuous neck and narrowed his eyes at his enemies. He stood no more than twenty feet from Jaimee, but he didn't attack her. What was wrong with him?

Jaimee gave a powerful heave to throw Lily off. Jaimee tried to break free, but she and Lily were locked together too tightly.

At that moment, a man rushed out of the chaos and crammed his arms between Lily and Jaimee. "Knock it off, both of you!" Liam thundered. "You are not enemies! Stop fighting each other!"

He gave an almighty shove and pried the two women apart. He held them at arm's length against their combined efforts to attack each other.

Another rumble drew Jaimee's attention to the black dragon, but it wasn't there anymore. She glanced past Lily in time to see the dragon implode on himself. He shrank and transformed into a powerfully built man in a dark red kilt.

He strode into the estuary and crossed it coming straight toward Jaimee. She braced herself to defend herself against him, but he was totally unarmed. What the hell was he doing walking into battle like this?

Another exploding ball of burning tar pounded down into the Creighton forces nearby. The noise made Jaimee, Lily, and Liam all glance over and the whole battle surged toward them as another flank of attackers swarmed the planes from the north.

They came out of the mountains where the blue dragons appeared, but these fighters wore black kilts and none of them wore shirts or shoes. The Buchanans overran the Creightons in a second with Colton in the lead.

He took one look at the cluster surrounding Jaimee and veered toward her. He raised his saber to attack.

Lily reacted in a heartbeat and sprang between Colton and the unarmed guy who had been a black dragon a moment before. Lily raised her weapons to block Colton from reaching that man.

Jaimee read the whole situation in the blink of an eye. This man must be Grant Ritchie, the Creighton prince. Lily had turned her back on the Last Division to marry this man.

Grant spun around to face Colton, too. Grant braced himself and squared his shoulders. If he shifted back into a dragon, he could incinerate Colton without even trying.

Jaimee flew across the ground so fast she even surprised herself. She launched herself between Colton and Lily and Jaimee smashed Lily's saber out of her hand.

Jaimee lunged forward aiming her saber at Lily's face. Jaimee didn't think twice. She would cut Lily to shreds before she let anyone lay a finger on Colton.

The next second, the battle surged back toward the Boundless. The shriek of cats punctuated the din, and before anyone could move, the Buchanans shattered the Creighton line all over again.

A dragon screeched overhead and Jaimee glanced up to see one of the blue dragons plummeting from the heavens. A massive spear impaled its body and more flaming balls of tar pelted out of Icemeet targeting the last two dragons still in the air.

The Buchanans collided with her and Colton's forces wheeled to join the fray. Jaimee leapt into the melee and attacked Lily even more ferociously.

Lily whipped around to close with Jaimee, but she never got there. Grant charged Lily from behind, pinned her arms to her sides, and hauled her backward across the Boundless.

Jaimee pursued them as far as the water's edge, but the combined Buchanan force surrounded her so thickly that Jaimee couldn't reach Lily again.

The Buchanans pulled up at the edge of the estuary. The Clansmen cheered and roared, shook their weapons at their retreating enemies, and hollered insults at the Creightons.

Grant set Lily down on her feet on the Kald side. He leaned close to her ear and yelled at her, but she was too busy glaring at Jaimee. The two women locked eyes across the Boundless. Jaimee would storm over there to attack Lily again, but Grant didn't give her a chance.

He took hold of Lily's arm and pulled her away. He had to yell at her for at least another minute before Lily finally walked off.

The Creighton army set up guards on their side of the estuary. Colton and Reid went through the Buchanans doing the same thing. The two Clans faced off with just a few dozen yards of water between them.

The Buchanans kept yelling rude remarks at their enemies, but the Creightons didn't reciprocate.

Colton came over to Jaimee and startled her out of her thoughts by calling into her ear. "Get up to the fortress, lassie, and check on the defenses. We'll need to rearm for the next attack." He tugged her sleeve. "Go on, lass. I'll handle things here. Dinnae stand here gawping."

She looked up at him and his dark eyes told her he understood. She looked back toward Kald, but Grant and Lily were long gone. There was no one here but common soldiers.

She tore herself away and Duncan accompanied her up to the fortress walls. Colton was right. Icemeet's defenses were dangerously depleted, but it was all worth it. At least ten dragons lay dead on the planes.

She got busy rearming. She gave orders for new projectiles to be made and all the catapults repositioned. Duncan led a party down to the planes to retrieve the spears that proved so deadly against the dragons. They worked a thousand times better than Jaimee hoped. Those spears had turned the tide in the Buchanans' favor.

She finished all her work, but she still didn't leave the parapet. The Creightons and the Buchanans arrayed their guards on either side of the Boundless. They lit fires and she could even hear Buchanan voices drifting up the mountain. Loud talk carried on the evening air and laughter broke out in the Buchanan camps.

Lily was over there somewhere on the other side of the estuary. Was she planning to kill Jaimee the same way Jaimee was planning to kill her?

Jaimee went over every detail of the battle in her mind. She couldn't stop replaying the moment when Lily raised her weapons against Colton.

A fresh wave of hatred gripped Jaimee's heart. She would destroy anyone who threatened Colton. She didn't give a damn anymore who it was. She would kill her best friend rather than let anyone touch him.

Chapter 18

Colton spotted Jaimee the moment he walked into Icemeet's great hall. Clan Buchanan usually reserved this hall for special occasions like weddings and Clan Chief succession ceremonies.

Now wounded fighters crowded the floor. Their makeshift beds lay side by side with barely enough space between them for the attendants to move around.

Jaimee squatted next to a pallet at the far end of the room. Louisa went over to her and tried to hand something to the man on the floor in front of Jaimee. The patient didn't move and Jaimee took whatever it was instead.

Lousia left them alone and Jaimee leaned in close to the injured man's face. She picked the man up and Colton recognized Bryce.

She cradled Bryce in one arm while she held a cup of water to his mouth. Then she laid him down and squeezed his arm.

Colton crossed the hall and stopped next to Bryce's bed. Bryce was gazing up at Jaimee and struggling to keep his composure. He pressed a thick wad of bloody fabric to his ribs and cold sweat saturated his face, hair, and bare chest.

Bryce's eyes swiveled over to meet Colton's. Bryce tried to change his expression and failed. "Laddie...."

"Easy, man," Colton murmured. "Lie quiet."

"Ye.... dinnae.... lie down.... lad...." Bryce choked out the words in between broken gasps. "Ye.... hold.... our land...."

"Och, aye," Colton whispered. "Ye ken I will right enough."

"Ye......become...our Chief.... Dinnae.... let ought.... stand in yer....in yer way, lad...."

Colton swallowed hard. Jaimee might not understand what Bryce meant, but Colton did. Colton could only become Chief once he took a mate.

Bryce took his hand off his bandage and groaned through locked teeth. His head lolled over to Jaimee. "Lassie...."

"Take it easy, pal," she told him. "Don't strain yourself."

Bryce ignored her. He pulled his dirk from his belt and pressed it into her hand. "Ye...take this...lassie.... Ye...use this....to defend .... our Clan...."

She looked down at the blade.

"Promise me," Bryce hissed.

She looked up and locked onto his gaze. Her eyes glistened with moisture. "I promise."

Bryce lolled the other way and snarled up at Colton. "Promise, lad."

"I promise," Colton breathed. "I swear it by Almighty God."

Bryce collapsed back on his blankets. His eyes rolled up in their sockets and he let out his last gasping breath. His body went limp and he collapsed.

Colton stared down at him and struggled to suppress the seething emotions threatening to erupt out of him. Bryce could only have meant one thing.

Jaimee could only defend Clan Buchanan if she stayed at Icemeet. She wouldn't be able to do that if she went home. She gave Bryce her promise before he died that she would do it. She must understand what that meant.

And then there was Colton's promise. Bryce exacted Colton's promise that he would become Chief and let nothing stand in his way.

Bryce must have meant that Colton shouldn't let the differences between himself and Jaimee stand in the way of mating with her. Bryce must have meant that Colton should mate with Jaimee to consolidate his leadership over the Clan. What else could Bryce have meant?

Colton couldn't look at her. He couldn't stand to see any sign from her that she understood what it meant—or that she didn't understand. He couldn't face the uncertainty. How exactly was he supposed to do this when she had always been so adamant about going home?

She remained bowed next to Bryce's bed. She stared down at the dirk in her hand. Did her people hold the same value for promises and giving one's word as one's bond? Did she realize what she was agreeing to when she made that promise?

A commotion broke out behind Colton. He turned around to see Alastair in the doorway. The big Highlander towered over Louisa and some of the other maids. He thundered at the top of his lungs and Colton saw right away why.

Burns covered most of Alastair's face, one arm, and one side of his chest. His tartan had stuck to the burn and the maids were trying to remove it so they could treat his injuries.

He spun around and lashed out his big arms while he roared in excruciating fury. He almost punched one of the maids, but she sprang out of the way just in time.

Colton saw what he had to do, but Jaimee sprinted past him before Colton could move. She darted between the assembled wounded and reached the door just as Louisa and two other maids went running for cover.

Alastair didn't see Jaimee. He didn't see anything but his own pain and rage. Jaimee headed straight for him, but he shifted before she got there. He wheeled back toward the hall and transformed in a split second.

The tiger landed on all fours on the floor and crouched there yowling at everyone in sight. The maids scurried to get as far away from him as they could. Only Jaimee kept pressing toward him.

The tiger whipped the other way and hissed at her. She froze in her tracks and Alastair coiled himself to spring. He looked absolutely awful with half his fur scorched off.

She took a few slow, deliberate steps nearer. He flattened his ears against his head, bared his fangs, and hissed up at her, but she didn't stop. "It's okay, Alastair," she murmured. "You're safe now. We can put something on your burns and make the pain go away. Let me help you."

He flattened himself to the floor, shrieked, and glared up at her with furious eyes. She eased out of the hall, picked up a jar of ointment from the floor where one of the maids had dropped it, and held it out to Alastair. "You know what this is, don't you? Let me put this on your burns. It will make the pain go away."

She folded her legs and sat down on the floor ten feet away from him. She held out the jar where he could see it, but he only hissed at her again.

She hooked her finger into it, picked up a blob of the ointment, and held that out to him, too. "It will only take a second, Alastair. No one is going to hurt you. Let me help you.... just a little bit."

She leaned forward and brought the ointment toward his head. He screeched louder and swiped his claws at her hand, but he didn't try very hard to scratch her.

She froze, and when he returned to his crouched position, she scooted a little bit closer. "That's it. Nice and easy. I know you're hurting. You're home now. You can rest now."

She touched the ointment to his head and he let out another piercing shriek, but he didn't retreat. He hunkered there hissing and spitting while she spread the ointment on his head and back. She spread it over the exposed, burned skin and the cat started to relax.

She pushed herself back to a safe distance. "You can shift now, Alastair. Once you do that, we can finish taking care of you."

The cat glared at her and then shot a hateful hiss into the hall. He hissed at Colton, but Colton didn't move. Alastair always liked Jaimee. Colton couldn't do anything for Alastair that Jaimee wasn't already doing.

A second later, Alastair shifted back into a man and gave a ground-shaking roar when his tartan reappeared on his shoulder. He kept bellowing, baring his teeth, and rolling his eyes in pain.

Jaimee got to her feet and approached him. She started talking to Alastair, but Colton couldn't hear her over Alastair's enraged bellows.

Jaimee talked to him while she spread more ointment on his chest and face, but she couldn't get him to quiet down. He must be in agony.

She finally led him into the hall and sat him down in a chair by the door. She didn't ask him to lie down. She knelt down in front of him and waved to Louisa, who peeked at Alastair from behind the door.

Jaimee finally convinced one of the maids to give her a pair of scissors. Jaimee started cutting off Alastair's tartan, but a large section of it still stuck to his shoulder. Colton didn't want to watch and Alastair's excruciating yells became more pained with every cut of the scissors.

The other patients were getting agitated and some of them started calling out for the maids. Colton couldn't let Alastair disturb them so he went over to the pair. Colton motioned to Jaimee and Alastair. "Come along, laddie. We'll find ye a room of yer own."

Alastair didn't hear him. He just kept roaring. He didn't move until Jaimee took his elbow and led him out of the hall.

Colton took them to the kitchen and Jaimee parked Alastair on the bench at the kitchen table while she finished cutting as much of the tartan away as she could. She finally stood back and reapplied as much of the ointment as she could.

"Let the burn dry!" she yelled at Alastair over his tortured bellows. "Once it forms a scab, you can take a bath and soak the rest of the fabric off."

Alastair gritted his teeth and snarled at nothing, but he was starting to quiet down. The ointment was doing its work.

Louisa came in and nodded to Jaimee. Colton pulled Jaimee away, but he didn't take her back to the hall.

He stopped her in the corridor outside. "Ye need to sit ye down and rest yerself, lassie. Ye cannae work yerself into an early grave looking after everyone else."

She covered her face with her hands and let out a long, shaky breath. "I never thought I'd have to go through this again. I thought it was all behind me. I don't think...." She straightened up, tried to shake it off, and failed. She looked down at the floor and tears welled up in her eyes. "I don't think I can do this."

"Aye." Colton put his arm around her shoulders. "Ye've had yer share for one day. Come along and we'll go get ye something to eat. Ye dinnae have to save everyone else when ye're barely on yer feet."

He steered her to the dining hall where the Clan usually ate together. Most of the uninjured Clansmen and archers sat around on the benches eating and talking, but the atmosphere was much more subdued than usual.

None of the raucous laughter, jokes, or singing enlivened the hall now. A few people talked in low tones, but mostly everyone just concentrated on eating.

Colton guided her to a bench and sat down opposite her. No one made any fuss about either of them. They were just rank and file Clansmen like everyone else.

Someone passed Colton a platter of roasted meat, potatoes, and vegetables—the same food everyone ate every night. Tonight was no different except that Colton and Jaimee seemed to be sitting apart from everyone else.

She chewed her food mechanically and didn't look up at anyone. She didn't share the Clansmen's bawdy sense of humor, nor did anyone engage her in conversation the way they did on a dozen other nights.

She tore off a piece of bread and bit it off before she looked up at him. "Did you see the way that man crossed the Boundless?"

He tried to shrug the question away. "What man? I saw hundreds of men crossing the Boundless. One's as good as the next."

"You know who I mean. It was Grant Ritchie, Lily's husband."

"What if it was?"

"He was unarmed. He walked into the battle with no way to defend himself."

"Then he's the biggest fool on either side of the line."

"He shifted before he crossed. He could have killed us all, but he didn't."

"He didnae attack because he saw ye locked up with Lily. He didnae want to hurt her."

Jaimee shook her head, but she couldn't argue with him. She didn't know what to think.

"What do ye care about Grant Ritchie? He's our enemy. We'll skewer him along with all his lizard kin."

"I guess I'm not thinking about him." She pushed the food around on her plate. "I can't stop thinking about Lily."

Colton pretended to look around. "That reminds me. I havenae seen that snake Liam since the battle. Ye'd have had her if he hadnae separated ye two."

"I just can't believe she's fighting for the Creightons," Jaimee murmured. "Everything I thought I knew about the Last Division is coming apart at the seams."

"How do ye mean?"

"She was as dedicated to our mission as anyone. She was the one I never had to worry about. She threatened to kill Liam when he came around and told us we were being called to leave Ironforge. Now she's here." She shook her head, but the cloud hanging over her didn't dispel. "I just don't get it."

"Did ye see the way she jumped in to defend Grant?" he asked.

"Yeah. I saw."

"She must think a lot of him. That explains why she married him instead of trying to find a way back to yer own time."

She studied the piece of bread in her hand. She didn't seem to recognize it for what it was. "I guess she figured out what I'm just figuring out now. I guess she had a few more weeks to put two and two together whereas I'm just now waking up to the fact."

"What fact is that, lass?"

She looked up and locked her eyes on him, but she wasn't fighting back tears anymore. "That our life at Ironforge was really nothing more than a living death. We were never more than corpses living entombed year after year in the pain of the past. I didn't understand that before today, but I understand now. I even understand why she jumped in to defend Grant."

"*Ye* jumped in to defend *me*, lassie," he pointed out.

"Yeah." She broke eye contact and went back to looking at her bread. "I did."

He almost asked her straight out if she understood the promise she made to Bryce. As if in answer to his thoughts, Louisa came into the dining hall just then. She came over to Jaimee and Colton, set Bryce's dirk on the table next to Jaimee's plate, smiled at her, and left without a word.

Jaimee looked down at the blade for a second and then picked it up to study it. Her expression changed and she stood up, put the dirk into her belt, and stepped over the bench. "I'm not hungry. Are you sticking around here for a while?"

He got to his feet to match her. He wasn't particularly hungry, either, not after what he saw in the hall. "I'll walk ye upstairs, lassie. We're both tired."

They headed for the stairs and didn't speak until they got to her bedroom. He halted outside her door. "Ye must sleep a bit, lassie. We dinnae ken when the Creightons will launch another assault."

She stared at him for a minute. He was just starting to wonder if she heard him at all when she stepped toward him and took his hand. She didn't say anything. She pulled him to face the other way and drew him down the corridor.

She opened his bedroom door and towed him inside. He thought she might want to continue the meal they were having when the assault started, but she didn't go near the table.

She looked up into his eyes and smiled. That smile twisted his heart with a pang of exquisite agony. She understood. She knew exactly what she promised Bryce. She knew what the dirk meant and she knew what it meant that she defended him against Grant and Lily.

She let her fingers slide out of his and she walked into his room—his bedroom. She'd been here a handful of times already, but this was different.

She walked over to his bed, pulled off her jacket, draped it on a nearby chair, and sat down on the fur throw covering the mattress. She sat facing the window and she gazed out at the mountain peaks falling into darkness.

He almost couldn't survive the feeling of crushing pain in his heart when he understood what she was doing. She was moving into his room. She was making it her own. She wouldn't leave it—not in that way.

He gulped down the lump in his throat. He didn't think he could take the pain of going near her, now that he knew he had won her.

How did he do that? He didn't do anything and yet here she was, in his room. She was relaxing into spending the night here as though this was her room, too. It *was* her room. It was their room.

She kicked off her boots, took the dirk out of her belt, and laid it on the same chair with her jacket. She looked down at something in her lap that Colton couldn't see.

He had dreamed about this moment, but he didn't think he would feel this way when it actually happened. He thought he would be thrilled, delighted, exhilarated. Now he only felt sad—not that she was here. He was ecstatic that she was here, but the pain of losing Bryce and so many others weighed heavily on him.

He never let himself feel that weight until now. She was here and she made him feel it because she shared it.

He didn't know the moment he strode over to her. It just seemed the most natural thing to do the same way her coming into his room and making it her own was the most natural thing for her to do. What else in the world was there for either of them to do?

He halted in front of her and she looked up at him. Her eyes hid nothing from him. He saw everything and knew everything in her eyes, but he still hesitated to cross that last barrier holding them apart.

"Are ye sure about this, lassie?" he whispered.

She nodded. "I'm sure."

He didn't need to hear anything else. He cradled her beautiful face and kissed her. Her breath warmed him and her smell enveloped him. Even that seemed so ordinary and natural. It was in the order of things. It was meant to be.

She wrapped her arms around him, and this time, there would be no separating, no parting ways to go to separate rooms. She was here and she would stay here forever. He knew that now.

He kissed her harder and her tongue met his. He moved in and their combined weight fell back on the bed where the furs swallowed them.

Chapter 19

Colton pushed himself up on his arms so the covers fell down to his waist. He seemed so much bigger, now that Jaimee was in his bed and they were both naked.

He picked up a pitcher of water from the night table, poured some into a cup, and drank it. "Do ye want some, lassie?"

"Sure. Thanks."

She rolled onto her back waiting for him to pour it for her. The mattress under her felt strange. A thick feather cushion made it soft and inviting, but whatever supported it underneath felt like no mattress she'd ever slept on before. She made a mental note to find out what it was.

He handed her the cup and she propped herself on her elbow to drink it. Colton leaned back on the pillows and jostled her arm. The water splashed up her nose and she coughed. She accidentally sprayed water all over herself and the sheet underneath her.

"Aargh! What are ye doing?" Colton roared. "Ye've saturated the bed! I'm mated to a heathen!"

"What are you complaining about?" She ran her wrist across her nose. Half the water was gone. "The wet spot is on my side so I'll be the one sleeping in it, not you."

He laughed and ran his fingertips through her hair. "In that case, ye can spill yer drink all over the place."

"You're a real prince, aren't you?" She downed the rest of the water and stretched across him to put the cup back on the table.

She had to spread her body over him and he took the opportunity to nuzzle into her neck. "I'll dry ye off with me tongue, lass. Ye'll be warm and dry any moment now...."

She dug him in the ribs. "Don't turn this into another wrestling match. You know that won't end well for you."

"Ye dinnae think so?" He lunged off the bed, seized both her wrists, flipped her, and pinned her down while he rolled back on top of her. "We'll see about that."

She laughed and pretended to struggle while he nibbled down her neck toward her chest. "Don't push your luck, pal."

He gave her a nip on the shoulder and toppled sideways to lie down next to her. "Ye count yer blessings it's after midnight or I'd have to teach ye a lesson."

"You wish," she growled, but she cuddled close to his side and buried her face in his chest.

She felt nothing but relief now that they had actually sealed the deal. She thought it would be a serious, earth-shattering experience, but it only confirmed how comfortable they were with each other. Nothing could be simpler and more natural.

He ran his fingers through her hair and started massaging her neck. "Now that we're mated, I must take ye to meet me father."

She shot up fast. "Really? You mean it?"

"Aye. It isnae a question. It's required."

"But what about...." She glanced toward the door. She didn't want to mention Liam. Colton read her mind. "It's just ye and me, lassie—no one else."

She settled back down thinking fast. Liam wouldn't be happy when he found out Jaimee went to visit Neill without him present.

Then again, Liam would be even less happy when he found out that Jaimee and Colton were mated for life—on purpose this time. This was no accident like Liam and Edeena.

"Father's meant to approve all our mates, but he'll say naught about ye. He isnae active in our Clan at all."

"Why not?" she asked. "What happened?"

"He's been in seclusion ever since he lost Ilisa."

"What do you mean—he lost her? How did she wind up in Tyrekirk in the first place?"

"I dinnae ken. He winnae speak on it. He winnae even say her name. He doesnae see or speak to anyone if he can avoid it."

"That's weird. I wonder why."

"He went the same way when me mother died. We didnae think he'd come back from that loss, but then Ilisa came along and brought him back. I havenae seen him so happy as when she was with him....and then she was gone. She vanished out of Icemeet one day. It wasnae a full three years later before we found out the Laird was holding her a prisoner in Tyrekirk."

She leaned back to study him. "So Ilisa isn't your mother? She's your father's second wife?"

"Aye. Didnae ye ken?"

"How would I know?"

"Didnae ye see how different Duncan is from the rest of us?"

"Duncan! What do you mean? What about him?"

"Reid, Edeena, and I are from me mother—Father's first wife, Caitrin Buchanan. Duncan is Ilisa's son. He's her only son."

She sank back down on the pillows where she could see him. "He looks like you. I never would have known."

"Not a bit of it. He couldnae be more different."

"How do you figure? He has dark hair and dark eyes like you. If one of you was different, it would be Reid. He's blonde—and Edeena has red hair. You and Duncan look the most alike."

"Och, no! He's the picture of Ilisa. When I was young, I thought Father went into isolation because he couldnae stand to see Duncan each day. It was too painful a reminder of Ilisa."

"Don't you think that way anymore?"

"Not at all. Now I'm older, I understand it better."

"You understand what?"

"I understand now how it feels to lose yer mate. He went the same way when Mother died. No one wants to live once they've lost their mate. Man or woman—it doesnae make a bit of difference. Ilisa brought him back and then, with her gone, he went down the same way, only it was worse the second time because she was still alive somewhere—somewhere he couldnae find her. That would be a thousand times worse than the mate dying."

She stared at him letting the full power of what he said sank in. He never told her before. He let her believe he would be alright if she went back to Ironforge, but he must have only said that to spare her the guilt of making her own decision.

Colton would have been like his father. He would have been half alive. He would have been reduced to a ghost wandering through life wondering where she was. He would have been better off dead than to be separated from his life's mate. He would have wished he was dead.

She winced when she thought how close she came to leaving him like that. She breathed another long sigh of relief that she'd finally made the decision. She would never go back on that.

She rolled onto her back and folded her elbow under her head. "So when do I get to meet your father?"

"First thing in the morning."

She jumped up so fast she made the mattress bounce. "What?"

"Aye. As soon as possible. I'd take ye right now, but he'll be asleep at this hour." He pretended to look around. "I wonder what time it is. It cannae be far off from dawn."

"That soon?" She gulped.

"Dinnae trouble yerself, lassie." He put his arm around her and pulled her down. "Father's harmless. He winnae hurt ye....and I'll be with ye. He's a broken old man. He maynae even talk to ye at all. It's naught but a formality."

She settled into his chest again. She had been hoping to get some sleep tonight, but it didn't look like it was going to happen. She and Colton had been fooling around for so long.

Now she couldn't sleep if she tried. She was going to meet the reclusive Neill Buchanan. He was the real Clan Chief around here even if Colton did the heavy lifting.

This was the final river she had to cross. Once she met Neill, Colton would be declaring to the whole Clan that Jaimee was his mate. She would be an official member of this Clan, for better or for worse. There would be no going back—as if she needed something else to confirm it.

Colton kissed her on the head. His chest rose and fell with his breathing. Everything about him radiated masculinity. She trailed her fingertips through the dark hair on his chest. Heat pulsated off his body and warmed her so she never got cold.

"Ye dinnae regret ought, do ye, lassie?" he breathed.

"Nothing," she whispered. "Do you?"

"Not at all. I havenae ever felt happiness like this."

She kissed his skin and snuggled her cheek deeper into the cleft of his chest. His heartbeat thumped against her ear. "What will the rest of your Clansmen say?"

"They'll say I'm a clod for waiting so long."

She buried her face in his shoulder to stifle her laughter. "You can tell them I'm a little thick when it comes to love."

"I'll tell them no such thing. At any rate, they all ken ye planned to go home at some stage. They'll understand."

"I wish Bryce was still alive. I wish he was alive to find out."

"He already kenned, lass." He kissed her hair again. "He kenned before either of us."

"Yeah. I guess he did."

Chapter 20

J aimee paced up and down in a corridor she'd never seen before. It was on the very back side of Icemeet and faced directly toward the mountains. Hardly any sunlight made it to this keep.

She couldn't understand why anyone in their right mind would want to live here. Only someone who wanted nothing more to do with life would choose to live here. That pretty much summed up Neill Buchanan.

He was Chief of his Clan, but he had been living in seclusion for years and rarely spoke to anyone, including his own children. Now Jaimee was going to meet him, not as a guest in this fortress, but as Colton's mate for life. Was she ready for that?

She might not be ready to be Colton's mate, but at least now she might finally get some answers about Lady Ilisa Buchanan. Maybe now Jaimee would finally find out if Lady Ilisa Buchanan was the same person as Lady Rhona Armstrong.

She rubbed her hands together fighting to control her nerves. Reid and Duncan had been tasked with keeping Liam far, far away while Colton took Jaimee to meet his father. No one wanted Liam to interfere in the interview. Jaimee wanted that least of all.

She still hadn't dropped that particular bomb on Liam yet and she wasn't looking forward to it. She could imagine Liam's reaction when he found out about Jaimee mating with Colton for life.

A nearby door opened and Colton came out. He was dressed in his most spotless clothes and he looked amazing except that he was obviously as nervous as she was.

She rushed over to him. "What did he say?"

"He didnae say ought. He never does, but he's ready to meet ye now." Colton pressed both hands on her shoulders. "Are ye ready, lass?"

She nodded. "He doesn't bite, right? This can't possibly be worse than fighting Bryce."

"Father winnae fight ye. I'd be surprised if he even looks at ye. Come along."

He opened the same door and led the way into what had to be the biggest, fanciest, most palatial apartment in all of Icemeet.

Jaimee had had a few opportunities to see some of the rooms the other Clansmen used. Most of the single guys lived in a kind of barracks on the opposite side of the fortress. The single female archers had a giant shared apartment with several bunk beds in every room.

Mated couples had their own rooms, but most shared a single large bedroom not nearly as nice as Colton's. Their younger children lived with them until they got old enough to move into the barracks or the archers' apartment.

Only Jaimee and Colton shared a room as big and as nice as his. They only got the luxury because he was destined to be Clan Chief after his father died and was already doing the job now.

This apartment was lightyears better than any of the others. Several bedrooms led off in different directions from multiple giant interconnected sitting rooms. All the bedrooms stood open and Jaimee could see that they were all immaculately maintained. She could also see at one glance that they hadn't been used in a very long time.

Colton shut the apartment door softly so it made no noise. Even the latch clicking sounded unnaturally loud in the stillness.

Colton made his way through three massive sitting rooms, each one at least twice as large as his own bedroom. He halted in the very last one and Jaimee stopped short when she saw a disheveled man seated in an armchair in the corner.

Large windows gave a view of the mountain slopes outside. It would have been an impressive view if the mountain didn't block the sun, but Neill Buchanan sat with his back to the window. He faced the corner where he would be certain not to see anything, including anyone who happened to enter his apartment.

Colton and Jaimee stopped in the middle of the room. Jaimee shot a quizzical glance at Colton and he nodded. This was his father, the Chief of Clan Buchanan?

Neill wore a kilt like the rest of his Clansmen, but he didn't radiate the kind of hidden wild ferocity of the other Buchanans. He sat slumped, bowed, and totally unresponsive.

Jaimee inched forward. What should she do? Should she talk to him? Should she introduce herself? She could see right away that he wouldn't appreciate that or any other part of her visit. He wanted to be left entirely alone.

She snuck around the chair with Colton at her side. They both looked down at Neill's face and she realized that he wasn't that old at all. He had to be at least forty to have four fully grown children, but he wasn't as wrinkled or decrepit as Jaimee expected.

He had the figure of a man who might once have been as bulky, powerful, and intimidating as Colton. Neill had probably been as reckless as Duncan, but all of that was in the past.

God only knew how long Neill had been sitting here like this, utterly insensible to the world around him. Did he even know that his Clan was at war against the Creightons? Did he care?

Colton pulled up a chair at his father's side. Colton took hold of the back of it and inclined his head in a way Jaimee had come to understand. It was Colton's way of telling her to sit down.

She did and he brought over a second chair for himself. He rested his hand on top of his father's hand. "Father.... this is the lassie I told ye about. We're mated for life so she'll be me wife when I become Clan Chief after ye."

Neill didn't move. He blinked at the wall.

Colton cleared his throat. "Will ye give us yer blessing, Father? Ye ken we need yer approval before we can be lawfully joined."

Nothing. Colton and Jaimee exchanged glances. Now what?

Jaimee leaned forward. She stretched out her hand to touch Neill, too, but she stopped herself. "It's a pleasure to meet you, Sir. I've heard a great deal about you and it's an honor to join your Clan. I hope I can do you and Colton proud."

Neill blinked once. Was she supposed to take that as an approval? Colton fidgeted. This must be so much harder for him than it was for her.

She glanced up at him and threw caution to the wind. "Excuse me for saying so, Sir, but we're still trying to find your wife, Lady Ilisa Buchanan. Colton has sent spies into Kald and we think Lady Ilisa is being held a captive in Tyrekirk."

That got through to him. Neill turned and fixed his dead, unseeing eyes on her. He blinked again, but he showed no emotion and he didn't speak.

"Do you know why the Creightons would want to hold her as a captive? Does she mean something to them or did they just want to hurt the Buchanans by taking her away from you?"

He still didn't speak, but now she knew for certain that he was listening and that he understood every single word.

Colton didn't move. Jaimee expected him to intervene and stop her from questioning his father about Lady Ilisa, but Colton sat motionless and said nothing. Jaimee definitely took that for an approval and she forged ahead.

"My friends and I came here to find Lady Rhona Armstrong. Is there any possibility that Lady Ilisa and Lady Rhona could be the same person?"

Neill kept staring at her listening and saying nothing. What was wrong with him? He might not care about his children, but he must care enough about Ilisa to want to find out what was happening to her.

She glanced over at Colton again, and when she turned back to Neill, he was already swiveling his eyes back to the wall. He went back into his inert stupor and wiped her and Colton from his awareness.

"We'll leave ye to it, Father," Colton told him. "Thank ye for meeting us. We'll let ye ken when we're to be married."

He stood up and Jaimee copied him, but she couldn't stop staring down at the man in the chair. Was this the fate of any Buchanan who lost their life's mate? This was worse than death. It was living death.

Colton put her chair away and took her hand. He led her back into the corridor outside and shut the door.

"Wow!" she breathed. "He's a mess."

"He's been like this for decades—ever since Ilisa disappeared."

"How long is that?"

He shrugged. "Twenty years I'd say—ever since Duncan was born."

"Are you saying.... she got kidnapped right after he was born?"

Colton nodded. "Aye. She wasnae with us more than five years at the most."

Jaimee frowned at him doing some quick mental calculations. "How did your father meet her? Did she live in Icemeet before they got married?"

"She didnae live here. She came to visit from one of the western fortresses and they struck up an acquaintance."

"So...do you remember them getting together?"

"Aye. I wasnae more than five meself at the time, but I remember. I remember what he was like before he married her. He was.... well, he was like this, wasnae he? He came back to life when she arrived."

"Wow!" She passed her hand across her eyes. "That is not how I pictured meeting the in-laws would go."

He furrowed his brow at her. "What does that mean?"

"Nothing. Are we done here?"

"Aye. We can leave now."

He led her back toward the main keep, but they hadn't gone very far before Reid and Duncan came to find them. "Is it done?" Reid asked.

"Aye," Colton replied.

"Any change in him?" Duncan asked.

"None at all. He's always the same."

"I asked him about Lady Ilisa," Jaimee told them. "That got a reaction out of him, but he didn't say anything. He definitely paid attention, though."

"What did ye ask him?" Duncan asked.

"I just told him that we found out Ilisa was in Tyrekirk and I asked if he knew why the Creightons wanted to capture her. Then I asked if there was any connection between Ilisa and Lady Rhona Armstrong."

Reid shrugged. "If he didnae speak, then it's as good as if ye hadnae asked at all."

"I guess you're right, but at least I asked."

"He's too far gone to care about her or anyone else," Duncan snapped. "He's as good as dead himself. We'd all be better off if he snuffed it and left Colton to do the job."

"Dinnae ye speak of yer own father that way, laddie," Colton returned. "He's our Clan Chief no matter the state he's in and we'll all pay him the respect he's owed as long as he's alive under our roof."

Neither brother replied and Duncan looked away. He clenched his jaw biting back what Jaimee assumed must be some very biting remarks about his father.

Jaimee didn't blame him. Losing his mother must have been hard enough on Duncan. Now his father had been absent and unresponsive for just as long. Neill would have left Duncan an orphan when he was just a baby. That had to be hard on anyone.

Colton hooked his arm around Duncan's neck and pulled him into a rough, brotherly embrace. Colton cupped Duncan's cheek and pressed Duncan into his shoulder before letting him go. Then Reid clapped Duncan on the back.

He didn't push them away. He let his head lie on Colton's shoulder for a brief instant before all three brothers straightened up. It was a moment of affection and comfort that would have made Jaimee uncomfortable if it had happened any other time since she arrived at Icemeet.

Now it felt like another honor that they were letting her see them in this unguarded display of intimacy. They let her see their vulnerability and the rugged support they gave each other in their parents' place.

Reid, Colton, and Edeena must have suffered the same way when Neill checked out of his family life, not once, but twice. Colton was only five when his father married Ilisa, so he must have been much younger when his mother died.

Colton, Reid, and Edeena must have really needed a mother and a father. They got that when Neill married Ilisa and then they lost both for the second time when the Creightons kidnapped Ilisa.

The question plagued Jaimee's mind again. Why did the Creightons take Ilisa? Did the Creightons know somehow what a devastating blow they were dealing to their enemies? Was that why they snatched the Clan Chief's wife—to cripple Neill's family?

Colton faced his brothers. "I want ye two to meet me for a council of war. Ye must come, too, lassie, and Liam and Edeena."

"Och, no!" Reid snapped. "Not that trollop!"

Jaimee thought he meant Edeena and she almost protested him calling his own sister such an offensive word, but Colton cleared the matter up. "I dinnae fancy him any better than ye, but we cannae plan our counteroffensive with Edeena without inviting him as well. None of us want him around, but he's Edeena's mate and he's a wizard in his own right. He may prove useful in the end."

"If he doesnae betray us all, ye mean," Duncan growled. "I'd sooner cut his throat as share our plans with him."

"He hasnae done ought to betray our trust so far...." Colton raised a hand to stop Reid from interrupting. "Apart from binding Edeena—which was unintentional."

"If ye believe him," Reid countered.

"We have no reason not to believe him," Colton replied.

"I did see him try to break the mate-bonding spell," Jaimee told them. "It was when we were locked up in the vault. She came down to visit him and he tried to break it then. I believe him when he says he never meant to bind her."

"That does us no good at all, lassie," Duncan fired back. "They're bonded whether we like it or not. We're stuck with the nupty."

She almost laughed at the expression, but the three brothers' stern looks stopped her. "What do you want to do at this council of war?"

"We must change our strategy. We must switch it up from everything we did yesterday. The Creightons will expect us to repeat our victory. We must keep them guessing." Colton motioned to the others. "Come along. I dinnae fancy hanging about Father's apartment. It gives me the shivers."

Chapter 21

C olton pointed to a map on the table on his desk. "We came from the west last time, so we must plan flanking offensives coming from the north and from the east."

"How can we attack from the east?" Reid countered. "There's naught there but the estuary and the sea."

"It's simple," Colton replied. "We hide our men here behind the mountain. When we launch our offensive, our men come out from behind the mountain, move up the estuary, and assault the enemy on the planes.... here."

He traced around the map showing every direction to the planes. The Boundless offered the Creightons their only avenue into Buchanan territory. That left three directions from which the Buchanans could counter any invasion force.

"We'll post archers here." Edeena pointed to a different spot on the northeastern peaks. "We can hide there ahead of time and attack from a direction they winnae expect."

"How would you hide the archers there?" Liam countered. "You and the archers would have to go out there and sleep in the rocks starting now. That's the only way you would be in place when the Creightons attack."

Colton didn't answer him. Colton came into this meeting determined not to say a single word to Liam if he could possibly avoid it. Reid and Duncan also kept their eyes on the map and on Colton. They didn't acknowledge that Liam had spoken.

"We'll plant yer crossbows here and here, lassie," Colton went on. "We can target the dragons better from there. They'll be more maneuverable."

Jaimee took a deep breath. She'd been so deep in thought since they came back from visiting Colton's father. He knew she was dwelling on something. Maybe now she would finally get it off her chest.

"I've been thinking. Grant Ritchie crossed the Boundless unarmed. He risked his life to get near us in as non-threatening a way as possible. I'm starting to think he might have been trying to talk to us."

"Ye're barmy!" Reid countered. "He didnae fancy torching his wife. It's as simple as that."

"He could have decimated our men with one breath without putting her in danger, but he didn't. What if we contact him and offer a rapprochement? We could get him to tell us what's happening with Lady Ilisa."

"There'll be no rapprochement," Colton snapped. He heard himself being overly harsh with her, but he had to shut this down immediately. "The Creightons are our sworn enemies and he's the one arming for their next incursion. He's the biggest and the baddest of them second only to the Laird himself. We winnae treat with him nor any Creighton."

She cringed at his tone, but she didn't argue. It was more important than ever that she be seen to agree with everything he did and said now that they were mated.

An upwelling of pride overwhelmed him when he saw her holding back the protests she obviously wanted to make. She restrained herself perfectly. He couldn't be happier to have her at his side.

He couldn't say the same about Liam, though. "What about Lily? We could contact her. Maybe she can get to the bottom of this and broker some peace between the two Clans."

"There'll be no peace," Colton clenched his teeth and locked his eyes on the map so he wouldn't have to look at this traitor. "I dinnae care who it's with nor who negotiates it. We winnae communicate with them nor negotiate with them nor treat with them nor ever speak to them on ought connected with peace. We'll kill any of them that sets foot on our land and that includes yer sister. If ye cannae stomach that, then ye'll go the way of all our enemies. Is.... that.... clear?"

He forced out the last words and dead silence answered him. At least Liam had the brains not to push Colton any further. Colton was at the end of his patience where Liam was concerned.

No one moved or even breathed for a second until Colton shook himself, let out a long sigh, and pointed at the map one more time. "Edeena, ye'll station yer archers on the rocks as ye say. Ye can ask for volunteers for who'll go out now and hold the line until the Creightons strike."

"Aye," she agreed. "I'll havenae any shortage of takers, I'm sure."

"Duncan, ye'll take the eastern beach and Reid the northern flank. That leaves ye to the west, lassie, and me in the fortress for the front assault. I think that's all unless someone has anything else to add."

He glanced around the group making sure not to make eye contact with Liam. Colton didn't trust himself not to do something drastic if Liam opened his mouth a second time.

Reid, Duncan, and Edeena nodded. Jaimee stood off to one side studying Colton with an expression he couldn't read, but he couldn't spend any more time on this. They'd already been discussing their strategy for over an hour.

Reid and Duncan started talking to each other about how they were going to divide up their Clansmen into the different flanks. They wandered out of the room and Liam and Edeena followed shortly after.

Colton turned to Jaimee, but she only squeezed his arm and let herself out of the room, too.

Colton propped his hands on the table and bent over the map, but he couldn't see it anymore. He had too much on his mind, but Liam's behavior overshadowed everything else. Colton had been waiting since Liam's first appearance for that eel to step out of line.

Colton could see Liam gearing up for something. Colton just didn't know what it was and he didn't want to wait until Liam blindsided him with it to find out.

He pushed himself upright, rolled up the maps, and put them in his desk. Piles of work waited for him to attend to them, but he also had his own work to do getting ready for the next battle.

He was too agitated to sit down and shuffle papers so he strode out of the office. He planned to go to the courtyard and find his brothers.

He didn't want them to take the best men and leave him hamstrung with the dregs, which they were certain to do if he didn't participate in dividing them up. At least he could rely on Jaimee to make sure they left him a proper fighting force.

He headed down the corridor toward the stairs, but he pulled up short when he heard voices coming from around the corner. He eased forward to listen and he bristled when he heard Liam and Jaimee arguing.

"Don't you think it was less than prudent to get yourself mated to one of the Buchanans when our mission obviously lies in Kald?" Liam was saying.

"You're one to talk," she fired back. "You're mated to one of them and at least I can say I did it on purpose. I didn't fall out of a tree and end up mated to Colton by accident. Anyway, I'm not convinced our mission lies in Kald at all."

"How can you say that when your meeting with Neill didn't turn up anything useful?"

"Just because Neill didn't tell me what he knows doesn't mean he doesn't know anything."

"If he won't talk, then it's a dead end. We should follow up our other leads which are all in Kald, not here."

"Well, I'm not so sure I'm on board with the mission anymore anyway. My life is going in a different direction."

"You got that right," Liam countered. "You should be loyal to the President and the United States and now you've gone over to the enemy."

"Don't give me that line of crap," she spat. "I gave the US Military the best years of my life and what did I get for it? I owe myself something now. If that means falling in love with a good man and maybe having a life and a family for once, then that's what I'm going to do. It's a hell of a lot more than you'll ever have considering the way you're acting, Liam."

"Okay, fine, but don't you at least care about finding out what this whole Lady Rhona thing is all about? Do you really plan to just drop the whole mission and forget about it?"

She hesitated, and when Colton dared to glance around the corner, he saw her studying Liam with her head on one side.

"Did you ever think maybe the President and Felix Margoles gave you incomplete or incorrect information? Maybe the President is wrong about Lady Rhona or maybe he deliberately deceived us for some reason of his own."

Liam gasped. "How can you even think that?"

"Oh, wake up, Liam!" she countered. "Lady Rhona doesn't even exist. Everyone says so. Grant and Elliot Ritchie worked as guards in Tyrekirk for years and they never heard of her which means she can't be a Creighton. None of the Buchanans have ever heard of her, either. Something isn't right with this mission. So far, we have only the President's word that Lady Rhona is even real. Maybe he had some other reason to send us back in t ime."

Liam lowered his voice to a deadly murmur. "You really have gone over to the other side, Snowflake. You aren't who I thought you were."

"I'm glad we got that straight. It's what I've been trying to tell you all along."

"Why would the President deliberately deceive us when it's his own ancestor he sent us here to protect? How can I trust you, now that your loyalty is suspect?"

She snorted at him. "I haven't been able to trust you since you first showed your face at Ironforge, so I guess we're even now. You lied to Lily to get her into a dangerous, compromised situation without knowing the risks and then you lied to me to do the same thing to me. As far as I know, you're a tool for Felix Margoles trying to use the Last Division for some underhanded reason."

"Don't you dare!" he hissed. "Don't you dare accuse me of that!"

"I just did, so what are you going to do about it?"

He glared at her and gritted his teeth. "I see how it is. I can see we're on opposite sides now."

"Good. That's exactly where I want to be."

He scowled at her for another few seconds pursing his lips like he wanted to say something else. Then he whirled away and stormed off down the corridor.

Her shoulders slumped and she buried her face in her hands. Colton held himself back from going to her even though this aching pride and craving for her threatened to tear him apart.

She proved herself far more in that conversation than she ever did in the courtyard or on the mountain. She was becoming a woman he couldn't imagine living without. She told his father that she wanted to do Colton and the Clan proud. Colton was never prouder of her than he was right now.

He wanted to stand off in the shadows and admire her fortitude, her loyalty, and her determination in the face of incredible odds, but he didn't get a chance to.

She tore her hands off her face, threw back her head, and turned in the opposite direction from the one Liam had gone. She turned toward Colton and started walking before she spotted him standing at the corner watching her.

She pulled up short and stared at him as the puzzle pieces clicked together in her brain. Then she crossed the remaining section of corridor to where he stood. "Did you hear all that?"

"Aye. I heard."

She heaved a massive sigh and glanced over her shoulder in Liam's direction. "What are we going to do about him?"

"Ye leave him to me, lassie. We've more important things to think on right now."

Her expression softened and she grimaced. "I'm sorry about this. I feel like I've let you down."

"How have ye let me down? Ye've done all for me, lass. I couldnae ask for more than ye've done."

"It's him." She jerked her chin over her shoulder. "It's my fault he's here. It's my fault if he does something to...." She trailed off and winced again.

"Ye arenae responsible for what he does. Ye've done more than enough to rein him in. Ye leave him to me and go on with ye to the courtyard. Ye help the lads prepare for the next assault. That's more important than anything he does."

"Are you sure? I feel like I should do something about him...or to him. I feel like he's going to do something stupid and I should stop him before he damages us somehow."

"I told ye I'll be the one to deal with him. Ye go on. Ye've yer own work to do."

"All right." She sighed heavily once more and then leaned in and kissed him. "I guess I'll see you later."

"Aye. Ye can bet on it."

Chapter 22

J aimee ran her fingers through Colton's loose hair and savored the deep, passionate bliss of falling into his kiss. His mouth consumed her mind and wiped out every other thought but the rapture of being with him.

His hair fell over her and got tangled up with her own. It caressed her cheeks and neck as his body moved against hers. She released herself into the never-ending softness of his lips and tongue.

He reared off the bed and propped himself on his powerful arms. His chest and shoulders formed a protective rampart around her. She could shelter in this hollow where nothing could reach her or disturb her happiness.

She felt him stiffen and his muscles tensed down his stomach to where their bodies met. She arched into him and spun off into delirious passion as their desires quickened. She faded into a blurry dream where her body took over. She responded to him in magical ways that she didn't try to understand.

Her eyes drifted open and she reeled in the majestic power of him looking back down at her. His eyes hypnotized her into a trance where nothing existed but him. She gasped as he snatched one more kiss from her.

He slid his knee up the bed to push into her when a crash startled both of them. It came from downstairs followed by hushed voices talking fast.

He spun around and they both looked toward the bedroom door, but the sound was too far away for anyone to know what they'd been doing.

"It's nothing," she breathed and put her arms around his neck.

She pulled him down into another kiss. He tore off and dove down to bite her neck, but a second later, he drew back and straightened up on his knees. "It's nearly dawn anyhow. We've been at it all night again, lassie. We'll be getting up soon."

She glanced toward the window. He was right. The sky beyond the mountains was already turning grey. She could see every detail of the landscape out there.

She ran her fingers through her own hair and sank back on the mattress. "I guess it was asking too much that we take our honeymoon in the middle of a war zone." She shut her eyes and chuckled. "I should have known. That's just like me."

He stretched out on top of her and rested his head on her stomach. His arms kept moving and stroking her naked body, but he didn't rise again. "That's a second night we've gone without sleep, lassie. This cannae continue. We'll have to assign times to be together so we both get some sleep."

She smiled to herself and combed his hair out of his face. She rubbed his neck and shoulders while she hugged his head into her body. He made her indescribably happy. She would gladly go without sleep just to share these moments with him for the rest of her life.

"Are you sure you can do that with us sleeping in the same bed? Are you sure you can restrain yourself or do we need separate bedrooms?"

"I can sleep right here if ye let me." He started groaning and snuffling in a mock snore much louder than any normal person would have snored.

She laughed. "Don't you dare! You'll be asleep and I'll be awake all night."

"Eventually ye'll get so exhausted that ye black out."

They both laughed and then he sat up. "We may as well get out of bed and see what this day holds for us. It's only a matter of time before the Creightons make another mess of our territory. Each day brings us closer to the battle."

"You're right. I'd much rather spend every day and every night in bed with you, though."

He bent over and kissed her. "That makes two of us." He pushed his hair behind his ears and swung his legs onto the floor. "Come on, lassie. We can fool around all we like when this war is over."

"If it's ever over," she grumbled, but he didn't answer. He stood up, pulled on his shirt, and started buckling on his kilt.

She dragged herself out of bed and went over to the washstand. She washed her face, rinsed out her mouth, and started straightening her hair. She returned to the chair by the bed to put her clothes on when she noticed Colton watching her from the window.

"What's wrong?" she asked. "Do I have dirt on my face or something?"

"I want to talk to ye about Liam."

She groaned. "Do we have to?"

"Aye. I want to get rid of him to get him out of our lives forever. It's like ye say. I sense he plans to do something that may harm us."

"How do you plan to stop him? He's mated to your sister. If he's gone, she'll fall apart like your father."

"It's a price I'm willing to pay for the safety of me whole Clan."

"What are you going to do....and what do you need me for? You said you'd handle it."

"That's why I'm talking to ye about it, lassie. I want to send him forward in time to his own world, but I dinnae ken how."

"Do you plan to send Edeena forward in time, too?"

He shrugged. "If it comes to that."

"She's your sister. She belongs here."

"I dinnae ken about that, either. I dinnae trust him as far as I can throw him, and if she's determined to remain loyal to him, perhaps I cannae trust her, either."

"Wow!" she breathed. "That's big."

"Aye. Now I need ye to tell me about this time portal ye use to get back to yer own time. How does it work?"

"I'm not exactly sure. You saw that box that came through the portal with us. Liam does something to it, but I don't know how he does it. Besides, it must have malfunctioned when it sent us here instead of to Kald. If you or I tried to use it, it could wind up sending Liam and Edeena anywhere."

"Can ye find out for me, lassie? Could ye question him on how it works?"

"I could, but I would almost certainly raise his suspicions if I did. You heard our conversation yesterday. He knows I plan to stay here with you and he also knows I'm not following the mission anymore. He considers me his enemy."

"Aye." He turned away. "That's the rub."

"Do you still want me to talk to him about it?"

"I suppose not. As ye say, it will only tip him off."

"I can try to find out where the box is," she suggested. "I haven't seen it since we first came through the portal, so he must be hiding it somewhere.... but I am kind of busy with all the other stuff going on around here."

"Aye. If ye see or learn ought, ye tell me."

"Of course." She rose on her tiptoes and kissed him again. "I love you."

He pulled her in close against his chest. "Aye....and I love ye, lassie."

He kissed her on the forehead and they parted for the day. She headed for the courtyard and separated from him when he went into his office.

She pushed Liam and the box and everything connected to them out of her mind. The counterassault was much more important.

She reached the passage leading to the courtyard when Liam appeared from nowhere. He didn't come from the stairs behind her nor did he come from the courtyard. There was no other way he could have gotten here except by his own magic.

She stiffened at the sight of him. "Are you going to challenge me to a duel now? I hope you packed a lunch."

He dodged in front of her to stop her. "Look, Snowflake. I just want to say I'm sorry."

"For being an irretrievable ass? There's no apologizing for that."

"I'm sorry I questioned your loyalty. That was uncalled for."

"Uncalled for doesn't cover it," she growled.

"Just listen to me for a second, okay? I don't blame you for questioning this mission after everything that's happened. I would probably question it, too, if I was in your place, but you have to believe me. I saw the President's genealogy with my own eyes. Lady Rhona Armstrong is real. Her name is on his genealogy."

"Genealogies can be tampered with and faked, Liam. Use your brain."

He held up both hands. "I'm sorry I withheld information from you and Lily. I was under orders. You of all people should understand what that means."

She eyed him, but she couldn't argue with his point. "So what do you want me to do? I'm already mated to Colton and I won't go back on that. I'm sorry, but I can't be part of the Last Division anymore. My life is linked to the Buchanans now and I don't regret that at all. The President and the United States and the Army don't hold any power over me anymore."

"I understand." He spread his hands again. "I don't blame you. In fact, I envy you."

"I gotta go, Liam. We have a war to fight."

She started to walk around him again, but he stopped her. "I'm going to try to cross the Boundless and see if I can talk to Lily. Maybe she can tell me something that will further our mission."

"How the hell are you going to do that? There are two armies standing in the way."

"I'll figure it out."

"You would walk out on Edeena a second time?" She snorted and turned her back on him. "You really are as low as everyone says you are if you could abandon her now."

Chapter 23

Colton closed the door to the weapons storeroom and turned to his brothers. "Did ye talk to Connell the way I asked?"

Reid nodded. "Aye. He's put an undetectable spell on the blighter to stop him from using magic to leave Icemeet."

Colton turned to Duncan. "Have ye kept him under yer eye to ensure he isnae interfering with the preparations?"

"He doesnae interfere nor ought else. He doesnae do ought that I can see...other than skulk around in corners and whisper in people's ears."

"Which ears?" Colton asked.

Duncan shrugged. "None but Edeena and Snowflake as far as I can see. The rest avoid him."

"It isnae possible he's poisoning Snowflake," Reid countered. "She's been in the thick of fighting this war from the beginning. She's a mad woman."

"Aye," Duncan agreed. "We havenae any cause to doubt her loyalty, lad."

"I dinnae doubt her at all," Colton replied. "It's Edeena I worry on. Do ye ken her position?"

"I havenae asked outright," Duncan replied, "but she's been up to her neck organizing the archers, too. I'd lay any odds she's staunch."

"Aye," Reid added. "She wanted to volunteer to go out with the archers and stake out their mountain hiding place. She would have been there these last twenty-four hours if that slug hadnae convinced her to stay."

Colton gritted his teeth. "We must get rid of him one way or the other."

"There is only one way to get rid of him for good," Reid murmured, "only one way to break the mating bond and free Edeena from him forever."

"It's as likely to break her heart as free her," Colton countered.

"That's better than suffering him to lurk about turning her against us," Reid argued. "He'll be a millstone around our necks as long as he's alive."

"We have a plan, lad," Duncan whispered. "When the next assault comes, we strike in the confusion. We can finish him off and hide the body among the wounded on the battlefield. We can make it look like he fell in the fighting. Edeena never has to ken it was us."

"I dinnae care ought about him being an outsider," Reid added. "I never dreamed I'd say this about an alien, but Snowflake has proved us all wrong and we wouldnae say a word against her. Ye made yerself a perfect match there and we couldnae be happier for it. It's *him* we cannae stomach. He's a parasite."

"Aye," Duncan agreed. "Snowflake hates the war and she's working harder than the lot of us to win for us. He'll betray us and Edeena and the whole Clan the moment it suits him. He wouldnae have survived this long if it wasnae for Snowflake."

"We cannae make a move without yer say, laddie," Reid went on. "If ye say to hold our hand, we'll stand or fall on your word."

Colton looked back and forth between his two brothers. He didn't have to ask what they were talking about. He'd been thinking the same thing since Liam set foot in Icemeet.

Edeena would be free to mate again with one of her own kind as soon as Liam was dead. All three brothers heard her when she first came back from Kald. She never wanted this. She never wanted to mate with Liam in the first place. He forced it on her and the thought ignited Colton's fury every time he thought about it.

He finally nodded. "Very well. Ye carry out yer plan, but choose yer moment carefully. I'm trusting ye lads. Snowflake cannae see me hand in it at all."

"Of course, lad," Reid agreed. "We dinnae care to hurt her with this business."

Colton didn't know what else to say. Was he really plotting Liam's murder behind Jaimee's back?

He opened his mouth to speak when a loud bell started clanging right outside. It sounded exceptionally loud this close to the courtyard. He slapped his brothers on their backs. "It's the invasion! Go! Get it done and be off to yer posts!"

He whirled away and bolted into the courtyard with his brothers right behind him. The rest of their Clansmen barreled out of the fortress a second later. Colton got lost in the confusion of arming his men and seeing the others off.

Jaimee showed up a second later, but he didn't have a chance to say anything to her. She stood at the center of her forces shoving weapons into their hands and yelling orders at everyone.

She left to lead her party into a different part of the citadel. She would exit through a secret passage leading into the mountains. From there, she would go around to the western hills where she would spring a surprise attack on the Creightons from their flank.

Colton turned to his own men and started arming them and issuing orders. He caught a glimpse of Reid and Duncan vanishing into the stairs. They should have gone with their own men to their own posts, but instead, they went hunting Liam.

Edeena raced past Colton on her way up to the rocks to join the archers. Good. She wouldn't see her brothers attacking and hopefully killing Liam.

Colton turned to the battle. The gate stood open and he could see all the way down the mountain to the Creightons crossing the Boundless.

They were already engaging the guards posted on the Buchanan side. The clash of weapons echoed up the slope and dragons launched from Tyrekirk's upper turrets.

He raised his saber to call the assault when a flash of light caught his eye. It came from a high window four stories up the fortress. Three figures crossed the window and more flickers of light fired back and forth.

A single tall man stepped in front of the window facing off against two more armed men. Liam fired spells at Reid and Duncan, who deflected them with their weapons. A sudden explosion struck the window and the glass shattered.

Colton looked in on the fight unfolding before his eyes. He couldn't leave without seeing the outcome, but the noise coming from the planes escalated to a deafening thunderous din.

He waved his saber toward the battle. "Attack, lads! All in!"

His Clansmen roared their war cry and took off running down the mountain. He stood back by the gate and watched them out of sight before he dared to look up at the window again.

He barely caught a glimpse of Liam shooting another incantation at Duncan. A winding snake of light whipped around him, bound his arms to his sides, and hurled him backward.

His saber flew out of his hand and he crashed into the wall behind him. Reid charged Liam with his saber upraised. Liam coiled back his arm and unleashed a long, crackling whip of forked lightning. It snapped around Reid's ankles and flung him deeper into the room where the three men were fighting.

Liam looked around for another threat. Light and energy sparked from his fingertips and his eyes narrowed with deadly fury. Colton couldn't stand here waiting for Liam to spot him.

Colton raced through the gate and buried himself in the horde of Buchanans storming the planes. He forced his way to the front and Liam evaporated from his mind.

The Buchanans had bigger problems right now. The dragons stooped low over the battle and spat fire at the assembled Buchanans, but the dragons didn't try very hard to torch their enemies.

They belched a few puffs of flame and then climbed up toward Icemeet. They flew straight into the siege engines hidden in the rocks. The huge crossbows unloaded and hurled massive spears at the dragons.

They hit two of them and the creatures tumbled screeching and writhing to the rocks below. The archers sprang out of their hiding places and unleashed torrents of arrows on the Creighton troops.

"Forward!" Colton roared and charged for the Boundless to drive the enemy from his land.

The Creightons and the Buchanans met in a devastating clash of steel, and for a second, neither army could push the other back. They surged this way and that. Colton hacked at his enemies and struck down dozens of soldiers, but the Creightons held their ground with more men crossing the estuary by the second.

They started to force the Buchanans back onto the planes and Colton glanced toward the west. Jaimee should be coming around those mountains any second now. Then the Buchanans would overrun the Creightons and finish them off.

More arrows rained into the Creighton army. They started to weaken and the Buchanans lunged forward for another charge. Colton raised his saber to attack his next enemy when someone grabbed his arm. "Hey!"

He spun around ready to cut someone in half and glared at Liam holding Colton's saber arm down. Colton shoved him away. "Get yer hands off me, ye mapit!"

Liam dove right back in and bellowed in Colton's face. "Your brothers just tried to kill me! They attacked me in *your* house! Tell me you didn't plan this! Tell me to my face you didn't send them to get rid of me!"

Colton scowled at him. He seriously considered telling Liam the truth. Maybe then this fool would understand how much the Buchanans hated him.

At that moment, one of the Creighton soldiers roared and rushed Colton on his other side. Colton raised his saber to deflect the attack just in time, but the man turned out to be stronger than Colton realized.

Colton had to fight to his utmost just to stay alive. He parried several strikes until he finally lunged and skewered the guy through the chest.

Colton looked around for Liam and froze when he spotted the man he'd come to think of as his enemy. Liam wasn't on the Buchanan side anymore.

A gleaming halo of magical energy surrounded him as he strode through the Creighton ranks. He reached the Boundless and waded across it to the Kald side.

Colton gaped at him in horror. The traitor! Colton knew Liam's motives were suspect. Colton couldn't even be happy that his suspicious had been confirmed. Colton was vindicated, but at what cost?

A ground-shaking rumble shook the earth beneath Colton's feet, and before he could move, a massive tide of Buchanan Highlanders charged from the west with Jaimee in the lead.

She overran the Creightons on that side at the same time two more mobs of Buchanans attacked, one from the northern mountains and another from the east, but Reid and Duncan weren't with them.

Fergus led the charge from the north and Alastair dashed up the estuary from the east. The three armies met and dealt the Creightons a crushing blow as the full might of Clan Buchanan sealed their fates.

The sight electrified Colton and his men. They laid into the Creightons with every ounce of their strength. Colton drove the enemy into the estuary and back toward Kald.

The Creightons retreated and Colton pursued them halfway across the water. He drew to a halt with the water lapping his knees and he watched his enemies vanish inside the city walls.

He burst out laughing and turned back to his men. He raised his saber and bellowed in triumph. The whole Clan answered him and he saw Jaimee laughing farther up the plane.

She turned around and her eyes shone with so much love and compassion that he couldn't stand to keep away from her. He took a step....and froze when her smile drained away. She stared past him in stark horror.

He looked over his shoulder to see what the matter was. Then he turned all the way around clenching his saber in a death grip when a single black dragon launched from Tyrekirk's highest turret.

The creature stooped low over the city and picked up speed heading for the Buchanan side. It was Grant Ritchie, Laird Balfour Creighton's chosen heir.

The whole Buchanan force swiveled back toward the Boundless to face the dragon. Colton raised his saber to strike the monster down. The dragon narrowed his eyes....at h im.

Time slowed as the dragon streaked closer and closer. Colton could no longer deny that this creature was flying straight at him. The dragon locked his glowing eyes on Colton alone.

The dragon got bigger and bigger as he got nearer. He blocked out Colton's sight until Colton couldn't see or think of anything else. He faced Grant down with nothing but his saber and dirk. Would they be enough to defeat an enemy as big and powerful as this?

Colton crouched low timing his strike. He would have one chance at this before the dragon destroyed him. The dragon stretched his neck out in front of him flying fast and straight and sure. Colton eyed the dragon's neck for the best place to cleave the creature's head off.

A scream pierced Colton's iron reserve. Was that Jaimee screaming his name?

He raised his saber to bring the dragon down, but at the last second, the dragon thrust out his massive wings, braked his flight, and swung his clawed feet forward. He arched back his neck and those giant claws descended on top of Colton.

Colton swiped his weapons, but they only deflected off the dragon's armored scales. Sparks flew from Colton's blades and then the dragon landed on top of him.

The dragon pinned him under his claws and Colton hit the dirt. Black talons closed around him, and the next instant, the dragon ripped him off the ground and took wing.

Another hair-raising shriek erupted out of the Buchanan army, and this time, Colton heard it loud and clear. "Colton!" Jaimee shrieked. "Colton—NO!!"

Colton twisted toward the noise. He shifted back and forth a dozen times, but he couldn't break the dragon's grip. The dragon's massive wings thumped the air as Grant launched over the battlefield.

Colton arched his spine to the breaking point and the last thing he saw was Jaimee down on the ground. She screamed his name and tried to charge through the Buchanan ranks to reach the Boundless. Ewan and Alastair held her back and she fought them until the dragon swooped back to Tyrekirk taking Colton with him.

Chapter 24

J aimee stormed through the gate into the courtyard to find it deserted. The Buchanans fled back to Icemeet after Grant Ritchie snatched Colton. Now the Buchanans didn't even have the heart to come out of their fortress.

She shot a terrible look around just to make sure the guards were still on duty on the parapet. Other than them, the whole Buchanan army had taken shelter inside.

She marched down the passage and blasted into the central foyer. Where were they hiding? She wouldn't let them huddle under the covers when they had a war to fight.

Jaimee's despair at losing Colton vanished the moment Grant returned to Tyrekirk. Jaimee watched him take Colton inside the castle ....and then Jaimee saw Lily standing on the highest turret.

Murderous rage burned in Jaimee's heart for the woman who used to be her friend. Lily was the one responsible for this. She was the one who took Colton. Jaimee would never forgive her for that. Jaimee would get her revenge on Lily if it was the last thing she ever did.

She barely registered that she was still holding her own saber and dirk. She wanted to kill someone. She wanted to kill anyone who stood in the way of her getting Colton back, even if that person was a Buchanan.

She stormed into the dining hall and pulled up on the threshold taking in the scene. Reid, Duncan, Alastair, Ewan, Fergus, Edeena, and a few others faced off against all their Clansmen with both sides yelling, bellowing, and arguing at the tops of their voices.

Jaimee stood there fuming trying to understand what the hell was going on, but she couldn't hear a word over the noise. She listened for a second, but this wasn't getting anywhere.

She looked around for some way to get their attention and spotted a large iron kettle sitting on one of the tables. It was empty.

She swung her saber at it and vented all her rage on it. She smashed her saber into the metal and it made an almighty clang. That sound rang through the hall and everyone turned around.

The assembled Clansmen stared at her for what seemed like an eternity. No one moved until Duncan finally broke away and strode toward her. "Och, lassie! Ye're back! We worried ye were lost on the planes."

"What the hell is going on?" she demanded. "What the hell do you people think you're doing in here when we have a war to fight? Colton is still out there. We have to get him back."

"Och, aye," Reid replied. "That's what we were just discussing."

"Discussing! You call this discussing?" She scanned the crowd on the other side of the room. "What could possibly be more important than getting Colton back?"

Reid shuffled his feet and Ewan chimed in. "With him gone, it's Reid as should be taking over as Clan Chief. These cowards dinnae fancy following any man into battle against the Creightons." He sneered at the assembled people who obviously didn't agree with Reid taking over.

Jaimee inched forward and glared at everyone one person after another. Her knuckles whitened on her weapon. She had to struggle to keep control of herself.

"Which one of you is that spineless that you want to hide in here while Colton is a prisoner in Tyrekirk? Which one of you wants to tell me to my face that you'd rather snivel in your beds while the rest of us risk our lives getting him back?"

No one answered her. Reid, Duncan, and the others on this side swiveled around to stand next to her. She could see the whole thing plainly now. These brave few had been trying to convince their Clansmen to do something—anything—and the rest didn't want to.

"We need a plan, lassie," Duncan began again. "We need a much bigger force to get inside Tyrekirk and take Colton back."

"We don't need to get inside Tyrekirk. We can use other methods."

"How?" Edeena asked. "We've never crossed the Boundless before. We'd be fighting street to street just to get near the castle and the Creightons have the whole place rigged with magic."

Jaimee faced her and some of her rage started to fade. Edeena didn't know yet. She couldn't if she was still functioning. "We'll find a way to get Colton back. Make no mistake about that.... but Liam is gone, Edeena."

Edeena gasped out loud. "What? When? How?"

"He crossed the Boundless during the battle. He's gone over to the Creighton side. He told me he was going to try it. I just didn't think it would be so soon."

"NO!!" Edeena screamed. She charged Jaimee brandishing her fists.

Jaimee instinctively raised her weapons to defend herself, but Alastair caught Edeena before she could attack.

"Ye did this! Ye turned him against me!" Edeena shrieked. "Ye did this! Ye took him away from me!"

Alastair wrestled her out of the hall, but not before giving Jaimee a knowing glance. Edeena kept screaming all the way to the stairs. Her voice echoed far away until it vanished to nothing.

Jaimee turned back to find everyone looking at her, including Reid and Duncan. Exhaustion and desperation were starting to take a toll on her. She kept trying to come up with some way to bring Colton back, but he wasn't here.

Was this how the Buchanans felt when they lost their life's mate? She didn't want to live without him. Colton had been trying to make her understand ever since she met him.

She didn't understand until right now—not fully. She didn't know the mind-destroying catastrophe of losing part of her living soul.

Reid and Duncan looked back at her with pinched expressions and she realized with another gut-wrenching pang that they felt sorry for her. They knew how she felt.

She could fall apart like Neill. She could go out of her mind with grief like Edeena, but that wasn't going to happen.

She gritted her teeth wrestling herself under control. It took all her willpower not to go over to Kald right now and start slaughtering everyone in her path.

Her voice shook with rage and every nerve stretched to the breaking point putting words together into some order that made sense. "We're going to get Colton back. We're going to win this war and we're going to make the Creightons pay for what they've done."

"How do we do that?" Fergus asked. "Just tell us what to do, lassie."

She gulped down rising anguish. She had to bury it under a black tide of fury so she didn't lose her mind. "We can't use any of the tactics we used before. Liam is with the Creightons now and he heard all our preparations."

"Bastard!" Duncan hissed. "We should have gutted him the moment he showed up on our doorstep."

"That doesn't help us get Colton back," Jaimee returned. "Ewan, I want you to bring all the siege engines back inside the fortress."

"That'll take hours," someone in the crowd called out. "We've already spent two days moving them up there."

Jaimee spun around. "Who said that? Who wants to come out here and tell me to my face that we can't do this?"

No one moved. She paced up and down the line of faces. She woke up this morning loving this Clan and everyone in it. Now she couldn't think of anything but killing anyone who dared to question her.

She came pacing back the other way and Fergus stepped out of the way to let her through. "Listen to me very carefully, all of you. Colton is still your Clan Chief. These three brothers have been sending search parties over to Kald for decades trying to find Lady Ilisa Buchanan. Do you think we're going to turn our backs on Colton after only a few hours?"

"No, lassie," Reid replied, but he was the only one who dared to speak.

"Each of you owes Clan Buchanan your loyalty and your effort. You owe Colton your blood and your sweat and your strength, and as long as he's in Creighton hands, you owe Reid and Duncan. Anyone who isn't prepared to fight for this Clan can walk out that door right now—and you better hope and pray the Creightons take you in because we will never stop hunting you and all the rest of this Clan's enemies."

Another deadly silence fell over the hall. Jaimee shuddered from the tension racking her nerves. She had to keep going. She had to keep fighting and killing and destroying. She would fall apart completely if she didn't.

She turned back to her core of loyal supporters. "We have to retool the siege engines. We need to increase their range so we can start bombarding Tyrekirk."

"Bombard...Tyrekirk!" Duncan gasped. "Is that even possible?"

"It's possible. We just need strong enough siege engines. Maybe when our projectiles start falling inside Kald the Creightons will start to take us seriously. Edeena is right. Fighting inside the city isn't practical, but we need to take the fight to their front door."

"What about the enchantments?" Fergus asked. "If the Laird has bewitched the castle to withstand any attack, projectiles from Icemeet willnae touch Tyrekirk."

"Dinnae question Snowflake's orders!" Ewan boomed. "Ye heard what she said, ye traitor!"

"Stop it!" Jaimee snapped. "No one is a traitor for asking questions and Fergus raises a good point. We'd need to strengthen our siege engines anyway. We need to make them stronger and more accurate so we can take out more of their dragons. Their dragons are their only real advantage. Once we get rid of them, we can annihilate the Creightons down to the last man—starting with that big black bastard, Grant Ritchie."

"Aye, lass," Reid replied. "We'll pay them back for this. Dinnae ye concern yerself with that."

"And if the castle is bewitched to withstand any assault?" Fergus asked and got another dirty look from Ewan.

"Then we'll send another party into Kald to plant explosives around the castle walls. We'll blast the place to smithereens until we find a way in."

Everyone stared at her with huge eyes. She saw herself teetering on the edge of madness, but she didn't care anymore.

Reid opened his mouth to answer when a door slammed somewhere. Jaimee glanced toward the threshold expecting to see Alastair coming back.

Instead, young Gavin Buchanan skidded into view outside the hall. He lost his footing and crashed down on the floor before he scrambled to his feet. He staggered into the hall, cast one frightened look around, and faced Jaimee. "Lassie.... there's a messenger.... coming across the Boundless...."

"A messenger—from Kald?"

"Aye," Gavin panted. "He's demanding to speak to Snowflake under a flag of truce."

"Flag of truce, my ass!" she growled and stormed out of the hall. "Show me where."

Reid, Duncan, Ewan, Fergus, and several archers flanked Jaimee on her way back outside. Gavin went in front and led her up to the parapet.

She looked down the mountain toward the Boundless. The sun was going down and it gleamed on the water and on Tyrekirk. God, she hated that place!

Gavin pointed down at the estuary. "There, lass."

A single man stood on the Kald side of the river. He held two white flags, one in each hand. He yelled up the mountain and his voice carried on the evening breeze. "I carry a message from Lady Lily Armstrong to Snowflake of Clan Buchanan! I carry a message from Lady Lily Armstrong to Snowflake of Clan Buchanan! I carry a message..."

"Be quiet, fool!" Jaimee bellowed. "We can hear you just fine. State your business."

"I carry a message from...."

"I'm Snowflake, you dope!" she roared. "What's the message?"

"Lady Lily Armstrong wishes to discuss terms for the return of Colton Buchanan, Clan Chief of...."

"What terms?" Reid called down.

"Lady Lily Armstrong wishes to meet with Snowflake of Clan Buchanan at high noon tomorrow here, on the banks of the Boundless. Lady Lily Armstrong and Lord Grant Ritchie Armstrong offer their pledge of honor to safeguard Snowflake's safety during negotiations...."

"More negotiations!" Duncan snarled under his breath. "This is some trap or other."

"You haven't told us what the terms are," Jaimee called down. "What do the Creightons want in exchange for Colton's return?"

"Lord and Lady Armstrong wish to discuss terms in person with Snowflake tomorrow at high noon here on the...."

"To hell with it," Jaimee muttered. "He won't tell us anything."

"He's naught but a messenger boy," Reid added. "He doesnae ken nor care about any terms."

Jaimee raised her voice to yell down the mountain. "Tell Lord and Lady Armstrong that I'll be there to hear their terms."

"Yes, me lady!" The messenger started to turn away.

"Ye cannae trust them, lassie!" Duncan hissed. "This is a trick. They'll snatch or kill ye along with Colton."

"I doubt that," Jaimee called down to the retreating messenger. "Tell them I'm offering no pledge that I'll agree to their terms. Tell them I make no guarantees about anything."

"Yes, me lady!" the messenger repeated and vanished inside the city walls.

"Duncan is right," Reid told Jaimee. "Ye'd best ignore this offer."

"Don't worry. I don't plan to negotiate anything with anyone, but if I can get near enough to Lily, I might be able to kill her while the Creightons' guard is down. In the meantime, as long as they think we're negotiating under a flag of truce, we can attack them and wipe them out for good."

Chapter 25

A loud slam made Colton jump. He spun around ready to defend his life, but he couldn't get out of this room. A magical field blocked half of it and held him in this corner. He couldn't do more than pace back and forth across fifteen of floor.

He stiffened when a square-shouldered man with brown hair strode into the room. A short, curvy woman dressed in trousers accompanied him and they halted just beyond the field that kept Colton confined here.

He gritted his teeth when he recognized Lily Barnett and Grant Ritchie. "I hope ye're both right with the world as ye winnae survive this stunt very long. Do ye have any notion what me Clan will do to ye for taking me?"

Lily stepped closer to the field. "We didn't bring you here to harm you, Colton. We want to talk to you."

"Aye, ye're all a pack of talk and no teeth. Ye dinnae dare face us on the ground for fear of getting yer eyes scratched out."

"Will ye hold yer noise and listen, man?" Grant cut in. "We dinnae want any war with yer Clan. We brought ye here to make peace with ye."

"Peace!" Colton snorted. "It's a fine way of making peace, ye launching one invasion after another onto our land, killing our people, and bombarding our fortress with yer dragons. I dinnae need enemies with friends like ye."

"We never wanted to launch any invasion against you," Lily told him. "Laird Balfour was the one who did all this. We want to join forces with the Buchanans to bring down the Laird."

"Ye're in the same house with him," Colton countered. "Ye bring him down yer own selves. He's yer headache, not mine."

"Laird Balfour was the one that stole Lady Ilisa from yer Clan Chief," Grant went on. "If ye want revenge on anyone, it's him."

"He isnae the one that stole *me*, is he? Do ye think me Clan will forget yer actions today? I think not."

"What can you tell us about Ilisa's relationship with Neill Buchanan?" Lily asked. "He's your father, isn't he? How did Snowflake get to Icemeet? Did she go there to find out Ilisa's connection to your Clan?"

"I'll tell ye naught. I'd spit in yer eye if this infernal magic didnae stop me. Ye can chirp all day long. Ye havenae business even saying her name to me."

"Who?" Lily asked. "Do you mean Ilisa?"

Colton turned his back on them. He didn't want to talk to them about anything, especially not about Jaimee.

He gulped down rising panic. He couldn't be stuck in Tyrekirk while she was back at Icemeet. He had to find a way to get back there. His life wasn't worth spit without her.

"Please listen to us, Colton," Lily went on behind his back. "Lady Ilisa was Grant and Elliot Ritchie's mother. She gave birth to them before she crossed the Boundless to marry Neill Buchanan. She died two months ago when...."

Colton whipped around fast. "She's dead?"

"Aye," Grant murmured. "The Laird's wizards attacked me and she stepped in front of me to protect me."

He gave them a sick, sadistic grin. "If she's dead at Creighton hands, then me Clan will never stop seeking revenge for me father's wife."

He turned his back on them again willing himself to think. Lady Ilisa was dead and now he was a prisoner in her place. The Creightons held Ilisa a prisoner for twenty years despite all the Buchanans' efforts to find and free her.

How long would it take Jaimee, Reid, and Duncan to find and free Colton? Would they be able to do it at all?

"Listen to reason, man," Grant urged. "We only helped the Laird organize this battle so we could talk to ye. We had to work inside the castle to find a way to bring him down. Help us defeat him and we can end the war."

He didn't turn around nor did he speak. He would never say another word to them again. He hated them for taking Ilisa, for taking him, but more than anything, he hated them for separating him from Jaimee.

She'd be working to bring him home. She would never rest until she freed him. He knew that. He could rely on her heart.

She loved him. She said so. She gave everything to his Clan. She wouldn't fail him now.

"Did Snowflake tell you about the Last Division, Colton?" Lily asked.

Colton's heart twisted. He didn't want Lily or anyone else even talking about Jaimee. She was his alone. He cherished her in his heart. He wanted to destroy anyone for even thinking about her or saying her name.

"Did she tell you that we swore never to marry or love for the rest of our lives?" she asked.

Colton clamped his eyes shut to block her voice out of his head. Where was Jaimee right now? When would he see her again?

He had to hold out hope that she was searching for him. He had to cling with all his might to the promise that he would see her again. He would go out of his mind if he didn't hold that thought in his mind at all times.

Grant murmured low under his breath. "Come along, lassie. He winnae talk to us again tonight. Leave him alone."

Neither of them moved for a second and Colton felt both of them looking at the back of his head. A moment later, footsteps walked away and faded, but Colton only heard one set of feet leaving the room. One of them was still here.

"Ye'll be hungry and tired, laddie," Grant told him. "I'll send ye a meal and give ye somewhere to sleep. I cannae let ye leave the castle yet. Me grandfather doesnae ken ye're here or he'd kill ye for certain. We must keep ye hidden until we can come to some understanding on how to deal with him. Ye dinnae believe I'm not yer enemy. I hope ye'll come to see I want to defeat the Laird as much as ye—maybe more. It was he who killed Lady Ilisa, not us."

Colton still didn't turn around and he didn't answer. He shouldn't let this man's tone weasel into his mind, but Colton found it difficult not to listen.

It had to be a lie that Ilisa had two sons before she came to Icemeet. That was impossible, especially since Grant was one of the dragons. A Buchanan couldn't give birth to one of those lizards.

The next moment, Grant walked away and left Colton in silence. He slumped with a broken sigh, but he had to straighten up right away when some wizards reentered the room.

They did something to their magical field. Four men stepped through it and carried a bed into the room. They set it up near where Colton stood and then they brought in a small table and laid a meal on it.

The wizards stood guard through the whole procedure, and when they finished, they re-established the field closer to the door. They left Colton with more space, but he was still a prisoner.

He paced around for a long time, but his nerves got the better of him. He couldn't keep pacing all night long....and then he remembered.

He hadn't slept in two days. He'd been too busy enjoying his nights with Jaimee...and now she was gone.

Exhaustion and despair robbed him of his willpower to continue. He couldn't stand the thought of eating anything, so he stretched out on the bed and fell asleep instead.

Chapter 26

Jaimee halted under the big Icemeet entrance gate. Reid stood at her right and Duncan was on her left. Ewan, Alastair, and Fergus followed them into the sunshine and all six looked down the mountain toward the Boundless.

The Creightons had set up some kind of pavilion right next to the estuary. Tiny people moved around under the canopy.

"Look at them scurrying around down there," Alastair snarled. "They're the most affected wee toffs I ever laid eyes on."

"Colton isnae with them," Duncan murmured. "They're all wearing Creighton tartan."

"All except that muckle laddie at the back," Reid pointed out. "He's wearing Armstrong colors."

"It's Grant," Jaimee muttered. "He isn't as much of a coward as he seems."

"He's no coward at all if he came across the water unarmed in the middle of the battle," Reid replied.

"He wasnae brave enough to take Colton as a man, though," Alastair countered. "He wouldnae dare pull a stunt like that without the dragon in him."

"What time is it?" Jaimee asked.

"Five minutes until noon," Fergus replied. "Ye'd best be going if ye mean to, lassie."

She started down the mountain with these five loyal souls at her heels. They surrounded her in a guarding posture and accompanied her to the water's edge.

The whole Buchanan fighting force stood armed and ready for battle on the planes. The archers waited on the rocks above Icemeet and all the Clan's strengthened siege engines aimed toward Kald. If the Creightons broke their pledge, the Buchanans would be ready to strike back with a vengeance.

Jaimee and her entourage filed between sturdy Clansmen who all stood with drawn blades and glared across the water toward the pavilion. Not one person from Clan Buchanan stayed behind.

She halted on the Buchanan side of the estuary and squinted up at the pavilion. Grant and Lily stood up there along with Liam and a few other people Jaimee didn't recognize. They didn't concern her. Only Lily mattered.

"You guys stay here," Jaimee murmured to her companions. "Keep an eye on things, and if anything goes wrong, don't hesitate to launch our assault. Don't hesitate to cross the estuary if you have to."

"Aye," Reid breathed. "Dinnae ye concern yerself with us. Just finish this."

"Ye shouldnae go over there alone, lassie," Duncan insisted. "Ye need some guard. Let me come with ye."

"We've already talked about this. If anyone comes, they won't let me near enough to Lily to kill her. I have to go alone. I can take her in a fight. I just have to get close enough. Remember what I said and launch the assault as soon as I give the signal."

She started forward and strode into the water. She would finish this, all right. She would finish it right now.

Bryce's dirk stuck out of her belt. Jaimee didn't need any other weapon and she was secretly pleased to see that Grant and Lily were both armed, too. Good. They weren't so stupid as to think she would meet them without protecting herself.

She crossed to the Kald side and climbed the stairs. She stepped under the pavilion canopy that shaded the parties from the sun.

"How are you doing, Snowflake?" Liam asked.

She wrinkled her nose at him and turned to Grant and Lily. "Where's Colton?"

"He's back in Tyrekirk," Lily replied. "We wanted to talk to you before we send him home."

"If you harmed a hair on his head, we'll hunt you down and I'll personally make sure you both suffer the painful, miserable death you deserve."

"We didnae harm Colton," Grant countered. "We only wanted to talk to him. We want to make peace with the Buchanans."

"And while we're at it, I plan to make sure you both suffer the painful, miserable death you deserve for taking him in the first place. Whatever you have to say, save your breath."

"At least hear what we have to say," Lily insisted. "We're friends. Can't we just talk to each other and come to an understanding?"

"We aren't friends," Jaimee snapped back. "I don't know if we ever were, but we sure as hell aren't now."

"Why?" Lily's voice cracked. "What happened to you in Icemeet?"

"That's none of your business. It's enough for you to know that I'm not a part of the Last Division anymore...." Jaimee dragged her eyes up and down Lily's body. Jaimee hardly recognized Lily. "I can see that you aren't, either, so don't give me any claptrap about loyalty to the President and the US Military or anything like that. It means nothing to me anymore."

"So you're loyal to the Buchanans instead?" Liam interjected. "Do you even realize how stupid that is? You're a modern woman and they're.... they're heathens. Reid and Duncan tried to kill me before the last battle. That's the kind of people you're signing up to defend."

"It's too bad they didn't do it," Jaimee snarled. "You're a foul traitor and I'll finish the job the very first chance I get."

"That's enough of that," Grant interrupted. "We didnae ask ye here to exchange threats and insults. Colton is safe in Tyrekirk and we'll return him if ye'll only listen to us."

Jaimee turned around to threaten and insult him again, but something in his direct gaze stopped her. "What guarantee can you give me that Colton is alive?"

"I give ye me word of honor as a man that he hasnae been harmed at all since I took him from the battlefield. I give ye me word of honor that I didnae take him to harm him or to deprive ye of his presence. We tried to reason with him and he wouldnae listen at all."

Jaimee snorted. "I bet he didn't."

"Hear what we have to say." He held her gaze with an unnerving steadiness that reminded her of the Buchanans. "That's all I ask."

She measured him in a split second. He might be a Creighton and an Armstrong, but she believed him when he gave his word on Colton's safety.

She crossed the estuary ready to kill Lily and Grant if she could get away with it. Now that she came face to face with Grant, she found that she couldn't. He was something completely different than she expected.

"Fine," she snapped. "Say what you have to say, but I can promise you that I won't listen to a word you say until I see with my own eyes that Colton is unharmed."

"We had no intention of harming him," Lily insisted. "How could you think that, Snowflake?"

Jaimee sneered at her. "You squawk all you want. *Your* word doesn't mean shit to me."

Lily gasped, but Grant held up his hands. "Come back to Tyrekirk with us. Ye can see Colton yerself and we can talk there. Just hear what we have to say. Give us a chance to convince ye that we arenae yer enemies"

Jaimee pricked up her ears. He was inviting her inside Tyrekirk. This was better than she hoped.

She made a snap decision to go along with this. She would pretend to cooperate, and once she got inside, she would kill both of these idiots. She might even get lucky and kill the Laird, too.

"Fine, but I'm not making any guarantees that I'll agree to your terms."

"Of course," Grant replied. "If ye come, we'll extend our pledge to guarantee yer safety until we can return ye to yer Clan."

She studied him for another long moment. He didn't hesitate to call the Buchanans her Clan. Could it be that he understood that part, too? He never once balked at giving her his assurance about Colton's safety. He didn't think her attachment to Colton and the Buchanans was stupid.

Jaimee's vendetta against Lily still gnawed at her guts. She would never trust Lily again as long as she lived, but Jaimee believed Grant. His word was good to her—for now, at least.

"Wait here," she told him. "I'll be right back."

She turned on her heel and crossed the estuary again. She pulled up in front of Reid and Duncan. "Ye didnae give the signal, lassie," Duncan hissed. "What's amiss?"

"Nothing. I'm going back to Tyrekirk with them."

"Och, no, lass!" Reid exclaimed. "Ye cannae! It's insane!"

"Colton is back at Tyrekirk and they've given me their pledge that he's safe and that I'll be safe until I bring him back home. They say they'll release him if I just listen to what they have to say."

"Ye cannae believe them!" Duncan countered. "They're full of hot air."

"It doesn't matter. Colton is in Tyrekirk. Even if they're lying and they don't intend to free him, I'll be inside the castle. I can get him out. This is our best chance to get him back quickly. I'm going with them, even if just to satisfy myself that he's all right. I have to. I have to see if he's...."

She looked over her shoulder to cover up the break in her voice. She had to see Colton again. She didn't give a damn about the consequences. He was alive in Tyrekirk and she would hazard any danger to find him.

"What do ye mean for us to do, lass?" Reid asked. "Do ye mean for us to stay here and wait for ye to come back? Ye could be gone another ten years."

"Stay here. Maintain the standing army just in case the Creightons try to pull something. Guard our land and don't let them cross the Boundless again."

"Let me come with ye, lass," Duncan breathed. "We want Colton back as much as ye."

She smiled at him and squeezed the back of his neck in a playful shake. "Somehow, I don't think you want him back as much as that. Hold your ground and defend the Clan."

She turned away, walked back to the pavilion, and straightened up in front of Grant and Lily. "I'm ready."

Chapter 27

Colton barely opened his eyes when a door slammed out of sight. He'd been hearing the same sound nonstop for hours. It didn't mean anything.

He adjusted his position on the hard wooden bench. He'd been woken roughly by soldiers dragging him out of the soft bed Grant had given him. They had dragged him here and thrown him in this dungeon cell. Now he knew what he put Jaimee through when he first locked her in the vault at Icemeet.

He tried to go back to sleep, but his eyes popped open when he heard voices nearby. Some of them were female voices.

He froze and his nerves threatened to break when he saw Jaimee walking toward him beyond the bars. He didn't want to believe his eyes, but this racing feeling in his heart didn't lie. She was here. She came for him.

He rose to his feet and adrenaline shot through his veins when he saw her flanked by Grant and Lily. The three of them halted in the middle of the dungeon.

Jaimee's eyes glowed with excruciating agony and she fought to keep her features under control. Her face overflowed with so much love that he couldn't stand it. He gulped holding back the urge to rush to her, but the bars blocked his way. She was out there and he was in here.

"Are ye satisfied now?" Grant asked. "Ye can see he's unharmed."

Jaimee didn't turn around. "Leave us alone for a while."

Grant nodded to someone behind him. A young man stepped out of the shadows. He snapped his fingers and the bars vanished. Now nothing stood between Jaimee and Colton.

Grant steered Lily and the rest of his people out of the dungeon and the same door slammed somewhere. Silence descended over the cell—or what used to be a cell.

Jaimee charged him and threw her arms around Colton's ribs. She crushed him and turned her face up to kiss him. "You're all right! I was so worried about you!"

He fought back emotion stroking her cheeks and kissing every part of her face and hair and neck. "Ye're here, lassie! I feared I'd never see ye again."

"I couldn't leave you in here. I'm going to get you out and take you home. I promise."

He pushed her back and feasted his grateful eyes on her face. His heart cracked with so much love that he thought he might die. "Ye should have come. Ye shouldnae have put yerself in danger."

"I had to! It's okay. They just want to talk. Then they say they'll release you, and if they don't, I'll be inside here. I'll kill them all and take you home. It's that simple."

He held her at arm's length. He struggled not to devour her right here and now. "Listen to me, lassie. Ye cannae negotiate with the Creightons. I winnae allow it. It's a matter of our Clan honor. Whatever it is they want, ye must burn the whole of Kald to the ground rather than give an inch of ground."

"Don't worry." She cracked a wild grin. "I'm only doing this to get you free. Then I'll rain terror and vengeance on their heads. No one wants them dead more than I do."

He grabbed her and kissed her more deeply and passionately. His chest ached from desire and desperation. He needed her so badly. He needed all of her. He couldn't bear the thought that she would leave in a few minutes.

She collapsed into his arms and her mouth opened so their tongues met. She hugged him close against her and held nothing back. They might be alone in his room at Icemeet.

He opened his eyes and watched her while he kissed her. The sight of her overwhelmed him with so much emotion. How did he come to love her so much?

She straightened up and their eyes found each other. She swallowed hard and her voice strangled in a ragged croak. "I.... I don't want to leave you alone."

"Ye must, lassie." He petted her cheeks and allowed his fingertips to trail through her hair. The satin sensation brought back so many memories of their time in his room. "Ye do what ye must and we'll deal to these bastards once I'm free."

She looked down at the floor and nodded, but he could plainly see her struggling to hold herself together. "It's just.... hard. I can't stand being away from you."

"It's the same for me. That's the way with life mates. It's torture to be without ye, but we'll be back together soon. Ye'll see."

She kissed him again. "I love you."

"Aye, and I love ye as well. Ye're me whole life, lassie—ye and me Clan."

Her eyes darted around at nothing. She opened her mouth to say something else, but no sound came out. She looked so desperate and upset at the idea of leaving him that he had to kiss her again.

"It will be all right, lassie," he breathed. "We're together even when we're apart. Ye ken that."

She nodded down at the floor.

"Ye're right here." He picked up her hand and placed it on his heart. "Ye'll always be here. It doesnae matter how far apart we are. No one can take ye away from here."

She fell against him and rested her head in that hollow place at the center of his chest. He cupped her head and pressed her ear against his heart. He prayed that she could hear how much his heart ached for her. He never wanted to let her go.

She finally pulled herself out of his arms. She straightened up with tears brimming in her eyes. "I won't leave without you. I swear it."

"I ken ye winnae, lassie." He kissed her. "I have complete faith in ye."

She kissed him one last time and stepped back. His arms weighed a ton without her in them. His skin and bones burned as she moved farther and farther away.

She crossed some invisible barrier in the middle of the room and the bars rematerialized where they were before. They blocked Colton and Jaimee from reaching each other.

She froze on the spot still staring at him. Her cheek and lips quivered fighting down emotion. Her voice jumped all over the place when she choked out one last, "I love you," and raced away.

He stared after her. He would give anything to go after her, to hold her and kiss her one more time, but the bars locked him in. He was stuck in this cell while she was out there fighting to free him.

He shuffled back to the bench and sat down. He held himself together as long as she was here, but the full catastrophe of losing her hit him hard now that she was gone. She was so close and yet so far away.

He buried his face in his hands and let out a shaky breath. He couldn't fall apart now. He had to stay strong, but the anguish in his heart wouldn't stop plaguing him.

She was in there—in the deepest, darkest corner of his heart. She would always be there, but her love tortured him as long as she remained out of his reach.

Chapter 28

J aimee paced back and forth in the bedroom Grant and Lily gave her for her stay in Tyrekirk. The high windows gave her a view across the Boundless in the opposite direction.

She could even make out Reid and Duncan moving around among their Clansmen. The Buchanan army was still out there. If the Creightons thought this view would dishearten her, they would be sadly mistaken. It only strengthened her resolve to take revenge and finish these bastards for good.

Her brief meeting with Colton reignited her murderous fury against Grant and Lily. How dare they imprison Colton in a dungeon cell? Didn't they know he was basically Chief of Clan Buchanan? How dare they?

Seeing him, touching him, kissing him, and hearing his heartbeat against her ear fired her determination to get him out of here, no matter the cost. She had to take him home to Icemeet. She couldn't leave without him and she couldn't face another day without him near her. She really must be a Buchanan if she felt this way about her life's mate.

She turned to pace back the other way when someone knocked on her bedroom door. Whoever it was had some nerve pretending to be polite when she was little more than a prisoner here herself.

The knock came a second time. The sound irritated Jaimee. "What do you want?" she snapped.

The door opened and Jaimee's hand flew automatically to her dirk when Lily walked in. Lily's eyes flicked to the weapon. She stood up a little straighter, but she didn't say anything about Jaimee threatening her.

"Do you have anything you need?" Lily asked.

"Everything except Colton....and your head on a platter. When can we get this over with so I can find out that you and what's-his-name are full of shit?"

Lily spread both palms. "Just listen to me for a minute, okay? Just hear what I have to say and then we'll send you and Colton back to Icemeet."

"I'm listening." Jaimee crossed her arms over her chest. She wasn't holding onto her dirk anymore, but that could change at a moment's notice. "Say what you have to say."

Lily took a deep breath. "It's like this. Lady Ilisa Buchanan was a Creighton. She was Laird Balfour Creighton's oldest daughter. She had two sons with her husband, Camdyn Carmichael. Laird Balfour threatened to kill Grant and Elliot, so Ilisa arranged for a wizard to conceal their identities. She did it to protect their lives and she gave them to a maid in the castle to raise as her own."

Jaimee let the words sink in. She didn't want to believe them at first. Lady Ilisa Buchanan—a Creighton? That couldn't be possible.

"Laird Balfour tried to find the two boys because he knew they'd be strong enough to take the Seat of Armstrong from him. When he couldn't find them, he threatened to kill Ilisa, too, and she ran away. She ran to the one place she knew Laird Balfour wouldn't be able to find her. She went to Icemeet."

Jaimee turned away. She didn't want Lily to see the effect this story had on her.

Turning away only brought her face to face with the window and the view beyond. Holy living Christ! If this story was true, it would be the most explosive revelation in history. It would blow both Clans apart.

"Grant and Elliot grew up thinking their mother was a maid," Lily went on. "Neither of them ever found out they were directly in line to inherit the Seat of Armstrong.... until two months ago. Grant got into a fight against the Laird's wizards and he shifted into a dragon. He's the Laird's grandson. Both he and Elliot are, and now that Ness Creighton is dead, the Laird has made Grant his heir. We're only cooperating with him so we'll be close enough to find a way to bring him down. Neither of us wants war against the Buchanans."

Jaimee hardly heard her. If Lady Ilisa was a Creighton, that meant Duncan was part Creighton and part Buchanan. He was part dragon and part Highland tiger.

Maybe he wouldn't be both. Jaimee couldn't know for certain if Duncan would be able to shift into a dragon. He could definitely shift into a tiger. Jaimee had seen him shift with her own eyes.

Maybe his tiger nature would block him from shifting into a dragon. Maybe that's why no one found out yet that he was half and half. Maybe he couldn't. Maybe he never would.

Did Neill know? He must. That must be why he stayed hidden all the time. Maybe he didn't trust himself to participate with the rest of his Clan without giving away the secret.

Jaimee's mind spun. She had to keep this to herself. The President must have sent Liam and Lily back in time for something connected with Duncan, so what was it?

If it was true, Duncan would be in line to inherit the Seat of Armstrong, too. He would be Laird Balfour's grandson the same as Grant and Elliot. Duncan would be Grant and Elliot's brother.

A hybrid between the Creightons and the Buchanans would be able to unite the Clans. Duncan would be able to end the war.

A Buchanan—on the throne of Armstrong? Holy mackerel! That would be something to write home about. The evil wizard the President sent them here to stop must be Laird Balfour. Laird Balfour must be launching these ill-fated wars to stop Duncan from robbing the Laird of his power. It all made sense now.

No one had found out yet who Lady Rhona was, if Lady Rhona existed at all. Jaimee determined to find out more when she got back to Icemeet. She had to get both herself and Colton out of this castle first without Laird Balfour finding out the truth—or anyone else for that matter.

Lily came over to Jaimee's side. "Can you tell me anything about Lady Ilisa's time at Icemeet? Did anything happen there that could help us find out what's been going on?"

Jaimee turned around very slowly. She had to be careful here not to give anything away. She still didn't trust Lily, especially not with something as explosive as this.

"Are you absolutely certain that Lady Ilisa was a Creighton?" Jaimee asked. "Do you have iron-clad proof of that?"

"Absolutely!" Lily exclaimed. "I saw her shift into a dragon with my own eyes. Grant and I were standing right there. The wizards attacked Grant and Ilisa jumped in front of him to protect him. She lost her life saving his. She told him the whole story with her dying breath. There's no question in my mind that she was his real mother. Anyway, it isn't possible that he could be a dragon if his mother was a maid. Only the Royal Family can shift into dragons."

Jaimee shook those thoughts out of her head and walked away. She couldn't be near Lily with all these conflicting ideas crowding her mind. Jaimee needed to think.

"What's wrong, Snowflake?" Lily asked. "What's going on? What can you tell me about what Ilisa did at Icemeet?"

Jaimee turned around to face Lily. Jaimee had no idea what she would say. She only knew she had to get Lily out of this room before Jaimee's brain exploded.

At that moment, the door burst open and a butler in a tuxedo entered without knocking. He bowed to Lily. "Excuse the intrusion, me lady, but His Lairdship calls yer guest to his audience hall immediately."

"What?" Lily gasped. "What does he want with her?"

"I'm sure I dinnae ken, me lady. It's His Lairdship's wish to speak to yer visitor in person."

The butler bowed himself out of the room and shut the door.

"Great," Jaimee huffed. "I'm looking forward to giving that fool a piece of my mind."

She started for the door, but Lily jumped into her path and stopped her. "Wait, Snowflake! You can't go."

"Why not? Someone has to tell this jackass where to stick it."

Lily straightened her arm to hold Jaimee back. "You don't understand. Laird Balfour is the most powerful wizard in the whole country. He probably plans to use his magic to get information out of you."

Jaimee froze. If Laird Balfour did use magic on her, he could find out about Duncan. Jaimee couldn't let that happen. She whirled away. "I'm getting out of here. I'll grab Colton and...."

"You can't, Snowflake! The Laird will only track you down with magic, and if he can't retake you, he'll kill you. You have to meet with him. Just take Liam with you. Liam can use his magic to protect you.... or at least stop the Laird from finding out what you know."

Jaimee checked herself and stared down into Lily's bright eyes. Lily didn't know what Jaimee knew and here was Lily trying to make sure the Laird didn't find out, either.

Jaimee's world teetered on its axis. Lily really was trying to protect her. Lily was trying to protect the secret even if she never found out herself.

Jaimee leaned back and her shoulders relaxed. "All right. I'll take Liam with me."

Lily's countenance cleared and she smiled for the first time. "Grant and I will come with you. The Laird might try to hurt you or kill you if he can't get the information he wants. You'll stand a much better chance with us there."

Jaimee opened her mouth, checked herself, and had to think twice before she said, "Thanks, Lily."

"Sure." Lily headed for the door and the two women fell in side by side crossing the room.... the way it used to be.

Jaimee pushed those thoughts out of her head. She couldn't let her guard down around Lily. This might be another trick.

"You said you wanted to cooperate with the Laird to try to stop him," Jaimee began. "Won't he turn against you if you protect me?"

"Let's hope it doesn't come to that. If Liam can block him from squeezing information out of you, you might get out of the audience hall without getting into a fight."

Jaimee snorted. "Keep dreaming, girl."

Lily shot her a wild grin on the side. "None of us in the Last Division ever thought we'd be fighting in a place like this, did we?"

Jaimee pulled up short and towed Lily to a halt. "Hold it. I have to tell you something, Lily."

"Okay. What is it?"

"I'm mated to Colton for life. I'm not part of the Last Division anymore."

"I know....and I know the Buchanans mate for life. I figured that when you jumped in front of him to defend him."

Jaimee held up her hand. She had to get the rest out before Lily put herself in danger for Jaimee's sake. "I'm grateful for your help, but I can't begin to trust you as long as you're holding Colton as a captive. I can only go along with this if you promise to free Colton."

Lily's smile evaporated, but she didn't stiffen or brace herself. "I understand and I don't blame you. You can rely on Grant's word, but I can't speak for the Laird. I wouldn't trust him for all the money in the world. Just let us get you through this meeting and then Grant and I can help you get Colton out of the castle."

"I want to see him first—here." Jaimee waved to the room. "Show me you're sincere that you never meant him any harm."

Lily puffed out her cheeks and nodded. "All right. I'll see what I can do."

Chapter 29

C olton got to his feet when the dungeon door opened for the second time. He narrowed his eyes at Grant. "Where's Snowflake?"

"I'm taking ye to her now." Grant drew near the bars. "I want a word with ye first."

"Save yer breath. If ye arenae here to release me altogether, I dinnae care to see yer ugly face." Colton glanced behind Grant toward the door. "Where's yer confounded wizards? Ye winnae take me anywhere without them."

"I left them behind so I could speak to ye without them present."

Colton snorted. "Do ye think they will nae hear every word ye say? They have magic, ye nupty."

Grant broke into a smile and immediately bit it back. "Just listen to me, lad."

"I'm not a lad for ye to call me one. Mind yer mouth if ye dinnae fancy it smashed to a bloody pulp."

"As ye wish. Now listen. I gave ye a bed and a meal and all. I did it to show I meant to bring ye here as a guest. I brought ye here so we could speak man to man about ending this foul war."

Colton spread both arms and waved at the dungeon around him. "Why am I *here*, then? I was enjoying that bed when yer men hauled me down here. Ye dinnae treat all yer guests this way, I hope."

"Will ye stow yer noise and listen?" Grant snapped. "Ye get a rein on yer own mouth before ye start throwing insults about."

Colton checked himself. This man was no fool and he wasn't the slightest bit put off by Colton's attitude. Grant had been trying to talk sense to Colton since his arrival in Tyrekirk. Maybe Colton should listen just long enough to hear what it was Grant wanted.

"I had naught to do with bringing ye down here," Grant told him. "I would have left ye in that room until we'd had a chance to talk. It was the Laird that brought ye here. I didnae mean for him to find out ye were ever here, but he discovered somehow."

"Another wizard trick, I'll wager," Colton countered. "Ye arenae the brightest spark, are ye?"

Grant compressed his lips once and let the comment slide. "He's found out yer here and he's called Snowflake to his audience hall. He means to question her with magic."

Colton froze. He couldn't let these bastards threaten Jaimee, but how could he stop it?

"Lily has arranged for Liam to protect Snowflake with his magic, but she insists on seeing ye first."

"If ye lay a finger on her...."

"Will ye shut it for ten seconds, lad!" Grant hissed. "Lily and I are going with them in case it comes to violence. We've done all we can to prevent this. Dinnae ye see that? Open yer eyes. We arenae yer enemies. It's the Laird we all have to worry on."

Colton frowned at him trying to understand what he was hearing. "Ye...and Lily.... what do ye think ye'll do against a wizard as powerful as him?"

Grant shrugged and glanced behind him. "Maybe not much, but we'll at least get Snowflake out of the audience hall alive. It may cost much, but it's enough."

"Ye'd......ye'd risk yer lives....to protect her?"

"Aye, man! Dinnae ye see I brought ye here to reason with ye? We've been searching for months for a way to defeat him. We cannae stop him from bringing Snowflake before him and we cannae stop him from questioning her. We can only find some way to slow him down. Lily and I have done naught else for weeks now."

Colton turned away. He wasn't hearing this. He couldn't start thinking of the heir of Armstrong as anything other than his mortal enemy.

Why was Jaimee going along with this? If Grant was right, then they could all do little more than try to stay one step ahead of the Laird.

Colton turned around to find Grant looking at the floor. His eyes darted around like he was thinking fast, too. Could he possibly be telling the truth?

"If ye're serious," Colton began, "then take me to see her and dinnae delay it any longer. Ye've kept me from her long enough."

Grant nodded and went back to the dungeon door. He returned with the young wizard that removed and replaced the bars when Jaimee came down here last time.

The wizard removed them for the second time. Nothing stood between Colton and Grant anymore and the two men came face to face. Colton considered attacking the man who stole him across the Boundless, but Colton decided to wait on that. He could always kill Grant later.

The wizard hung back watching the two men, no doubt to defend Grant if Colton tried anything. Grant waved him away. "Off ye go, laddie. Leave us alone."

"But me Laird...." the wizard began.

Grant glared at him and the wizard retreated. He took off and shut the door behind him.

Grant faced Colton and spread his arms. "Go on. Ye ken ye want to."

Colton measured Grant up and down. Grant wasn't as big as Colton, but he was still carrying plenty of muscle. He could do some damage even without turning into a dragon.

Colton checked within himself. He could shift into a tiger whenever he wanted to. He had tried a few times since Grant brought him to Tyrekirk. The castle's magic blocked him, but it had vanished now.

He could shift right now and probably kill Grant before Grant had a chance to shift and defend himself. All the things Grant had been saying came back to nag Colton's mind. He wanted to find out more before he finished off his one source of information in this madhouse.

He shrugged. "Maybe another time."

Grant laughed. "Anytime ye say."

He turned away and headed out of the dungeon like they might be friends or something. His manner disarmed Colton. Colton was having difficulty remembering why he wanted to kill this man.

Grant held the door open for him and they climbed the stairs. They entered a normal-looking corridor and Grant halted by a random doorway. He nodded at Colton. "She's in here. She's waiting for ye."

Colton hesitated. "Just like that? No guards or naught?"

"Not a bit of it. She's called down to the audience hall in an hour. I'll be back then to take ye downstairs. Ye two'll be alone 'til then."

Grant bumped Colton's shoulder in a friendly way and walked off. He left Colton standing there in the corridor, totally unguarded. He could walk away. He could probably go all the way back to Icemeet, but he only had one reason to go back there.

He pushed the door open....and saw her. She spun around from the window, and the next instant, she was in his arms. She attacked him kissing him, stroking his face, and wrapping her arms around his neck.

He tried to keep up with her ravenous kisses. She seized his mouth with devouring kisses and shoved her tongue into his mouth. She ran her hands over every part of him that she could reach.

"Lassie...." he gasped between kisses. "Easy, lassie...." but she wouldn't go easy. She smothered him with her mouth and hands.

He finally forced her off and held her still. "Let me look at ye for a moment. Ye can kiss me all ye like after that."

Her features twisted in anguish. "I have to go before the Laird."

"Grant told me all. Ye dinnae think it's a good idea, do ye? Is there any way around it?"

"I don't think so. I think he wants information about the Clan—Clan Buchanan, I mean."

"There's naught to tell. He can use his magic to see all he wants to ken."

She shook her head and now she pulled out of his arms of her own accord. "I have to meet him. I found out a few things...."

"What things?"

"I can't tell you—not now. He could be listening, and if he finds out...."

Colton scowled at her. "So ye're keeping secrets from me now? Did they do ought to ye, lassie? Did they find a way to break our bond?"

"No!" she shrieked. "Never! Please. You have to trust me. I'll tell you everything as soon as we get out of here, but I don't want to tell you as long as we're inside these walls."

"And what's to stop him from searching yer mind once ye're in front of him? Ye dinnae ken his power. None of us does."

"Liam will...." She held her finger to his lips to stop him from saying it. "I don't trust him, either, but he's doing this for Lily. It's our best chance to stop the Laird from finding out what I know."

"So ye do ken something. Is that what ye're telling me? Ye ken something he wants to ken—something about our Clan. Is it something about our defenses? Does he want to ken how to defeat us?"

She gulped. He saw her fighting her desire to tell him everything.

She finally inhaled a deep breath. "Please, Colton. If you ever trusted me, trust me now. I'm doing this for the good of our Clan. I wouldn't keep anything from you otherwise and I swear to you, on my honor, I will tell you everything as soon as we're safe. I don't dare tell you now in case he finds out."

"Is it as important as all that?"

"Yes. I really wish I could tell you, but if I don't go before the Laird now, he might try to capture us another time when we won't have Liam there to help us. Please. I love you. I don't want anything but to spend the rest of my life with you defending our Clan. Please trust me. I'm begging you to trust me just this once."

Now it was his turn to take a deep breath. "I dinnae like this, lass, but if it means that much to ye, I can wait."

"Thank you!" She lunged for him and kissed him again. He felt the secret hanging heavy between them. It tormented him to have this between them—whatever it was.

He trusted her, though. If it was as important as that and she really thought that keeping the secret would protect their Clan, he could put it off a little longer.

She tried to engage with him and kiss him, but the secret quelled some of their passion. She leaned back and her eyes found his. "Do you still love me?"

"More than ever, lassie," he choked. "I only wish I kenned ye were still mine."

"I am." Tears welled up in her eyes. "If you feel that way, I'll tell you now."

He shook his head. "I'm trusting ye, lass. Ye'll tell me after we get out of here."

"I swear I will." She picked up his hand and laid it over her heart. "Right here. You're right here no matter what."

He couldn't stand that. He crushed her in his arms. He couldn't even kiss her. He had her heart and she had his.

All his doubts crumbled and he buried his face in her hair. He didn't want anything but to hold her for the rest of the hour. He knew he could trust her. He knew she belonged to his Clan for good and all. Why did he question her?

This horrid castle eroded his confidence somehow. It got into his head. Maybe that was the Laird's magic, too.

He straightened up, but she didn't try to kiss him. She held herself in reserve. She must be waiting until she could fulfill her promise.

He couldn't keep his hands off her. He grabbed her and pulled her in. All his passion for her erupted as never before. He clenched his fists in her clothes. "I need ye," he snarled in her ear.

She gasped and her body quivered. He cast one glance around and spotted a couch to one side. He lifted her off her feet and carried her toward it. If this was the last time he ever saw her, he better make it count.

Chapter 30

J aimee leaned and kissed Colton long and slow and deep. His strong fingers clenched in her hair and he crushed her mouth in a torturous kiss before they both pulled off.

She stared deep into his eyes and saw everything that had passed between them. They were still locked together for all time. Nothing could break that bond now.

"I'll see you soon," she whispered.

"Aye. Not soon enough."

"I love you," she breathed. "As soon as I do this, I'll come and get you and we'll go home."

"Aye, lass. I'll be counting the moments."

She kissed him again and they both stood up from the couch where they'd just spent the last hour. It was one of the most beautiful hours of Jaimee's life and now it was over.

Lily, Liam, and Grant waited for them across the room. Colton took Jaimee's hand and led her over to them. "I'm ready to go."

Grant opened the door and all five of them exited into the corridor. The same young wizard from the dungeon waited for them there and Colton stiffened at the sight of him.

"Tristan will take ye back downstairs," Grant announced.

Colton squeezed Jaimee's hand and walked off with the young man. That left Jaimee alone with Lily, Liam, and Grant.

She made sure to keep Lily and Grant between herself and Liam. He was supposed to be protecting her from the Laird's power, but she didn't want him anywhere near her. She would never trust Liam again.

"What can I expect when I see the Laird?" she asked Lily.

"I honestly have no idea," Lily breathed. "I wish I could tell you. I guess he'll try to question you, and when he doesn't get the answers he wants, he'll use his magic—whatever that is."

Jaimee studied her friend on the way down the corridor. "So he's never used his magic on you?"

"God, no! Then again, it isn't like I know anything he wants to know. I already know all the incriminating secrets he might want to hide from the world.... but no, he doesn't use that kind of magic on me—on either of us."

Jaimee shot a glance at Grant and then at Liam. She could ask Liam what spells the Laird would use on her, but she didn't ask. She didn't want to talk to him at all.

Grant halted in front of a pair of enormous double doors. "This is it, lassie. He's in there waiting for ye."

"You guys are coming in, right?"

"Of course," Lily replied. "We'll be with you all the way."

Jaimee glanced over at Liam again. She would have liked to get his assurance that he could block the Laird's magic, but she still couldn't overcome her aversion to him.

He read her body language without her saying anything. "Don't worry. I'll be there and I'll make sure he doesn't get inside your head."

"How will you do that?" she asked before she thought to stop herself.

He shrugged. "It's a pretty simple spell to block your mind from intrusion."

"Won't he be able to overcome it if it's that simple?"

Liam smiled. That smile made Jaimee sick. "He won't be able to overcome it *because* it's a simple spell. He'll be expecting something complex if he's expecting anything at all."

"We're trusting you, Liam," Lily added. "Don't play games with Snowflake's safety. If you aren't sure, tell us now."

"I'm sure. Don't worry about it."

"Ye saying that doesnae put anyone's mind at rest, laddie," Grant snarled. "Ye're too cavalier about the Laird. He can squash yer magic with not a thought."

"I bet he can't."

"Ye're betting with Snowflake's life," Grant countered. "If ye cannae take this seriously, I'll fetch Tristan to take yer place."

Liam's smirk vanished. "He's just a boy."

"He's a boy I trust a sight more than I trust ye."

Liam glared at Grant and Grant glared right back at him, but at that moment, the big doors opened from the inside. Jaimee didn't see anyone in the hall who might have opened them. The place was deserted except for an ancient man with long white hair.

He stood on a raised dais at the far end of the hall. He gazed out of high windows at the situation across the Boundless.

He turned around and grinned at the party as they entered. His grizzled features and crooked grin gave Jaimee the creeps. He oozed menace and insidious power.

She didn't want to go in there, but whatever invisible force opened the doors drew her to him against her will. She stopped in front of the dais and he floated down the steps toward her.

"Och, aye!" he breathed. "The latest visitor from the future. What is yer name, lassie?"

She gulped. Was he using his power to probe her mind yet? "My name is Snowflake."

He gave a twisted, gruesome laugh. "Ye're a liar just like yer friend here. Dinnae tell me anything so ridiculous. What's yer real name?"

His laughter infuriated her. She thought of something insulting to say back to him, but at that moment, she felt a delicious wave of peace, warmth, and happiness sweep over her. It wiped away all thought and all care about keeping any secrets from anyone. She just didn't care anymore.

"My name is Jaimee Abernathy," she replied.

The Laird smiled and nodded. "Good lass. You've been in Icemeet a few weeks now, I see."

"Yes."

"Ye've mated with the Clan Chief's son—Colton Buchanan is his name."

"Yes."

"And ye've met with the Clan Chief—Neill. Ye've met him to gain his approval of yer mating bond."

"Yes."

The words fell out of Jaimee's mouth without her even trying. She didn't think. She just blurted out the truth.

"Now tell me all ye ken about Lady Ilisa Buchanan's children. Tell me all Neill told ye about the children she had with him."

Jaimee opened her mouth to tell him all about.... Her breath caught in her throat and she stopped. She knew something important about Lady Ilisa's children. She knew exactly what he was asking, but she couldn't for the life of her remember what it was.

She scrambled in her brain trying to remember. The warm, peaceful feeling got stronger by the second. It built to a burning, punishing agony, but no matter how much she struggled and rummaged in her brain for the right facts, she couldn't remember.

"I.... uh...." She glanced over at Grant and Lily. They watched her holding their breath, too.

Liam stood off to one side studying her with his head on one side, but he couldn't help her, either.

She turned back to the Laird....and something snapped. The peaceful feeling vanished. Her mind cleared. She remembered everything, but he couldn't penetrate her mind anymore.

She knew now that Liam had fulfilled his side of the bargain. He protected her by burying the memory so deeply that she couldn't even remember it. Now the Laird would never be able to steal it from her.

She squared her shoulders at him. "I don't know anything about Lady Ilisa's children. I only know Neill's children. I don't know anything about their mothers."

His smug grin evaporated. "Ye're a liar."

"I'd rather be a liar than a madman. What is it you want from me?"

He paced up and down in front of her and she could see him trying to regain his composure. "Ye'll arrange Clan Buchanan's capitulation in this war and turn over all Icemeet's resources...."

"I don't think so," she cut in. "Clan Buchanan will never capitulate."

"Snowflake!" Lily whispered. "You promised in exchange for Colton's release."

"I agreed to come here and hear what you had to say in exchange for Colton's release. I've done that. I never promised to negotiate on the war and I certainly never agreed to capitulate. I would never do that. No Buchanan will ever do that. Clan Buchanan will never lie down—ever."

"You speak for Clan Buchanan?" the Laird demanded. "You arenae any Buchanan."

"I'm as Buchanan as any of them and I can guarantee that any other Buchanan will tell you exactly the same thing. You killed Lady Ilisa—or you had her killed. It's the same thing. Now release Colton. We're leaving."

The Laird's scowl turned upside down and he cackled with sadistic glee. "I kenned ye'd say something like that, but I never agreed to release him or ye. I kenned ye wouldnae cooperate or see reason so I arranged to deal with the traitor meself."

"What traitor?" Jaimee's blood ran cold when she realized what he was talking about. "You mean Colton?"

"He's a threat to the kingdom. I cannae allow him to live, so I've ordered his execution. He's on his way there now."

She gaped at him in mounting horror. A threat to the kingdom? Could it be that the Laird thought Colton was the hybrid? He must or he wouldn't think Colton was a threat.

The Laird must think Colton was Lady Ilisa's son. The Laird wanted to know who Neill's childrens' mothers were. Laird Balfour must be totally ignorant about Neill's family. He must think Colton, Reid, and Edeena were Ilisa's children, too. He didn't know the truth about Duncan.

None of that meant anything right now. Colton was in danger if he wasn't dead already.

She spun on her heel and stormed out of the hall. The Laird laughed at her behind her back, but she ignored it. He didn't matter anymore.

Grant and Lily pulled up next to her outside the big double doors. "Phew!" Lily breathed. "You didn't tell him anything important."

"Forget that!" Jaimee snapped. "Where's Colton?"

"Ye mean..."

"He's on his way to face execution! Where are they taking him?"

"He'll be down in the courtyard with the...."

Jaimee didn't wait around to hear anymore. She whirled away and took off running.

Chapter 31

F our guards attacked Colton and dragged him out of his cell. He kicked and fought, but they pinned his arms to his sides so he couldn't move. He bellowed in fury and managed to rip one arm out of their grasp. He landed a few telling blows, but more guards came out of the woodwork to subdue him.

Four more men got on his legs and lifted him off the ground. They buried him under a dozen bodies and started carrying him out of the dungeon. This couldn't be good.

He flew into an even more furious rage and thrashed for all he was worth. He tried to shift, but the Laird's magic still bound him. They got onto the stairs and descended another five levels. Now he knew they were going to do something really bad.

He roared out all his indignation and wrath and exploded wrenching his body in all directions. He almost got them to drop him head downward on the stairs, but at that moment, something wrapped tightly around his limbs.

Some magical spell immobilized him—all except for his head. He could still yell at them and he could still see exactly where he was going.

A guard near his shoulder kicked another door open and they lugged him into a stone courtyard. Colton's stomach plummeted when he saw a wooden scaffold set up in the sunshine. The rope noose hung in the center with a hooded hangman standing by.

Colton's nerves snapped and he struggled harder than ever. The magical restraints flexed under his efforts, but they didn't break.

He roared curses at his captors, but they didn't budge. They wouldn't even look at him. He searched frantically in all directions. Four wizards stood guard and they all aimed their hands at him.

Magical energy flowed from their fingertips to surround him, but he didn't recognize any of them. None of them was the young man who had been following Colton everywhere. These were strangers—not that it mattered who they were.

The soldiers hauled Colton up the steps. They stood him on his feet over a trapdoor right under the noose. There was no way out. He couldn't die like this—tied up like an animal.

The guards retreated to the ground, but they didn't leave. At least twenty of them blocked him from the only exit. He would have to fight his way through them even if he could somehow break these magical bonds. Besides, he was totally unarmed and he couldn't shift.

His heart hammered his ribs so hard that he couldn't breathe. This couldn't be happening. The Creightons couldn't be about to hang him like this. Where was Jaimee? What would happen to her after he died?

Anguish tore his heart in half. He would give anything to see her again just one more time, to kiss her once before he died. How did he know that the hour he spent with her would be his last? What forgotten instinct told him to make the most of it while he had the chance?

His heart stopped altogether when the hangman bumped into him from behind. The man wrestled the noose over Colton's head. The rope rested heavily on Colton's collarbone.

His mind scrambled for some way to make this not true. There had to be some way out, but he couldn't move.

The hangman returned to the lever and grabbed the handle. He locked his eyes on Colton. This was it. Colton was going to die right now.

That instant of realization and understanding fell over him with the weight of a heavy blanket. It wiped away all fear and Colton squared his shoulders. He looked straight ahead at the wall in front of him. He didn't see the soldiers or the wizards standing around.

The wizards didn't need magic to restrain him. Colton stood perfectly still and calm in the face of death. He would die as a Clan Chief should. He would die proud of his Clan and he would do his Clan proud by dying an honorable death. No one would ever be able to say that Colton Buchanan died frightened and struggling like a coward.

The lever thunked when the hangman pushed it taut. Colton didn't need to hear the moment the hangman pulled the handle. It would all be over in an instant and Colton wouldn't have to worry about anything anymore.

He straightened up for the moment of truth and the lever slammed back. The trapdoor dropped beneath him. Colton plunged through it and every muscle in his body relaxed. He closed his eyes. He didn't need to see anymore.

At that moment, a high-pitched whistle distracted him. He opened his eyes without meaning to, and for a second, he thought he might be dreaming. Jaimee stood before him as radiant and beautiful as ever. Her black eyes flashed and her satin black hair whipped in the wind.... but she wasn't smiling. She didn't even look at him.

The next instant, he landed hard on his feet underneath the scaffold with the open trapdoor swinging above his head and the rope still dangled from his neck. The frayed end bumped his arm.

He looked around in a daze and saw Jaimee rocket into the courtyard slinging two blades—a dirk and a short saber that Colton didn't recognize. Where did she get them?

Another dirk quivered in the wall behind the scaffold where it sliced through the rope. Jaimee whirled into the courtyard hacking, stabbing, and attacking everywhere.

The soldiers and wizards spun around to confront her and the magic binding Colton vanished in a blink. He could move, and even better, he could shift.

He launched himself at the soldiers from behind, shifted on the fly, and landed on a man's head. Colton twisted his body around the man's neck and ripped out the soldier's throat with one slash of his fangs.

Colton tasted blood and that taste drove him wild. He sprang off his falling victim and pounced on one of the wizards. The man was in the act of shooting spells at Jaimee. Colton hit him in the face and knocked him flat before shredding the wizard's eyes out.

Colton dispatched that man, too, and vaulted for the nearest soldier. Five of them surrounded Jaimee and the clash of weapons deafened Colton. Battle fury overwhelmed his mind. He landed on the soldier's back and Colton's claws hooked into the man's tartan.

The guy swiveled around trying to dislodge the tiger and Jaimee struck without mercy. She ran the soldier through and Colton sprang off for the next man in line. Colton and Jaimee coordinated their efforts fighting their way closer to the exit.

Jaimee backed up and yelled something to Colton, but he couldn't hear her over the noise. He reached the door first, but he couldn't open it in his cat form. He didn't dare to shift back. He was unarmed. He could defend himself much better like this.

She whirled backward, kicked out at the door latch, and it released. The door swung outward into the corridor, but before either of them could make their escape, three more soldiers lunged in to attack her.

Seeing her in danger broke a dam of murderous fury in Colton's being. He shot off the floor and soared for the nearest soldier's face. Colton extended his claws to catch hold of the man's head, but the guy ducked and Colton missed his mark. His claws sank into the guy's face and the man screamed.

That sound set off Colton's killer instinct like nothing else. He gouged with his fangs and kicked out his hind paws. His feet slashed downward into the guy's neck and blood gushed down his shirt.

Colton looked around for his next target when Jaimee's voice penetrated his rage-fogged brain. "Colton—come on! We have to get out of here!"

He jumped clear and saw what she meant. She had leveled two more soldiers and was holding the other seven at bay. Nothing stood between her and the exit.

He sprang off and landed at her side. She took another step back and crossed the threshold. They were out of the courtyard and back in the corridor.

She turned away and Colton followed her....and stopped when they came up against five more wizards blocking the corridor. There was no way out except to go back into the courtyard.

Colton coiled his legs under him to spring, but he could already see the wizards summoning their magic to bind the fugitives. Now they would send Colton back to the gallows with Jaimee along with him.

Jaimee crouched low and brandished her weapons at the wizards, but they all stayed well out of range. Neither Jaimee nor Colton would be able to get anywhere near them.

Colton yowled, flattened his ears against his head, and arched his back. He raised his hackles preparing himself to go down fighting when, without warning, a devastating tempest of fire erupted behind the wizards.

Colton hunkered low to the floor and Jaimee cowered as blistering flames licked the stone walls. The fire enveloped the wizards in a vicious inferno. Colton squinted into the light and heat. He couldn't see where the fire was coming from. He could only hear the crackle and screams as the wizards went up in smoke.

The fire blinked out in an instant and Jaimee and Colton stared at an absolutely massive black dragon huddled low in the corridor beyond. It was so unbelievably big that it only fit in the space by lying flat and hunched under the ceiling. It was Grant.

He couldn't lift his head or spread his wings. He couldn't even stand. His face pointed toward Jaimee and Colton and acrid smoke billowed from his nostrils. He growled low in his chest and narrowed his eyes at the two escaped prisoners.

Lily darted out from behind Grant's claws. She held a saber in one hand and a dirk in the other and she was dressed for battle.

She grabbed Jaimee's sleeve. "Come on! We have to hurry before the Laird sends more wizards."

Jaimee stared at her in stupid shock. "What are you doing?"

"Getting you out of the castle. We can't go out through the front. The Laird's magic will block you, but we know a different way out."

Lily dragged Jaimee toward the dragon. Colton didn't want Jaimee going anywhere near that thing and she held back. She resisted Lily's efforts to take her near the creature.

An instant later, the dragon shrank, straightened up, and turned into a man. The last fading trace of scales vanished beneath his skin.

The corridor was clear and Grant crossed the floor to Lily and Jaimee. "Follow me. There isnae a moment to lose."

Jaimee glanced over her shoulder toward Colton. His caution evaporated now that he was facing a man instead of a dragon.

Colton shifted and joined them. Grant and Lily led Jaimee and Colton deeper into Tyrekirk's underground tunnels. They entered another stairway and descended even further.

They came to a dank, damp tunnel barely big enough for a grown man to stand upright. Colton and Jaimee both had to hunch over.

"Where are we going?" Jaimee whispered.

"We're going deeper under Kald," Lily replied. "We have to get beyond the Laird's magic before we come back up the surface. He'll be able to see where we are even once we get outside. We have to get as far away from the castle as we can. Then we'll find a way to get you back across the Boundless."

Jaimee glanced over at Colton and he read her thoughts. Grant and Lily were helping Jaimee and Colton escape. So Grant was good for his word after all.

He had torched several of the Laird's wizards and now he was taking his life in his hands by defying his grandfather. That counted for a lot in Colton's book. He still didn't want to trust these two, but he didn't see that he had much choice considering the risks they were taking.

Jaimee and Colton followed Grant and Lily for miles under the city. Grant talked over his shoulder to Colton the whole time. "The Laird has launched an assault on Icemeet while we've all been occupied with ye. The bastard's a slippery eel if I ever met one. Ye two must get across as quickly as ye can and organize yer Clan to resist before the dragons take Icemeet itself."

"How do you know that when you've been with us the whole time?" Jaimee asked.

"Tristan told me. He's with us against the Laird. That's why I took him with me to see ye and assigned him to guard Colton. Tristan's a brick, but he's only one man. The rest of the wizards all stand and fall by the Laird. We cannae do much on our own besides wait and watch our chance." Grant halted at an opening where the tunnel exited into daylight. He squinted out at the city streets. "It's all clear. Ye must make a run for the walls."

"How far are we from the Boundless?" Colton asked.

"Only about thirty feet." Grant eased into the open and pointed up the street between two buildings. "Ye get over that wall there and ye'll have a straight run to the water's edge."

Jaimee turned to Lily. "I'm.... I don't know what to say. Thank you."

Lily beamed at her and squeezed Jaimee's shoulder. "Maybe now you'll realize that we're trying to help you."

"I'm sorry I doubted you, but...." Her eyes darted over to Colton. "We're still fighting on opposite sides in a war for blood. I don't know if we can ever be friends again."

"I understand." She retreated back to Grant's side. "You go home and take care of your Clan."

Grant extended his hand to Colton. "I dinnae ken when or how I'll ever see ye again, but I hope it will be on friendly terms."

"I dinnae ken about that, but I'm grateful for yer help." Colton shook his hand. "Thank ye."

Grant nodded toward the wall. "As soon as ye step outside, the Laird will see us and attack. Get over as quick as ye can and go. Dinnae concern yerselves with us. Understand?"

Jaimee nodded and inched toward the tunnel mouth. "We understand."

"Go!" Grant yelled and all four leapt into the open.

Colton could never understand how the Laird found them and attacked so quickly, but Colton had his orders. He grabbed Jaimee and charged the wall.

Grant and Lily turned backward. Explosions went off behind Colton's back and he heard male and female voices yelling. Something smashed into a wall near his head, but he didn't stop running.

He only slowed enough to make sure Jaimee stayed with him. They reached the wall and he crouched down to lace his fingers together. "Get up there, lass!"

She stepped into his hands and he propelled her to the top of the wall. She landed on her stomach and flipped over out of sight.

Colton took a fraction of an instant to glance back. He couldn't see Lily at all. The black dragon blocked the alley between two buildings and spread his massive wings on either side. He roared and jets of flame spat in all directions.

Spells and starbursts blasted on the other side and smashed the dragon all over his body. He reared on his hind legs as countless strikes pummeled his chest and face, but his bulk blocked Colton and Jaimee while they made their escape.

Colton fought the urge to rush back there and help him, but Grant made it clear what he wanted Colton to do.

Colton turned back to the wall, shifted, and sprang over.

Chapter 32

Jaimee crouched on the ground at the base of the wall. Her eyes darted across the Boundless, but neither the Creightons nor the Buchanans occupied the planes anymore.

The Creighton army surrounded Icemeet in droves. They besieged the fortress while dozens of dragons bombarded the citadel with fire.

Colton landed on the soft soil at Jaimee's side and shifted back into his normal form. "Bloody hell!" he whispered. "This is bad!"

"We'll have to fight our way inside."

"We cannae do that, lass. Christ Almighty, look at them all!"

He gazed up at dragons clouding the sky. They circled Icemeet pelting the fortress with steady concussions. The noise echoed all the way down to Kald where Jaimee and Colton hid.

"We'll just have to do our best," she replied. "Hopefully, when the guards see us coming, our Clansmen will open the gate and let us in."

She started to rise, but he grabbed her arm and pulled her back down. "Hang on, lassie. Ye arenae going anywhere 'til ye honor yer promise and tell me all. What's all this the Laird wanted to find out from ye about me Clan?"

She considered resisting. Every minute they stayed here put their lives in even more danger, but when she saw his eyes, she realized he was right. She made him a promise. She owed him an explanation.

She took a deep breath. This was going to be a lot harder than when Lily told Jaimee the story.

"Lady Ilisa was a Creighton," she began. "She was Laird Balfour's daughter....and she was already married when she got together with your father. She was married to Camdyn Carmichael and they had two sons—Grant and Elliot."

Colton froze and stared at her exactly the way she expected. Then he shook it off. "That's not possible lassie. Ilisa came from Easthollow. It's another Buchanan fortress in the mountains beyond Icemeet. She was as Buchanan as I am."

"That's what she told everyone so they wouldn't find out who she really was. The Laird wanted to eliminate her sons because he considered them a threat to his reign. Ilisa used magic to conceal their identities and she gave them to a castle maid who raised them as her own."

Colton shook his head again, but Jaimee was all finished taking it easy on him. There was no easy way to do this. She just had to get it over with.

"The Laird threatened Ilisa to tell him where the boys were. She fled to Icemeet and married your father—or pretended to. She had one son with him—Duncan. Don't you see, Colton? Duncan is a hybrid. He's half Creighton and half Buchanan. That's why Laird Balfour keeps attacking your territory. He wants to eliminate Duncan. Duncan could unite the two Clans and assume the Seat of Armstrong for the Buchanans. It all makes perfect sense."

"It makes no sense at all, lass," he countered. "Ilisa was no dragon. Ye didnae ken her as I did. We would have seen. We would have kenned. She couldnae live with us for so long with no one the wiser."

"What about your father? Why do you think he keeps to himself so much? He's petrified he's going to let something slip."

Colton shook his head again and turned away. "I can ae believe this, lassie. It's outrageous."

"Did you ever see Ilisa shift into a tiger? Can you tell me one time in all the years she lived at Icemeet when you saw her shift with your own eyes?"

"I cannae recall that, but I was only a lad then. Besides, she didnae go out to fight like the rest. She was a lady. She stayed indoors most of the time."

"Well, Grant and Lily both saw her shift into a dragon with their own eyes. She shifted to defend Grant's life. That's how she died and then she told him the story with her dying breath. She was his mother and he's a dragon. He wouldn't be if she was a Buchanan tiger."

He clamped his eyes shut tight. "Are ye saying, lassie.... that Duncan—me own brother—is a Creighton?"

"He's half and half. He's both. Don't you see? He's the secret to ending this war. He's the only one who can defeat the Laird and take the Seat of Armstrong from him."

Colton opened his eyes with a very different expression on his face. He turned toward the Boundless and snarled through gritted teeth in a deadly undertone. "The bastards! How did they keep this from him? How could they let him live so long without telling him? It's unforgivable! When I get back...."

Now it was Jaimee's turn to grab his arm and stop him from standing up. "Wait a minute. Just listen to me. You have to keep this to yourself....at least until we can talk to your father to confirm it. If your Clansmen find out, they might kill Duncan themselves."

"Do ye think for a second I'd let them lay a finger on me own brother? He's just a lad! He doesnae even ken what he is! I'd wager all I have on that."

"Just...hold on a second. Slow down. You can't just barge into Icemeet and start cracking heads."

"Why ever no? I'll crack any head that looks at him wrong. To think he's living all these years none the wiser! It's disgusting!"

"Whose head are you going to crack—your father's? He's the only one who knows. He could have been keeping the secret to protect Duncan from his own relatives."

Colton pinched his lips shut. He kept shooting venomous glares toward Icemeet, but at least he didn't argue.

"Just wait. That's all I'm asking," she breathed. "We have to talk to your father. We might have this whole thing wrong and Duncan might not be a hybrid at all. If you started shouting the news from the rooftops, you could put him in danger unnecessarily."

"The bastards!" he snarled. "How could they do this to him? I could kill them all for that."

"You're talking about your father. He's the only one who kept the truth from Duncan....and from all of you. Just promise me you won't say anything to anybody until we talk to your father."

"If ye think it's best, I'll play it yer way, lassie, but ye mark me words. If we confirm this, I winnae abandon the lad over some nonsense that doesnae concern him. It isnae his fault he is the way he is. He's blameless in this."

"I know he is. If I'm right, we can get your father to come out of seclusion to offer Duncan his protection."

Colton snorted. "Ye're dreaming, lassie. He'll never come out—never."

"Not even if it means saving Duncan's life?"

"I dinnae ken about that." Colton squinted toward Icemeet and grimaced. "He's been gone so long I dinnae like to depend on him for ought. He might as well be dead for all the good he does to any of us."

"We can only try. If he doesn't come out, at least Duncan still has you and Reid."

"And ye, lassie. The Clan'll listen to ye."

"They won't listen to me any more than you. You're their Chief."

"Ye dinnae ken yer own worth. They listen to ye a sight more than ye think. Ye stand with us, lassie. Ye stand with Duncan."

"Of course. You know I will. We won't let anyone harm him, but we have to make absolutely certain first. We can't just blast the news out there before we confirm it for sure."

"Aye." His expression cleared and he grinned at her. "Is that all? Is that the whole secret?"

"Isn't that enough? Do you really want there to be more?"

"Och, no, lassie! That's plenty for today."

She laughed in spite of herself. Relief made her shaky. Now he knew everything and the strain evaporated between them.

She leaned and kissed him. "I'm sorry I had to keep it from you. I didn't want to."

"I'm glad ye did, now that I ken what it is. I wouldnae want the Laird to find out about that."

"Thank you." She blushed and looked up the mountain. "Do you still think we can get inside?"

"Aye, but we cannae go through the gate. We'd let in the enemy if our Clansmen opened it for us."

"How do we get inside, then?"

"I ken another way, but it will be dangerous."

"It can't possibly be any more dangerous than going through the front gate."

"Dinnae count on it, lassie." He took her hand. "Come along."

Chapter 33

Colton hugged the wall making his way westward down the Boundless. The noise of battle coming from up the mountain escalated to a thunderous din. The dragons kept blasting away at the fortress, but they couldn't penetrate the thick stone walls.

Archers and siege engines up on the mountaintop fired countless arrows, spears, and bombs at the dragons and at the army assembled around the walls. The Buchanans hit a few dragons, but there were just too many of them to swing the battle the other way.

The army on the ground brought in more machines trying to ram the gate open, but they couldn't budge the giant stone across the entrance. Colton and Jaimee couldn't get in that way, either.

Colton took a position farther down the wall. He and Jaimee drew level with Icemeet, but the slope up to the fortress was even steeper here. It rose in a sheer cliff in some parts.

"How do you say we're going to get in there?" Jaimee asked.

"There's another entrance.... there." He pointed to a spot east of Icemeet.

"That's right underneath the crossbows! We'd be wiped out if we went over there. It's too close to.... well, everything."

"It's the only way in. There's another secret entrance forty miles to the west. We can trek through the mountains for the next week or so or we can do it this way."

She scanned the battle and her features hardened. Colton knew her well enough by now to know what that look meant. "All right." She raised her weapons. "Let's do this."

"I'll shift on the run, lass. I'll do me best to help ye, but ye must be prepared to fight all the way. Do ye understand?"

She nodded, but she didn't look at him. She narrowed her eyes at the mayhem going on across the estuary. "Don't worry about me. I'll be fine."

He didn't need to hear any more. He faced the battle and squeezed her hand. "Go!"

They both exploded into a dead run for the estuary. Colton shifted in a blink. He could cover the distance much quicker than she could, but she caught up when they reached the riverbank.

She waded in and clambered up the opposite side. He had to swim. He shouldn't have shifted so quickly. She didn't notice that he had fallen behind. She kept sprinting up the mountain running straight for the Creighton forces surrounding Icemeet.

Guards on the battlements saw them coming, but none of the Buchanans could do anything to help the pair. Colton reached the other side and streaked up the slope to Jaimee's side.

Colton plunged into the battle and veered toward the secret entrance. Jaimee didn't know where it was and checked her route, but at that moment, the Creightons noticed the new arrivals.

They rounded on Jaimee while Colton dodged and wove between their legs. Four soldiers surrounded Jaimee with their weapons raised to hack her to pieces.

Colton tried to rush back to help her when another soldier spun around and stabbed his saber straight into the ground where Colton had just been standing. He sprang out of the way just in time, but three more soldiers came at him from all sides.

They stabbed down at him and he had to keep leaping in all directions just to stay out of their reach. He couldn't get to Jaimee. She was on her own as more soldiers surrounded her from all sides.

A deafening explosion blasted into the Creighton army as one of the Buchanans' fireballs smashed the ground. It exploded spraying fire and burning tar in all directions. It hit several of Jaimee's attackers, but a blob of burning tar also smacked her in the chest.

She shrieked in pain, raised her saber, and sliced it off, but the damage was done. She cut off a section of her own shirt and left a bloody, festering burn right underneath her collarbone.

Colton rushed to her side, but more soldiers broke off their assault on Icemeet to attack the pair. Creightons blocked Colton and Jaimee from reaching their only way into the fortress.

Colton launched himself at a dozen guards. Jaimee bellowed in desperate rage and dove in hacking everywhere with her weapons, but she and Colton still couldn't get through.

The situation looked black when an ominous whistle broke the din. One of the Buchanans' spears whisked over the soldiers' heads and impaled a dragon swooping low to assault Icemeet's front entrance gate.

The dragon crashed to earth right in the middle of the army, but the spear didn't kill it. The dragon thrashed and writhed on the ground spitting fire everywhere.

A torch of flame leveled a dozen Creighton soldiers and an opening parted to let Colton and Jaimee through. She charged into the mix making for the cliff face.

Colton hesitated a second too late and the dragon belched another punishing spurt of fire directly toward Jaimee's fleeing back. The dragon's fire would incinerate her from behind.

Colton reacted on pure adrenaline. He launched himself at her and tackled her flat on her face just in time. Fire scorched his back, smoked his fur, and burned a wicked path of torture up his spine to the back of his neck.

He shrieked in pain and shifted back into a man without thinking. Jaimee twisted around to see what was wrong and her countenance went black when she saw the dragon contorting back in their direction.

She rocketed to her feet and Colton hit the ground shrieking in pain. She charged the dragon, dodged another vicious blast, and hacked her saber down on the dragon's neck. She chopped its head clean off and it finally fell limp to the ground.

That didn't help them get to safety, though. Colton cowered on the ground, too out of his mind with pain to move. Even thinking hurt.

Jaimee stumbled over to him hugging her injured arm against her stomach. Her saber arm hung limp at her side and her battle-mad eyes skipped all over the place.

The soldiers started to converge on her when the Buchanans downed another dragon. This one landed farther away and the soldiers had all they could do to cope with the creature's long neck and tail whipping everywhere. The dragon flattened twenty soldiers before the others got clear of it.

Jaimee staggered over to Colton and grabbed his arm. He screamed in agony, but she wouldn't let him go. "Get up, Colton!" she roared in his ear. "Get up now, damn it!"

He hauled him to his feet, but he could barely see straight. He tried to stand and his weight fell against her. She held him up and started lurching toward the cliff. Every step tormented him with unimaginable pain.

"Where's the entrance?!" she bellowed. "We can't get inside unless you show me!"

He dragged his brain back into focus and saw it. The soldiers were all reassembling at the gate. They had brought in some new battering ram, but they still couldn't move the big stone.

Jaimee cast one frantic look over her shoulder and scooted around the mountain. None of the soldiers were looking. Colton steered her into a crack in the cliff and they ducked out of sight.

"Keep...going.... lassie," he gasped. "Dinnae stop...."

She kept going and he allowed himself to drift to the edge of consciousness. He wasn't sure anymore where he was, but it didn't matter. She had him. She would get him home and relief flooded him. It almost felt sweet enough to wipe out the excruciating pain in his back.

A door slammed and startled him back to awareness. She barreled into the fortress and kicked the door shut behind them. They were outside his father's apartment, but she didn't stop.

She dragged him upstairs to the great hall, but when she tried to get inside, she found the place carpeted with wounded. She spun around and the stain of his arm tugging the burned skin on his back shattered his mind.

He groaned and almost passed out when she dropped him on a bench at the foot of the stairs. She raced away and vanished. He almost fell over, but she caught him when she came running back.

"I got the ointment..." she panted. "It will ease the pain."

"Lassie...." Colton choked back the words that wouldn't form.

"Don't talk!" she gasped. "Just.... keep still."

She leaned over him and started pulling his shirt aside. Everything she did blasted his mind apart with crushing pain....and then she started smearing the ointment on his back.

It tortured him even more....and then it started to work. The pain faded and he collapsed with his elbows on his knees. His head fell forward and he shut his eyes. He was alive and he was home thanks to her.

She didn't stop until she covered his back with the ointment. She finished and sank down on the bench next to him. "There. It's done."

He couldn't sit up. She rested her hand on his shoulder and looked around.

"Colton!" a familiar voice yelled.

He had to struggle to raise his head. He wanted to pass out. He hauled his vision into focus and found himself looking straight at Duncan.

Colton's heart dropped. How could he tell Duncan the truth? How could Colton tell anyone the truth?

Jaimee was right. The Buchanans might kill Duncan if they found out he was a Creighton, or worse, a dragon. Colton didn't think he could ever tell anyone, especially not Duncan himself. How could Colton inflict such a disaster on his own brother?

Duncan exploded in delighted laughter and rushed him. "Laddie! Ye're home! I shouldnae ever doubt ye, lass! Ye did it! Ye're home!"

Duncan held out his arms and tried to grab Colton, but Jaimee got to her feet. She dodged between Duncan and Colton. "Don't, Duncan. Don't touch him. He's injured."

Duncan blanched and looked down at Colton in horror. Then he burst out laughing again and clapped Colton on both shoulders.

Colton winced, but Duncan didn't notice. "Ha ha! Ye're home, laddie! It's a miracle." He charged over to the passage leading to the courtyard and bellowed down it. "Reid! Alastair! Colton's home! Come quick!"

"Dinnae, laddie," Colton croaked. "Dinnae fuss over me!"

"Go on with ye!" Duncan cackled. "We'll do a sight more than that. Reid! Reid! Come down here now!"

Jaimee sat down on the bench again and squeezed Colton's knee. He should have expected this, but he didn't feel like celebrating.

Men started streaming into the fortress. They crowded around and Reid shoved his way to the front. He tried to embrace Colton, too. "How did ye do it? How did ye get out of Tyrekirk?" His eyes darted over to Jaimee. "Ye're hurt, lassie." Then he laughed. "Ye made it home! It's a miracle."

Alastair, Fergus, Fletcher, and a dozen others burst in and the noise built to a rising tide of voices. Everyone wanted to hug Colton and celebrate his homecoming. They made a big deal about Jaimee, too. No one seemed to notice or care that both Colton and Jaimee were injured.

"We'll drive the bastards off our mountain now that ye're back," Duncan exclaimed. "We didnae ken ye'd ever make it back alive. Tell us what to do, lad."

Colton couldn't listen to this. He forced himself to stand up. His back didn't hurt as much, now that the ointment covered his burn.

He leveled his brothers with a penetrating stare, but Colton already knew what he had to do. The defenses didn't mean anything until he got to the bottom of this mystery.

He shoved between Reid and Duncan and left them standing there in stunned confusion. Colton walked away and left them wondering what was wrong.

Chapter 34

J aimee caught up with Colton in the corridor outside his father's apartment. She had used the Buchanans' healing ointment on her own burn, but it still hurt. It had eaten into the muscle of her arm and she couldn't move it.

She found Colton glaring at his father's apartment door. "Will he talk to you?"

"I'll make him talk. He cannae go on with this charade any longer. I winnae stand it."

He pushed past her, threw open the door, and stormed in. He smoldered with the barely suppressed rage that came to the surface when she told him about Lady Ilisa. Now the moment of reckoning was at hand and Jaimee didn't envy anyone who got in Colton's way.

He marched into his father's apartment and took a look around before he spotted Neill. The old man sat in the same chair facing the corner. He had probably been sitting there the whole time Colton and Jaimee had been in Kald. Neill had no earthly clue what was going on.

Colton barged over to his father's chair, seized it by the arms, and spun it around to face him. Colton leaned in and put his face right in front of his father's eyes. "Look at me, Father."

Neill blinked. He didn't focus on anything at first. He must be surprised that someone had the nerve to disturb his silence.

"We ken all about Ilisa being a Creighton princess," Colton snapped. "Now ye're going to tell us straight about Duncan."

Neill gulped, probably to get his voice working. "Duncan...."

"Do ye ken who I am?" Colton's voice started rising and he snapped loudly enough to make his father blink. "I'm yer son—Colton. I'm yer oldest son. Yer youngest son is Duncan—Ilisa's son. Pull yer head out of yer arse and answer me, Father. I winnae go or leave ye alone 'til ye answer me straight!"

Neill lowered his eyes to the floor. "I ken all about Duncan."

"He's a Creighton," Colton barked. "Say the words. Say Ilisa was a Creighton princess and Duncan is Laird Balfour Creighton's grandson. Ye've had it yer way hiding in this room for twenty years! Now ye'll do one thing for us. Ye've done precious little for us all this time, ye selfish piece of tripe!"

Jaimee couldn't listen to this. She crossed to Neill's chair and squatted down so her face came level with his. "Just tell us if Duncan can shift into a dragon. Did you ever see him shift? We know he can shift into a tiger. He shouldn't be able to do that if his mother was a dragon, should he? We only want to protect him. We don't know what the rest of the Clan will do if anyone finds out."

Neill glanced over at her and then up at Colton before looking away. The old man was coming out of his stupor. "Aye."

"What did you see?" Jaimee insisted. "Please.... Tell us anything we can use to help Duncan. It's a matter of life and death."

"He shifted.... When he was a baby." Neill's voice husked from lack of use, but he picked up speed the longer he talked.

"Did he shift into a dragon?" Jaimee asked.

Neill nodded. "He shifted back and forth from dragon to tiger and back again—dozens of times. He shifted every few seconds when he was firstborn. We didnae ken what to do. Ilisa was still in childbed. We sent all the maids away so they wouldnae see. We didnae ken what to do....and then, after a few days, he stopped. He took his human form and stayed that way. We stayed in hiding for weeks just to make sure. We didnae let anyone see him for fear he'd do it again."

Colton glanced down at Jaimee at the same moment she looked up at him. Their eyes met and they both knew. Duncan was a hybrid and he could shift from tiger to dragon and back again whenever he wanted. So why hadn't he shifted into a dragon before now?

Jaimee got the answer as soon as she thought the question. Duncan didn't shift into a dragon because he didn't know how to. He didn't even know he *was* a dragon shifter. He saw his brothers and Clansmen shifting into tigers so he did the same thing. It probably never crossed his mind to try to shift into a dragon. He might have lived his whole life without ever finding out.

Colton pulled himself together. "Ye're coming out to defend him. Ye're coming out to offer him yer protection as Clan Chief. Ye cannae leave him alone and unprotected with this. Ye're coming with me to inform the Clan and stand with Duncan against anyone who might harm him."

"I cannae, lad." Neill's voice faded to a whisper. "Ye dinnae ken what ye're asking."

"I ken right enough," Colton spat. "Ye'll do one thing for yer son or ye're no Clan Chief of mine. Ye're not a man if ye can sit here on yer duff and do bugger all while any man threatens yer own son. What on Earth is the matter with ye? Do ye care for yer own son less than I care for me brother? Ye're not man. Ye're a waste of flesh and no kin of mine."

Neill shook his head. He wouldn't look Colton in the eye. "I cannae, lad. It's too late for me."

"Ye can and ye will!" Colton roared. "Do ye havenae any honor at all?"

Neill didn't answer. He kept his eyes down and fell back into his brainless trance. Jaimee's heart contracted at the sight of the old man shutting down again.

"Ye bastard!" Colton snarled through clenched teeth. "It's bad enough ye've ruined me own life and Reid's and Edeena's into the bargain. Now ye'll sit here and do the same to Duncan. I hate ye and I cannae stand the sight of ye. I'll never set eyes on ye again as long as I live."

He stormed out of the apartment without looking back. Jaimee watched him go. Colton still wore the ruined jacket, shirt, and tartan he had on when he got burned. The tattered fabric hung off his big shoulders to reveal the ugly festering burn covering his back, shoulders, and neck.

He slammed the door extra hard and silence fell over the apartment. Neill stared straight in front of him without moving. He showed no sign that he had heard Colton's many insults. Nothing Colton said made a dent in the old man's armor.

Jaimee couldn't say anything to Neill that Colton didn't already say. If Colton's pain didn't call Neill back from his stupor, Jaimee couldn't do it.

She stood up. Neill didn't even look at her to acknowledge her existence.

She walked out of the apartment and shut the door behind her much more quietly than Colton did. The whole fortress seemed to fall silent so as not to disturb all the sleeping ghosts.

She didn't see Colton anywhere on her way back to the main part of the citadel. She walked into the foyer to find Reid, Duncan, Alastair, Ewan, and a few others standing around.

"What's the rub, lassie?" Reid asked. "Colton wouldnae even speak to us a moment ago. He pushed us aside and went upstairs. He winnae even go to look at the situation on the ground."

"What *is* the situation on the ground? Is the battle still going on?" She listened. "I don't hear anything."

"The Creightons are setting up to besiege us," Duncan replied. "They dinnae ken we have other ways to get in and out. We can hold out as long as we need to. Them camping outside our walls only makes them easier to hit."

He shot her a crazy grin. She did her best to smile back at him, but the sight of him made her sick to her stomach. She dreaded what would happen if word got out about him—or *when* word got out about him. It was only a matter of time.

He was such a kind, friendly, easy-going guy. This couldn't happen to a nicer guy. He was everybody's best friend and he'd been one of the first to show Jaimee real kindness since she got here. Why did it have to be him?

"Ye're injured, lassie," Reid repeated. "Ye should come into the hall and let Louisa take a look at yer arm."

"I can't. I have to go find Colton." She turned away.

"What's the matter with him?" Alastair asked. "It must be serious. I havenae seen him like this—ever."

"Aye," Ewan muttered. "He looked furious."

"I'll go talk to him." She headed for the stairs.

"Is he angry with us, lassie?" Duncan asked. "Is he not happy with our defense? We tried to hold the Creightons off as long as we could...."

"He isn't angry at you. He's angry, but not at you. He loves you guys. You know that. He'd do anything for you. He's angry that anyone could threaten you and his Clan. That's the only problem."

Reid and Duncan exchanged glances, but they didn't answer. Did they know how much Colton cared about them? They wouldn't doubt if they had heard him telling off his father a few minutes ago.

"You boys handle things outside," she went on. "If the Creightons aren't attacking, just leave them alone while we reorganize our defenses. Make sure all the archers get inside and then we'll start doing an inventory on the weapons we still have left."

"Aye, lass," Reid replied.

She put her foot on the first stair when Duncan called out, "Snowflake.... thank ye for bringing him home. We thought he was dead for sure."

She couldn't walk away from this. She'd come so far in such a short time. Her life would never be the same.

She went back down to the foyer and faced the men she'd come to consider her family—her true family—her Clan. She wasn't a part of the Last Division anymore.

"You guys don't have to call me Snowflake anymore. You can call me by my real name. It's Jaimee—Jaimee Abernathy."

"Are ye sure?" Reid glanced at his brother. "We dinnae want to trespass on yer privacy. We all respect ye as one of us."

She smiled at them feeling so much warmth and affection for them. "Thank you, but you aren't trespassing on anything. You guys are my Clan now. I want you to know who I really am. I made Colton promise not to tell anyone my real name when I first came to Icemeet. Now I want you to know. I don't want any secrets between us."

Duncan nodded. "It's an honor to have ye in our Clan, lassie. Ye'll make a proper Clan Chief's wife. None of us could ask for better."

"Thank you." She took a step forward and hugged him. Her arm screamed in pain, but she did it anyway. He deserved that and so did Reid, so she hugged him, too.

She pushed them back. "I better go talk to Colton."

"Will he be right, lassie?" Duncan asked.

"I'm sure he'll be fine. Just give him time. Things got a little hectic in Kald. He just needs time to process it all. He'll be all right in a little while."

Chapter 35

J aimee eased open the door to the bedroom she now shared with Colton. She wasn't surprised to see him standing at the window looking out at the mountains.

She didn't try to silence the door latch when she shut it. She walked up behind him. She would have liked to put her arms around him, but she didn't want to aggravate his burn, so she slipped her hand into his instead. "Are you okay?"

He dipped a single nod without taking his eyes off the mountains. "I'm just grand."

"Your brothers are downstairs wondering why you're so bent out of shape. They think you're mad at them for letting you down. They think they didn't defend Icemeet well enough for you."

He acted like he didn't hear her. "I'll have to tell them first. They have a right to ken the truth before I tell the rest of the Clan."

"Do you still plan to tell everyone?"

"I have to. I have to place him under me protection before anyone else finds out accidentally. If it got out and I was seen to be hiding it, the whole Clan would turn against me, too."

She sighed and rotated around in front of him to face him. "You're right."

"Ye said we'd make the announcement after confirming with Father. We've confirmed it. There isnae ought else to do. Now it's up to me to make the rest of the Clan accept Duncan. I'm the only one who can save his life."

She shrugged. "I just hate to do this to him, you know? I hate to be the one to ruin his life like this."

"I feel the same way." Colton turned his eyes to the mountains again and his features went hard and dangerous. "I could cut Father's throat for doing this—not just to Duncan but to me. He's throwing this all on me when it's his job to begin with."

"You're the Clan Chief your people deserve." She leaned in and kissed him on the cheek, but he barely noticed. "You're a much better Clan Chief than he'll ever be."

"He's a coward," Colton snarled. "He's a gutless old woman. I should throw him out of Icemeet to die in the snow. It's better than he deserves."

Jaimee almost answered when the door slammed open and Duncan staggered in. His eyes darted from Colton to Jaimee and back again. "Lad...."

"What's the matter?" Colton spun around and took several steps toward his brother. "Are the Creightons attacking again?"

"It's.... Father!" Duncan blurted out. "He's.... dead!"

Colton froze. He didn't move or speak. Jaimee stepped into the breach. "What happened, Duncan?"

"I dinnae ken...Louisa went to take him his dinner....and she just came back to the hall and told us. He's stone dead in his room. Some shock must have done him in."

Jaimee looked over her shoulder at Colton. He stood rooted to the spot staring at Duncan. Did Colton's mind snap? Did he blame himself that his last words to his father had been a string of enraged insults?

Jaimee had to do something. She grabbed Duncan's elbow and steered him back to the door. "Go back downstairs and try to keep everyone calm. Colton will be there in a minute. Go on, Duncan."

She pushed him out of the room and returned to Colton. She moved in front of him to make sure his eyes were still tracking right. "Are you okay?"

He turned toward the window and squinted up at the snowy peaks. "Good. I'm glad he's gone. He winnae stand in the way of me protecting Duncan now. It's down to me and Reid and no one else. It's for the best."

"Are you.... are you going to be all right?" she asked. "Aren't you worried that you telling him off was the shock that killed him?"

He turned to her and fixed his eyes on her with unnerving power. He was back. He was back to being the man she knew and loved. "I hope it was. I hope what I said was the shock that killed him. If he cannae stand to hear the truth, he's no good to the living any longer. Come along, lassie. We've a Clan to run."

He headed off to the door. "Wait!" she called after him.

"This cannae wait, lassie. We must organize the funeral and succession and all."

"Don't you think you should change your clothes first? Your shirt and jacket are in tatters and your tartan is ruined. Do you really want to go downstairs like this?"

He looked down at his hands like he only just noticed that he was walking around half-dressed. "Och, aye. Ye're right. Thank ye, lass." He shot her a flinty glare. "Ye arenae in the best state yerself, lass."

She looked down at herself. A section of her shirt lay dangling open where she cut it away from her burn. The burn looked even worse with the ointment smeared all over it.

Colton came over to her. "Come along, lassie. I'll see to ye. Ye cannae go downstairs the way ye are."

He led her over to the bed and sat her down on the mattress. He pulled off his tartan and then removed his jacket and shirt.

He tore into the shirt with his teeth and ripped it into pieces. "What are you doing?" she asked.

He handed her a large section of the thin linen. "Place this across me back. Cover the burn so me shirt doesnae touch it."

He turned his bare back to her and she pressed the cloth against his burn. The ointment soaked the fabric and formed a bandage. He pulled a fresh shirt over it and winced when he buttoned his jacket over it.

He spread his hands in front of her. "Do I look right enough now?"

She had to smile at him. "You'll do."

He laughed. "Now yer turn, lassie. Take off yer shirt."

She pulled it off and flinched when he covered her burned chest with another piece of his torn-up shirt. He handed her a clean shirt and brought her leather jacket from the chair. "Now ye look tidy enough to show yer face downstairs."

She snorted. "I think they've already seen me as messed up as I'm going to be."

He straightened up in front of her and cupped her cheeks in both hands. "Ye arenae a common soldier any longer, lassie. I'm Clan Chief now and ye're me lady. They'll all look to ye for leadership now."

"Even more than before?" she asked.

"Even more than before." He kissed her. "I owe ye me life, lassie. I couldnae be prouder to have ye by me side, now and always."

He lifted her lips to his mouth and she drifted into another daydream of their new life together, but they couldn't enjoy it right now.

He let her go and crossed the room to the dresser under a giant mirror. He took a fresh tartan out of the drawer and brushed an invisible speck of lint off it. "I dinnae have time to change now."

"Can you just go down in your kilt?" she asked.

"Aye. That'll have to do for now. Come along."

They left the room and found even more people crowded in the foyer. Most of the fighting men overflowed the room along with all the maids from the great hall.

More guards and Clansmen packed the passage leading to the courtyard. Some of the wounded from the great hall had come out to see the outcome of this unprecedented event. They leaned against the walls watching and waiting for Colton to show up.

All eyes turned to him and Jaimee when they appeared on the upper landing. Colton continued to the floor where his brothers waited for him.

He forced his way to the center of the throng. Bodies crowded close to him and everyone watched him intently waiting for his word, but he didn't speak. He didn't have to. He was their Clan Chief now. He was in charge of the whole Clan. No one would ever question that.

He made his way over to the entrance to the great hall and stopped in front of Louisa. Three other maids stood with her.

"I need ye lassies to clear all the wounded out of the hall," he told her. "We need to make room for the funeral. Remove Father's body from his apartment and house all the wounded there instead. There's plenty of space. Ye can take Father's body to the upstairs guest room. No one's using it. He can lie there until the funeral."

Louisa lowered her eyes to the floor. "Aye, lad. When would ye like to hold the funeral?"

"It's too late tonight and we've enough to do with the wounded and all. We'll do it tomorrow morning at ten o'clock." He turned back to the foyer. No one breathed listening to every word he said. "As soon as the funeral is over, Reid, Duncan, and I will meet to establish the matter of succession."

"There isnae matter of succession to discuss," Alastair blurted out from the back of the crowd. "Ye're our Chief now, laddie."

A dozen more people called out, "Aye," and many people nodded their agreement.

Colton only smiled at them. "I'm grateful for yer support, but we still need to discuss it. If any member of our Clan has any challenge to make to me succeeding Father, ye can raise it at the meeting or beforehand. Ye can address yer concerns to me, Reid, or Duncan. We'll consider every objection...."

"There'll be no objections," Ewan boomed. "We're all with ye, lad."

More voices rose to confirm his statement, and in a second, the whole mob crushed forward to surround Colton. The assembled Clansmen clapped him on the back and jostled him around as he made his way back to the stairs.

Many people bumped and slapped the burn hidden under his jacket, but he didn't flinch once. He accepted their congratulations and assurance until he got to the stairs.

He turned back to face them. "Thank ye all for yer support, but we must follow the traditional way to send Father off and bring in a new Chief, whoever may take that post. We'll hold the funeral tomorrow and then we'll see what's what."

People shouted up at him as he climbed the stairs and left them to carry out his orders.

Chapter 36

C olton entered the great hall with Jaimee on his arm. She elected to wear a traditional dress for the occasion and he wore his new kilt and tartan.

All his Clansmen wore their best, too, and Reid and Duncan flanked him as he arrived for his father's funeral.

Colton never realized until last night how much his father's isolation weighed on his mind. Being Clan Chief in every way but without the official title nagged at his mind.

He no longer had that problem and he never felt so relieved as he was when he received the news that his father was dead. His father had been an anchor weight dragging the whole Clan down. Now that was gone.

Colton never suffered the slightest twinge of regret or remorse that his words might have shocked his father to death. Hour after hour passed after he received the news and his relief and certainty only grew with every passing minute.

He had said words to his father that Colton had been thinking for years. He had never dared to tell his father what he really thought. Colton lived his whole life thinking his father was too delicate and too important for anyone to question his choices.

Colton had finally gotten those secret thoughts off his chest. He had told his father to his face that he thought his father was a coward and a waste of flesh. He had told his father that he hated him and never wanted to see him again.

If his father couldn't hear that after everything he'd done—after all the pain and agony he'd inflicted on his own children—then Neill's death confirmed everything Colton said. Every word Colton said had been true. Neill was a coward for dying rather than pulling up his socks and being the man his Clan needed—the man Colton and Duncan needed.

The crowd in the great hall parted to let Colton and his brothers through. The assembled Clansmen stood back and left an open corridor to the front of the hall.

Neill lay in state on a covered trestle table at the far end where everyone could file past him and pay their respects.

Colton's eyes rested on his father's dead body and he felt.... nothing. He told his father that he would never lay his eyes on his father again as long as he lived. Colton only attended this funeral because he had to. He wouldn't waste his time otherwise.

He halted next to the body. The maids had dressed Neill in his nicest dress kilt. He wore a spotless black jacket with a silver crest pin on his tartan. Someone had placed a saber on his chest with the blade running down the length of Neill's body.

They had closed Neill's dead hand around the hilt as though he was gripping his weapon. What a joke that was. Neill never defended his Clan. He left his children to fight and die in his place while he cowered in a back room with his face to the wall. He was the worst kind of coward.

Colton fought down rising anger. This man was no Clan Chief. He was no father. Colton was glad his father was gone. Now Colton could get on with the business of running this Clan—starting with the matter of Duncan's protection.

Colton made up his mind last night how he would handle this. He would be the Chief his father never was. The rest of the Clan better take notice because Colton had no intention of standing aside and leaving the hard decisions to anyone else. He would take the bull by the horns and get the job done the way it was intended to be done. He didn't give a damn anymore if anyone else approved.

Colton didn't look at his brothers, but neither of them moved toward the body. Did they feel the same way Colton did? He would probably never know.

He moved aside for the other mourners when a choking noise distracted him. He glanced behind him to see Edeena at the threshold.

She hadn't cleaned herself up and she looked awful. She hadn't combed her hair or washed her face in days. Dirt and grime darkened the hem of her dress. She must have fallen apart after Liam's betrayal.

Tears streaked her grubby face. She looked past her brothers to her father's body and, with no warning, she broke into a run. She charged the body and flung herself across Neill's chest, sobbing her eyes out.

Colton stood back watching her. He couldn't feel any sympathy for her. She should have let him get rid of Liam in the first place. She was the one who wanted Liam brought into the Clan so she could be properly mated with him. She would be free now if not for her dedication to the man who used her and ruined her life.

Louisa and some of the other maids came forward to comfort Edeena. They pulled her away from the body and took her off into the crowd. Now nothing remained but for

Colton to preside over the rest of the funeral. None of this meant anything to him until he could get his brothers alone.

He moved out of the way and took a position to one side. He faced the room and he, Reid, and Duncan stood there for more than two hours. Their Clansmen came forward one after the other to offer their condolences on his father's loss and to commit their support to Colton's succession.

He went through the whole process mechanically. He accepted their good wishes and thanked them for their support, but he didn't put much stock in it. He would see who supported him and who didn't after he told everyone about Duncan being a Creighton dragon. He would see who changed their loyalty when it really mattered most.

Jaimee stood at his side from start to finish. She didn't say one word to anyone through the whole funeral. She left him to handle his business entirely on his own, but her presence at his side strengthened him in ways he never could have imagined.

He never had to question her loyalty. She would be with him in the end. He wouldn't even care about the outcome because he would have Reid and Jaimee with him. They would never let him down, especially not over something as important as this.

At last, the long, painful hours came to an end and he could leave the hall. The maids came forward and wrapped Neill in his winding sheet. They knotted it over his chest with the saber still clasped in his hand. He would be buried with it for some sick reason.

Colton, Reid, Duncan, Alastair, Ewan, and Fergus carried Neill's body through one of their secret passages to a deserted part of the mountain. None of the Creightons came near here or even knew it existed.

They buried Neill among his ancestors and several people sobbed by the grave, but not as many as might have. Colton remembered his grandfather's funeral. Colton had only been four then. Nearly the entire Clan broke down in tears at the graveside. That man was a true Clan Chief, unlike his worthless son.

Colton stood by and stared down into the grave. He was burying twenty years of heartache and abandonment in this grave. Now he could finally start living, now that he no longer had this phantom lurking in one of Icemeet's back corners.

Colton experienced another wave of relief and happiness when he finally turned back to the fortress. The Buchanans returned to a feast laid out in the great hall, but Colton, Reid, and Duncan didn't go in there. It was time to bring the hammer down.

They went up to Colton's office and Jaimee halted on the threshold. Her hand slipped off of Colton's elbow for the first time since they left their bedroom this morning. "I guess I'll see you in a little while."

"No, lassie. Ye're coming with me."

She raised her eyebrows. "Are you sure? Isn't this a Clan matter between you and your brothers?"

"You're a part of this. I need ye to come and explain all to the lads."

"What if they don't want me there?"

"I want ye there. Come."

He pulled her inside. Reid and Duncan both jumped when Colton walked in with Jaimee. "She isnae a part of this, lad," Reid began. "The succession is a closed matter between the three of us."

"We arenae here to discuss succession unless either of ye or any other of our Clansmen has an objection to make." Colton shut the door behind him. "*Does* either of ye object to me succeeding Father as Clan Chief?"

"Of course not," Duncan fired back, "but this meeting is meant to be private."

"As I said, we arenae here to discuss the succession." He waved to a chair across from his desk. "Take a seat, lassie. Ye, too, lads. Sit ye down."

Jaimee sat down, but neither of his brothers did. They eyed him suspiciously as he went to his place behind the desk. "What's this all about, then?" Duncan asked.

Colton drew in a long breath and waved to Jaimee. "Tell them all, lassie."

She drew in an equally long breath. "I'm really sorry to tell you this, Duncan, but your mother was a Creighton. Lady Ilisa was Laird Balfour Creighton's daughter. She ran away from Kald and pretended to marry your father because Icemeet was the only place her father wouldn't be able to get to her. We have eyewitness statements from people who saw her shift into a dragon......and we have eyewitness statements from people who saw *you* shift into a dragon when you were a baby. You're a hybrid between Creighton and Buchanan. I'm really sorry, Duncan. None of us wanted to do this to you. We're only telling you so we can try to protect you from your Clansmen."

She blurted out the whole thing in a rush. She finished panting for air and sank into her chair as the tension left her body.

Duncan stared down at her, unmoving. He didn't react at all, but Reid sure did. "This is nonsense, lassie. Lady Ilisa came from Easthollow. She was a Buchanan through and through." He turned to Colton. "Tell her, lad. Tell her it isnae so."

"I'm afraid it is so." Colton turned to Duncan. "I'm sorry, laddie. I'd give anything to make it not so, but even Father said so. He saw ye shift into a dragon when ye were born. He kept ye hidden until ye didnae shift any longer and then...."

"That's impossible!" Reid bellowed. "It's a lie! Ye dinnae say ought against Father, now that he's dead and cannae defend himself."

Colton drew in a shuddering breath. "I'm saying naught against Father. He told me with his own lips that Duncan shifted into a dragon within hours of being born. I wouldnae put this on me own brother for anything." He turned back to Duncan. "I'm sorry, lad. I'll place ye under me own protection and any man that doesnae like it can go off and find another Clan. We winnae turn our backs on ye now. Ye have me word on that."

"This is bollocks!" Reid fired back. "What do ye stand to gain from this? Tell me that."

Colton rounded on his brother. He couldn't start off being Clan Chief by having Reid talk back to him, but it was Jaimee who spoke up. "We don't stand to gain anything except maybe saving Duncan's life. The Clan has to find out from Colton. That's the only way we can protect Duncan from his own Clansmen. Do you really think we concocted this to ruin Duncan's life? We're as upset about this as you are."

"I doubt that, lassie," Reid snapped.

"Dinnae ye talk to her that way," Colton growled. "Ye'll keep a civil tongue in here unless ye plan to go off yer own self."

Reid opened his mouth to answer and immediately shut it again when he saw Colton glaring at him. Colton had to make his stand as Clan Chief right here and now. He had to start with his own brothers.

Reid propped his hands on his hips and turned away grinding his teeth. Colton glanced over at Duncan, who still stood there like someone just hit him over the head with a hammer.

Jaimee stretched her arm toward him and took his hand. "I'm so sorry, Duncan. We had to tell you. We'll make it work. Colton and I will stand by you....and I'm sure Reid will, too."

"Ye're God damn right I will!" Reid growled.

"It isnae possible, lassie," Duncan choked. "It cannae be so! It cannae!"

"It is, darling," she breathed. "I'm so sorry. You have two brothers in Kald—Grant and Elliot Ritchie. You had another one—Ness Creighton—but he's dead now. I'm sorry you had to find out like this. It wasn't fair to you."

"It's Father's fault," Reid snarled. "He should have been the one to stand by Duncan all these years. What the devil is wrong with him that he stayed locked up all these years when he could be here to stand by Duncan's side?"

"I told him the same thing," Colton replied. "He wouldnae listen, but it doesnae matter much now. I'm Clan Chief and I'll be Chief of a Clan of four if it comes to that. No one is coming near ye, laddie. I winnae allow it."

Duncan glanced at Colton once and turned back to Jaimee. "Lassie...."

She started to speak again, but before she could get the words out, he folded into the chair opposite her, buried his face in his hands, and burst into tears. "It cannae be! I hate the Creightons! I cannae be one of them."

Colton couldn't stand the distance between himself and his brother. He strode around the desk and rested his hand on Duncan's shoulder. "Laddie....me own wee laddie...."

No one said anything for a minute while Duncan cried his eyes out. Colton gulped down a lump in his throat. He would much rather deal with Reid's righteous indignation than Duncan's heartbreak. Jaimee blinked back tears, too.

Colton didn't delude himself about what this meant. It was the death knell of Duncan's part in Clan Buchanan. He could never be a Buchanan again, no matter how much Colton, Reid, and Jaimee wanted him to be.

Duncan reared back so suddenly that he startled everyone. His swimming eyes skipped around the office not seeing anything. "I'll go off! I'll leave Icemeet. I cannae face the Clan like this."

"Ye cannae go anywhere, laddie," Colton told him. "Reid and I are yer best chance at survival now. The Clan would hunt ye down if ye left, and if they didnae get ye, the Creightons would."

Duncan searched the office, but Colton could already see his brother leaving rationality behind. His whole life just crashed and burned around his ears. He had nothing left.

Colton turned back to Reid, who was still fuming. "I need ye at me shoulder all the way, lad. Ye must stand with me against the whole Clan. Are ye ready to do that?"

"All the way," Reid countered without a trace of doubt. "If it's down to the four of us, so be it."

"Good lad." Colton clapped him on the shoulder and turned to Jaimee. "Lassie...."

Colton let his eyes slide sideways to Duncan and she nodded. He didn't have to say it. He waved Reid toward the door and let Reid out first. Jaimee remained sitting in the chair facing Duncan in his.

She smiled and nodded to Colton and he stepped out of the room leaving the two of them alone. She was the best person for him right now.

Chapter 37

Jaimee watched Duncan's eyes zip back and forth around Colton's office. She could read the thoughts running through Duncan's mind. He was planning to run away.

She leaned forward in her chair and clasped his hand. "It will be all right, Duncan. I promise. We'll work it out somehow."

"How can we work *this* out?" he choked. "There isnae any hope, lassie. No hope at all!"

"Don't lose faith just yet. Give Colton a chance to convince the rest of the Clan."

"Convince them!" he practically shrieked. "Convince them to stand a Creighton in Clan Buchanan! It's madness! It's insanity!"

Jaimee winced. "You might be right. Asking the Buchanans to accept a Creighton as one of their own is a tall order. It might even be impossible, but we have to try. You can't leave. You'd be dead in a matter of days. The Laird is looking for you. He wants to kill you and he has incredible magic. He would find you and finish you off. Colton and Reid are your only chance at survival."

His face contorted in agony. She expected him to fall apart again, but he instantly pulled himself together and wiped his expression. "Ye'll back me, lassie? Tell me ye'll back me."

"All the way, Duncan. Icemeet is your home. No one is sending you anywhere."

His features spasmed one more time and he pulled himself back from the brink with a massive effort. He nodded fast. "If ye say so, lassie...."

She squeezed his hand and stood up. "Come on. The sooner we make the announcement to the Clan, the sooner we can all get back to work."

She led him out into the corridor. She didn't see Colton and Reid right away, but when she approached the landing by the stairs, she heard their voices.

They stood together right inside the landing. They talked fast in hushed tones where no one downstairs could see or hear them.

They both broke off when they saw Jaimee and then Colton looked past her. She glanced behind her expecting to see Duncan, but he wasn't there.

Colton walked up to her. "Bring him to the upper gallery where we can address the whole Clan. We must face everyone with all four of us together." He glanced behind her again. "Do ye think ye can get him to come?"

"I'll try. He's pretty messed up."

Colton nodded. "I dinnae blame him. He's holding together better than I expected."

She went all the way back to Colton's office and found Duncan lurking inside the doorway. He kept peeking left and right. "Dinnae make me do this, lassie," he squeaked. "I cannae do this."

"You have to, sweetie." She took his hand. "If they see you scared of them, they'll finish you off for sure. You have to stand with Colton and Reid. Don't worry. I'll be there. Come on."

She towed him out of the room and up to the gallery. Voices bubbled in the courtyard below. The whole Clan must be out there waiting for Colton's announcement. They all thought he was going to address them as their new Clan Chief. None of them had any clue what was coming.

Duncan tried to break away when he saw Colton and Reid standing there waiting for him. Duncan tore his hand out of Jaimee's grasp and backed away. "I cannae do this, lassie. I'm sorry."

Colton strode forward before Jaimee could move. He grabbed Duncan and pulled him close. "If ye leave now, laddie, ye're a dead man. Do ye hear? This is the only way. Ye stay close by me and Reid. Dinnae fool yerself any about running away. Do ye hear? I'm yer Chief now if I wasnae before. I'll protect ye. I swear it, but ye must come and stand with us now. It's the only way. Come along."

He tried to pull Duncan onto the gallery where the rest of the Clan could see him, but Duncan recoiled shivering in terror and anguish. "They'll kill me, lad! Ye ken they will! Dinnae do this to me, Colton! Ye cannae do this to me! Please!"

"Dinnae look at them, lad," Colton breathed. "Dinnae look down into the courtyard at all. Do ye hear me? Look straight out at the sky and dinnae listen to ought that anyone says to ye. Become a statue. Become the mountain."

"How am I to do that?" Duncan whimpered. "How can I show me face out there?"

"I'm showing mine," Colton countered. "Reid and I are throwing our lives in front of ye. Ye can stand with us this once. Now come."

He snapped the last words with so much authority that Duncan had to obey, but Colton didn't leave it up to Duncan. Colton clamped his hand on Duncan's shoulder and steered him onto the gallery.

Jaimee followed, but she wasn't looking forward to this any more than Duncan was. The whole Clan might abandon Colton in a few minutes once they found out what he wanted them to do.

Colton planted Duncan at his side still gripping Duncan's shoulder in one powerful hand. Duncan's chest heaved fighting down panic, but he didn't break down. He trained his eyes straight ahead and wiped all expression from his face the way Colton told him to.

All eyes turned up to the gallery where Colton, Reid, Duncan, and Jaimee stood side by side in front of everybody. Jaimee knew every person down there, but she could count on one hand the number she felt certain would support Colton and Duncan.

She could count on Alastair, Fergus, Ewan, and maybe one or two others. That was it. The rest might raise the call to arms to wipe out the whole family. What would she do then?

Dead silence fell over the courtyard. Only the harsh, snowy wind howling through the rocks disturbed that ominous quiet.

Colton took a deep breath, threw back his broad shoulders, and drew himself up to his full height. "As there are nae any challenges to succession, I'm succeeding me father as Chief of Clan Buchanan."

Cheers erupted from the courtyard and many of the assembled Highlanders raised their weapons to salute him. They hooted and whistled and called out to Colton from the ground.

He held up his hand for silence and got it, but he only held up one hand. The other remained clamped on Duncan's shoulder in an iron grip. "I have an announcement to make to ye—a much more important announcement than me succeeding as yer new Chief. It has come to light that Lady Ilisa Buchanan was the daughter of Laird Balfour Creighton. She fled from Kald and took up with me father, Neill Buchanan. He fathered me brother Duncan with Ilisa, which makes Duncan half Buchanan and half Creighton. He's both a dragon and a tiger in equal parts."

Murmurs broke out on the ground beneath the gallery. All the goodwill of a moment before evaporated into thin air and the murmurs turned to grumbles.

Colton raised his voice even louder even though he didn't hear anyone protesting. "This lad is me brother and me father's son the same as I am. Any man, woman, or child who doesnae accept him in this Clan can pack off right now. We dinnae need any traitors in our midst. Anyone who winnae defend Duncan with his life can leave now and they winnae be part of any Clan I'm Chief of. Ye cowards show yerselves now! Show yerselves and walk out that gate to join our enemies. I hope ye enjoy the taste of blood for that's all ye'll ever get from us!"

He talked louder and louder until he bellowed the last words down at the crowd. He silenced the grumbling, but he couldn't silence the scowls and frowns staring back at him.

Jaimee cringed. She knew this would be hard, but this surpassed her worst nightmares.

Duncan stood impassive and unmoving through it all. He never took his eyes off the sky beyond the parapet.

Reid took advantage of the silence and yelled out in a thunderous yell. "Any man, woman, or child that stands against Duncan stands against me. Bring yer blades and hope to High Heaven ye're stronger than me for I willnae rest until I see the end of ye."

Jaimee stepped forward to the railing. "Any man, woman, or child that threatens Duncan will have to face all of us. We'll defend him with our lives, and if that means we're a Clan of four from today onward, so be it."

She called the words over the crowd with a lot more enthusiasm than she felt, but at least she got them out without letting her voice tremble.

Alastair shouldered his way out of the crowd, stalked to the passage entrance, drew his saber, and faced the crowd. "Any man here that wants to threaten Duncan can take his chance getting through me first."

Fergus planted himself at Alastair's side. "And me."

One by one, more Buchanans stepped out of line to join the Highlanders blocking the only route to the stairs. Thirty, forty, fifty men took their positions there.

They faced off against fewer and fewer people who stood opposite them. The women retreated taking the children with them. In the end, ten men remained standing out in the courtyard.

Several archers appeared on the parapet behind the last few recalcitrant protesters. The archers drew their bows and aimed down at the protesters from behind.

Jaimee braced herself for a bloodbath. Did Colton's succession as Clan Chief have to end this way?

One of the protesters spun away and stormed over to the gate. "I winnae serve in any Clan with a Creighton in it. Do ye ken how many we've lost at the hands of those lizards? Open the gate! I winnae stay in this madhouse a moment longer."

A few others turned away grumbling. They marched over to the gate. The guards on duty all looked up at Colton to see what he'd say.

He waved down at them. "Open the gate and drive these traitors back to the enemy where they belong!"

The guards got busy lowering the counterweight. The great stone barricade swung up and the ten protestors stalked out of Icemeet forever.

Alastair, Fergus, and the others advanced behind them with drawn blades and, almost as though it was meant to be, the protesters halted when they saw the Creighton army waiting on the slopes below them.

"Go on!" Colton roared. "Drive them out! Go, ye foul cowards! Go to the deaths ye deserve!"

Alastair and the others surged forward with a furious roar. They raised their blades to hack their former Clansmen to pieces. The protesters spun around to defend themselves, but it was already too late.

Alastair and the rest clashed with the protesters and forced them through the gate. The Creightons sprang to their feet in a blink and charged up the slope. They attacked the Buchanans closest to them, which were the protesters.

Alastair and his band pressed the traitors farther down the mountain and crushed their enemies into the Creighton line. The protesters had no choice but to turn back and defend themselves against the Creighton assault.

Jaimee watched the whole disaster unfold with a sinking heart, but it had to be done. Alastair signaled his men to fall back and they retreated inside. "Raise the counterweight!" Colton bellowed and the guards closed the gate with the ten protesters still locked outside.

Jaimee turned away feeling sick. She couldn't watch this. Colton took his hand off Duncan's shoulder, propped both huge arms on the railing and yelled down at his Clansmen. "Anyone who turns against Duncan can expect the same fate! That's me final word."

He whirled away and barged into the fortress. Reid, Jaimee, and Duncan followed a moment later. The clang of steel still echoed up the mountain from the battle going on. Jaimee went inside. She didn't want to hear the moment when that sound stopped. She didn't want to think about what it meant.

Reid passed her following Colton to his office. Jaimee turned to Duncan, but he wouldn't look at her. He kept glancing up and down and all around. He was a million miles away.

She took his hand and he didn't protest when she took him back to the men's barracks. He had been perfectly happy living here with the rest of the Buchanans for years.

As soon as she and Duncan walked in, she realized she couldn't leave him here. If anyone decided to stick around despite disagreeing with Colton's decree, they might cut Duncan's throat in his sleep.

She drew him back upstairs and took him to the upstairs guest room that had been hers before she moved in with Colton. The maids had cleaned it again after using it to prepare Neill Buchanan's body. The room was serviceable again.

She pushed Duncan into a chair, but when she faced him to talk to him, she changed her mind. She had already said everything there was to say and it didn't make any difference. She couldn't give him his life back. No one could do that.

She left him there, but this wasn't over—not by a million miles. She went back to the room she shared with Colton and got busy taking off her dress. She was already wearing her usual clothes when Colton came in.

"Back to work already, I see," he remarked. "Ye did look smashing in that dress, lassie."

She smiled ruefully. "I hope you got an eyeful because I'll probably never wear it again."

"Wear it at our wedding."

"When will that be? There's a war on, you know, and I have to get back to training the men.... though I don't know how I'm going to do that, considering how they feel about Duncan. He'll never be able to show his face among the men again."

"If anyone causes trouble, ye let me ken." He cocked his head and glanced at her. "How is he?"

"About as bad as you might expect. We need to keep a close eye on him."

"Aye. I'll keep him near me and Reid. If anyone tries anything, they'll have to get through us first."

"I'm not talking about that. He might try to take his own life."

Colton's head shot up and he scowled furiously. "Dinnae joke about that, lass."

"I'm not joking. He's desperate. He can't leave and he can't stay. He has nothing left. His whole life is over. I really feel bad for the guy. He's out of options."

Colton sighed and started taking off his fancy jacket. "Aye. I cannae say I envy the lad me own self."

She sank down on the bed and gazed down at the dirk in her hands. It was Bryce's dirk—the one he gave her right before he died—the one he gave her when he exacted her promise that she would defend Clan Buchanan to the bitter end.

Colton came over and looked down at the weapon. "Are ye all right, lass?"

She nodded and her heart spasmed when she looked up into his eyes. "Nothing will ever be the same after this. You know that, right?"

"Aye." He sat down next to her and put his arm around her shoulders. "Does it make ye change yer mind about all this?"

"Of course not. This is where I belong. I'm not going anywhere. This is my Clan now. Whatever happens to you happens to me."

He pulled her against him and kissed her hair. She nestled into his neck and experienced the warm flood of belonging, the belonging he gave her. Nothing would ever change that.

"Aye, lass. It's yer Clan now and no mistake."

She let her weight fall against him and he leaned back to stretch out on the bed. Whatever the future held, she knew where she belonged. This was the place she could always come back to, the place of ultimate safety and comfort—in his arms.

End of Book 2

Keep Reading

H ighland Heroes Series: Book 3: Clan Rebel

Only three members of the Last Division remain after Lily Barnett and Jaimee Abernathy disappeared into an alternate dimension beyond the time portal. Now Echo Boxwood and her two remaining comrades must travel back through time in a last-ditch rescue mission to save not just their missing friends but all of human history from disaster.

Elliot Ritchie has been trying to hide from the ghosts of a haunted past, but it all catches up with him when Echo shows up and offers him a temptation he can't resist. When a confrontation between him and the Buchanans goes disastrously wrong, Elliot will have to dig deep to find the courage, tenacity, and honor to make things right, not just with the Buchanans but with himself and his estranged brother Grant.

When Echo challenges him to seize the reins of his life, they'll both have to fight with all they have to build a world where war doesn't threaten to tear them apart and destroy the love they've worked so hard to win.

You can find it at your favorite book retailer.

Sign Up Once--Get all Theo Mann's free books including brand new releases

S ign Up Once--Get all Theo Mann's free books including brand new releases

Ian Wallace is tall, muscular, magnetically handsome, heroic, and passionately in love with the lady of his dreams--Lady Ada Ross.

Too bad he's just a character in a romance novel......or is he?

When Dayna Roberts finds a mysterious letter tucked between the pages of her favorite book, she decides to write Ian back to warn him of his enemies sneaking up on him. Little did Dayna know that one act would sweep her into a world of the past--a world of danger, intrigue, and powerful forces she never imagined possible. Disaster strikes when Ian's archnemesis Gavin Macauley intercepts her letter and conquers Grimlock Castle with Dayna inside it--but how could he intercept the letter when she wrote it in the twenty-first century?

If Dayna refuses to marry Gavin in Ada's place, he'll take drastic measures that could leave this whole mysterious world in ruins. Forget about Dayna finding a way to get back to the modern world. She'll be lucky if she survives long enough to escape from the castle. Is there any way out--much less a way to get back to the family and the modern life she knows?

Sign up at www.theomann.com to read it for free

About Theo Mann

I write 70 books per year—and yes, before you ask, all these books are my original creative work. Nothing written under my name is AI-generated or ghostwritten because I write better than AI and any ghostwriter out there.

People don't read fiction for entertainment or to escape from reality. People read fiction to see their humanity reflected in another person's character and story.

This is my promise to you. When you read my books, you'll see your own humanity reflected in the characters and stories. I take this commitment to my readers very seriously. My books are an intimate form of communication between us. I would never disrespect my readers by turning that over to a machine or another writer. This is my bond between me and you as my reader.

I write 20,000 words per day as my daily work output. If anyone with a public platform would like to challenge me to prove this in a controlled environment, feel free to contact me on this website's contact page.

I worked as a professional ghostwriter for fifteen years. Now I'm on a mission to set a Guinness World Record by writing 700 books over the next ten years and 1400 books over the next twenty years, all originally written by me. See my website for the full book list.

I'm also the author of *Proof for the Existence of God* and the *Crimes Against Fiction* blog. You can find all my nonfiction work at www.crimes-against-fiction.com.

If you have a story idea, or if you would like me to explore a series in more depth, or if you'd like me to explore a character by writing a spinoff series about that character or world, leave me a message on my website's contact page. I answer all reader emails, so ask me anything, tell me what you liked and didn't like, and let me know where you'd like your favorite series to go. I would love to hear your ideas and find out what you'd like to read next.

Find out more at www.theomann.com.

Also by Theo Mann (so far)